Praise for *The H*

"An homage to the richly folkloric A[...]
ing tapestry of myths from Mazari [...]
the Hazara people and their backgrounds." —*Publishers Weekly*

"Mazari and Hillman's collaboration reveals the rich culture of a region largely unknown in the West." —*Kirkus Reviews*

"This dazzling narrative is full of wonders and unfamiliar magic, shadows and lightening. The tales it tells are fascinating in their ordinariness and their strangeness. *The Honey Thief* is simply delightful to read on its own terms, but it also illuminates the real Afghanistan, that country many great powers have proved keen to invade but rarely to understand."

—Thomas Keneally, winner of the Man Booker Prize and author of *Schindler's Ark*

"The wisdom and enchantment of thousands of years are spun together in this vivid, beautifully written book. . . . A wonderful account of the past in fiction. [*The Honey Thief*] was a true joy to read." —Deborah Rodriguez, author of *The New York Times* bestseller *Kabul Beauty School*

"If a story is a recipe for how life should be, then Mazari's unforgettable stories—of wolves and warriors, beekeepers and musicians—hold the power to rewrite his country's past. Reading his recipes for traditional Afghan food feels like being in the kitchen with your favorite uncle. *The Honey Thief* is one of those books you'll want to read out loud so you can delight in Mazari's wise and funny voice."

—Annia Ciezadlo, author of *Day of Honey: A Memoir of Food, Love and War*

"A charming book . . . It's so good to see another side of Afghanistan—here we see a magical place, full of trials, certainly, but where we can observe the triumph of the human spirit. It has lessons for all of us in the West. How good to see the enormously rich vein of Afghan traditional storytelling tapped rather than the usual catalog of death and destruction we read of in the papers."

—Saira Shah, Emmy Award–winning filmmaker of *Death in Gaza* and author of *The Storyteller's Daughter* and the upcoming novel *The Mouse-Proof Kitchen*

PENGUIN BOOKS

THE HONEY THIEF

Najaf Mazari was born in the tiny Hazara village of Shar Shar, in Afghanistan's north. He herded sheep and goats as a boy, but later moved with his family to Mazar-e-Sharif, where he became a master rug maker. He was forced to flee the Taliban in 2000 and, after a long and dangerous journey, arrived in Australia, where he now lives.

Robert Hillman is an Australian novelist and biographer. His memoir of traveling in the Middle East as a teenager, *The Boy in the Green Suit*, won the 2005 Australian National Biography Award. He and Mazari have been close friends for almost a decade.

THE
HONEY
THIEF

NAJAF MAZARI
ROBERT HILLMAN

PENGIUIN BOOKS

PENGUIN BOOKS
Published by the Penguin Group
Penguin Group (USA) LLC
375 Hudson Street
New York, New York 10014

USA | Canada | UK | Ireland | Australia | New Zealand | India | South Africa | China
penguin.com
A Penguin Random House Company

First published in Australia by Wild Dingo Press 2011
First published in the United States of America by Viking Penguin,
a member of Penguin Group (USA) Inc., 2011
Published in Penguin Books 2014

Map illustration: Dimitrios Propokis

THE LIBRARY OF CONGRESS HAS CATALOGED THE HARDCOVER EDITION AS FOLLOWS:
Mazari, Najaf, 1971–
The honey thief : a novel / Najaf Mazari & Robert Hillman.
pages cm
ISBN 978-0-670-02648-7 (hc.)
ISBN 978-0-14-312539-6 (pbk.)
1. Afghanistan—Social life and customs—Fiction.
I. Hillman, Robert, 1948– II. Title.
PR9619.4.M37565H66 2013   823'.92—dc23   2012039997

Printed in the United States of America
1 3 5 7 9 10 8 6 4 2

This book is dedicated with great affection to

Robin Bourke, Norman Bourke, Jeanie Gibb,

Hakeema Mazari, Maria Mazari, and also to

Bruce Norman.

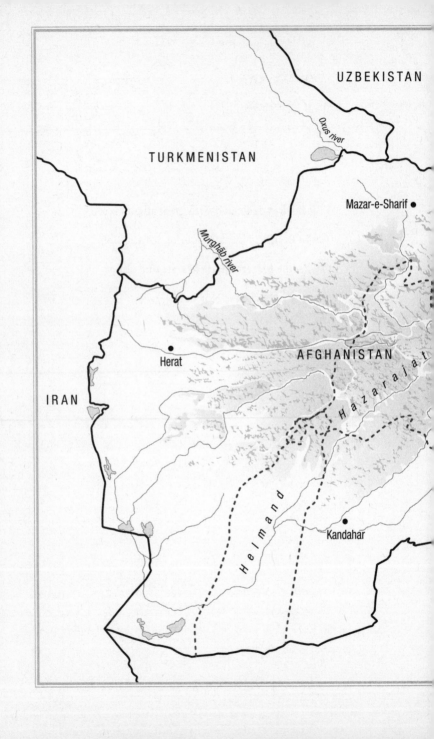

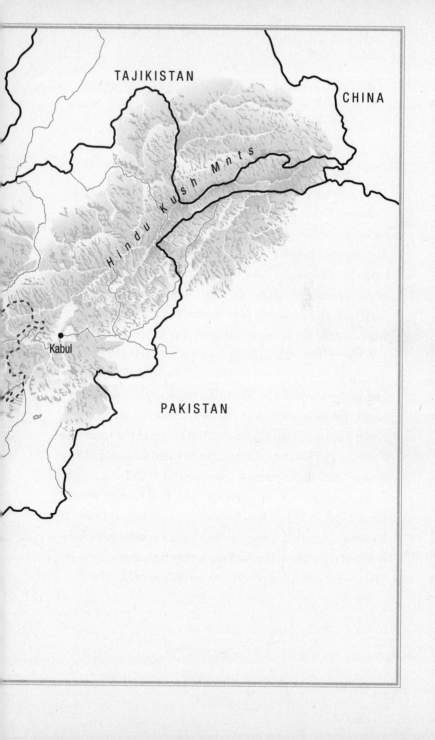

Acknowledgements

The authors wish to express their gratitude to the publisher, Catherine Lewis, and her dedicated team at Wild Dingo Press for their invaluable support in the development of *The Honey Thief*. We would particularly like to thank Hugo Britt and Katia Ariel for their painstaking editing of the manuscript and for the many improvements they suggested, and Susannah Low for her stunning design work. Special thanks go to Mustafa Najib, Abdullah Alemi and Major (Retired) Ali Raza for kindly agreeing to check the historical and political references throughout the book. The authors would also like to thank all of the following people for their advice and encouragement: David Baillieu; Julian Burnside; Dan Cudmore; Ann Dillon; Sally Godinho; Christian and Elisabeth Groves; Norm Groves; Bruce and Rea Hearn-Mackinnon; Jim and Caroline Hill; Walid and Nadda El-Khoury; Harry Kontos; Nancy Otis; Rod Parnall; Ahmad Raza; Hussain Sadiqi; Simon Stewart; Jessie Taylor; Dunstan Towning; Pamela Vincent; Lin Windram; Colin Young; all the wonderful people at the Asylum Seeker Resource Centre in Melbourne and Amnesty International Australia.

Contents

Note

The inspiration for the tales in *The Honey Thief* is derived from the long oral tradition of storytelling in Afghanistan. As in those tales of centuries past, a number of the stories in this collection are based on actual events, and some make reference to people who have played a role in the larger narrative of Afghanistan. The oral history of Afghanistan, preserved by storytellers in villages, towns and cities, is a living treasure. *The Honey Thief* is conceived as a tribute to the men and women who for many centuries celebrated in poems, songs and stories the experience of ordinary Afghans, their culture and wisdom.

The Honey Thief

1

Hazara

I was born in Afghanistan, but I only came to know where my country belonged in the world when I left it. I had seen maps of my homeland, of course, and I knew that Afghanistan had six other countries on its borders, but I took little interest in them. Then one evening, in a land of television sets far from Afghanistan, I saw a huge globe that rotated slowly, showing the weather for all the countries on earth. A young woman with dark hair and a green dress with silver buttons said that it would be dry in Kabul with a top temperature of thirty-nine degrees. I realised for the first time that Afghanistan is in the middle of the world, stranded there with no coastline, with no escape.

The sight of my native land on the television set fascinated me, but I must confess that it didn't fill me with pride. I had no desire to stand to attention and sing the national anthem. This had nothing to do with the fact that Afghanistan is only on the news when things are going badly there. It had nothing to do with the explosions that tear people apart in the streets; nothing to do with the American jets that fire rockets into houses from a great distance; nothing to do with harvests of opium poppies. No, it was because my loyalty is not to this land in the middle of the world, but to the small part of it in which my people, the Hazara, have toiled for their bread for eight hundred years.

Afghanistan is a land of struggle, more than most, but of all those who live there, none have struggled like the Hazara. Perhaps this is because we are a mystery people; no one knows for certain where we came from, and we have been resented for generations by those who live in Afghanistan in greater numbers than ourselves.

I say we are a mystery people, but only to others. We are not a mystery to ourselves; at least not amongst the Hazara I know. Many believe that we are the descendants of Genghis Khan's warriors who swept down from Mongolia eight hundred years ago and overran China, northern India and the whole of Central Asia. Scientists who have studied us say, 'Maybe.' They look at our faces, and see the same faces as those of the people who live in Mongolia today. They look at our customs, and see many that we share with the people of Mongolia. They look at our yurts, our tents, and see the same yurts that the people of Mongolia pitch on their plains. They look at a hundred different things, a hundred different signs, and the more they look, the more they see what ties the Hazara to the Mongolians. And then they say, 'Maybe.' They have to be cautious, in the manner of scientists. But we, the Hazara, we don't have to show the same caution. We know in our bones and in our blood where we came from. But does it matter? People are not theories. People are blood and bone, the eyes they see with, the hands they work with. Hazaras, who work with their hands, have lived in the land now known as Afghanistan for a very long time. There is no other land to which we belong.

A tribe is a world. I have described myself to people who are not of my tribe in this way and that, and usually I satisfy the person I'm talking to, and also satisfy myself, up to a point. I say, 'I am a pacifist,' and so place myself in a very large tribe of people who share at least one belief with me. Or I say, 'I am a businessman,' and the banker I am addressing knows that I can be relied on to keep an accurate account of what I buy and sell; that I make sensible decisions with my money. I say, 'I am a Muslim,' and the Muslim listening to me will make a dozen assumptions about the life I lead, most of them correct. When I meet a Hazara, I don't say, 'Nice to meet you, I am Hazara.' There is no need. We will greet each other in a different way to the way we greet people who are not of our tribe. We will be both excited and shy at the one time. Excited because we are brothers, shy because without even knowing my name, the man I am talking to can see deep into my heart. And if this man says, 'I have no bed for the night, I have no bed for the next year,' I will say, 'You have a bed in my house.' As we stand facing each other, hundreds of years of good news and sad news flow between us. We are made from the same clay; or rather, we have heard the same stories.

In the city where I now live, all the stories are in books. They are studied in the universities. I am not sure that these stories still pierce the flesh of those who hear them and make a life for themselves in the listener's heart. In Afghanistan, we have very few

3

universities and very few professors. The history of the Hazara is told in the fields, in our tents, in our houses. Many of the stories I heard when I was growing up, even those from centuries ago, came to life again before my eyes. I was told the story of Abdul Khaliq who was cut to pieces with knives because he would not submit to the enslavement of the Hazara people. Some years after I heard the story, I was running for my life from people who wanted to do to me what had been done to Abdul Khaliq, and for the same reason. I heard stories of Hazara chieftains who'd fought five hundred years ago to hold onto the small piece of Afghanistan that Hazaras hold sacred today. In my own lifetime, the great Hazara chief Abdul Ali Mazari fought with all his strength in the same cause and died because of the same small error as the chieftains of the past – by looking for a moment to the left instead of the right. I heard tales of the honoured eagles who came down from the highest part of the sky and took hares as they ran between rocks, and I saw the same thing when I was a shepherd in the mountains. My heart and my mind, my bones and flesh and all the organs of my body are bound together with the cords of the stories I was told. They made me Hazara, week by week, tale by tale.

This new land of mine is also the land of the Net; of the dot-com, Skype, Facebook, Google, Wikipedia, Twitter; of conference calls, direct debit, online banking. In the course of a day, I'm likely to employ all of these inventions and devices. A man I know well comes to my business premises, points at three rugs of great value and says, 'I can auction these at $25.50 minimum; that's each one, fifteen points to the gavel, ten to me. What do you think?' I take out my calculator, busy myself for two minutes, then reply, 'Fifteen to the auctioneer is steep. If he can make it 12.5, go ahead, ten points to you, of course.' I've embraced the digital world, and I've embraced arithmetic. But when the day comes to an end and I lock up my shop and prepare to drive my Corolla the ten minutes to the apartment where my wife and daughter are waiting, I always glance at the sky as I did a hundred times a day when I was a shepherd and try to work out the sort of weather I can expect the next day. If there are clouds in the sky, I take into account their height above the ground, the speed at which the wind drives them along and the exact direction in which they are heading. If there are no clouds in the sky, I look at the colour of the sunset, whether it is red or scarlet or orange or pink, because I will make a different calculation for each colour. Within my shop, it doesn't matter if the weather is hot or chilly, wet or dry or humid. And yet I cannot forget the habits of the shepherd. It is the same when I purchase honey in the supermarket. My brother, Gorg Ali, a beloved man, made the finest honey in the world, and he managed this by speaking to his bees, by pampering them, by searching for the place where they would be happiest. And so I still ask myself in the supermarket, 'But does this jar of honey come from bees who were loved?'

No, I cannot forget where I came from, the life I led when I was a boy and a young man, the people who stood close to me and told me the tales of my people. Some of those tales, like those of Abdul Khaliq and Abdul Ali Mazari, are known to every Hazara; others, like that of Esmail Behishti, himself a great storyteller, and Ahmad Hussein, the man who knew bees better even than my beloved brother, better than the bees knew themselves, are known mostly to the Hazara of the village in which I grew up. And some are known only to me.

When I open my shop, I am a businessman, no different to many other businessmen. And I am a citizen, no different to many other citizens. I take an interest in politics. I watch the news. I think, 'But is enough money being spent on education?' Or I might think, 'Is the earth becoming warmer? What is to be done?' I have a friend who comes from Uzbekistan, and he thinks such things as those that come into my own brain. I talk with my friend from Israel knowing that he has the same interests as me. I am alike to many people, millions, perhaps even, say, billions. But when I sleep, I am not the same. When I sleep, I dream like a Hazara.

2

The Wolf Is the Most Intelligent

of Creatures

He was an old man who lived in a village three hours' easy walk from the banks of the Murghāb River. In his life he'd had three wives and had outlived them all. Since he was so esteemed amongst the Hazara, he could have chosen a fourth wife but he preferred to live a widower with the family of his oldest son, Jafar Ali. He found enjoyment in the company of all his sons, all of his daughters and grandchildren but he liked the youngest son of Jafar Ali best, a boy by the name of Abbas. At twelve years of age, the boy had a quick mind and a ready smile. He had been to school in a town further south and could recite mathematical tables and measure angles. Abbas made it his job to sit with the old man over breakfast and bring him more tea when it was required.

Each morning, Esmail told the boy one of the stories for which he was famous. The first story he told was of a man whose hearing was so sharp that he could hear the sound made by cloud shadows as they passed over the land below.

'And what sound do the cloud shadows make?' asked the boy.

'A cloud moving fast makes a sound like this,' said Esmail, and he put his lips together and whistled softly, almost too softly to hear. 'But when the wind is light and the clouds travel slowly, they make a sound like a flower opening in the sun.'

Abbas smiled. He had a practical mind and he didn't believe that the stories he was told by Esmail were strictly true.

'My hearing is good,' he said. 'I can hear the sound of pebbles rolling when a red fox stumbles a long way off. But I have never heard a shadow.'

Nevertheless, he enjoyed listening to the old man. While they were being told, he believed the stories for the pleasure of it. The old man had tales to tell of horseshoe bats that flew across the sky in such numbers that they blacked out the light of the moon; of brown bears that held conversations with human beings; of snow leopards that sang songs.

When he'd finished a story, Esmail would ask the boy if he'd enjoyed it. The boy would say, 'A snow leopard cannot sing,' or 'Bears don't talk,' but he always said it with a smile. As he grew older, he understood that Esmail had such mastery as a storyteller that sometimes he would become fanciful just for his own amusement.

If the old man had only told stories of talking bears and singing leopards, he would not have built the reputation he had amongst our people, the Hazara. He was considered a man of learning, even though he had never been to school. Men came to him when they were troubled and listened to his advice. He spoke quietly on these occasions, sometimes standing, sometimes sitting. He carried a staff with him everywhere, made from the wood of a gundy tree and worn smooth all along its length. When he gave advice, he would tap the base of the staff on the ground, digging up the soil just a little, as if this helped him to concentrate. He gave advice on disputes between families, on marriages, on children who were growing up wild.

Nobody but Abbas ever questioned his advice. People saw he had a great power that he could use in a number of ways and they accepted everything he said. One day a man came to him to ask for advice about a woman he wished to marry, and since Abbas was then twelve years of age and much more than a boy, Esmail let him stay and listen. The man, whose name was Naid, was twenty-two. The woman he wished to marry was twenty and was considered very beautiful but also very lazy. Naid himself was anything but lazy. He was a carpenter and a house-builder and was always at work when the first light of morning came into the sky. Abbas could see that Naid was deeply worried about this marriage he was contemplating. Amongst the Hazara, there is hardly a worse vice than laziness. We have survived in the mountains of the Hazarajat by throwing ourselves into our work without complaint. In the mountains of the Hindu Kush, you work hard or die young. Women work as hard as men, or harder. Every meal must be thought about. Every purchase must be wise. A lazy wife is a catastrophe.

Young Naid told his story wearing a frown the whole time. He gripped one hand in the other and squeezed and kneaded it.

Abbas' mother Amalia served him tea which he drank very slowly, sometimes forgetting it was sitting before him. Often he pushed his hands against his temples and rubbed with his fingers. As Abbas sat watching, he could see only one answer that the old man could give Naid: forget this woman for she will be your ruin. Nobody supported Naid in his choice of a wife; his mother was full of scorn; his father said he was mad. And so Abbas was shocked to hear his grandfather say to Naid, 'Yes, marry her. Of course you must.'

'You believe so?' said Naid, who was as shocked as Abbas. He had been stooped over, sitting before Esmail, but as soon as the old man spoke he sat upright as if he'd been stuck with a prickle.

'Yes, that is my advice. Marry her. Buy a present for your mother to calm her temper. Ask your father for his blessing.'

'Then that is what I will do. My mother and father will accept the marriage once I tell them that you have approved. I thank you with all my heart. I honour your wisdom.'

When Naid had departed, Abbas said to the old man, 'That was a very strange thing to say!'

'Do you think so?' said the old man, and he gave Abbas a look that meant, 'There is more to this than meets the eye.'

'Surely you have sown the seeds of unhappiness for Naid.'

'Listen,' said the old man, and he made a gesture with his hand, touching one ear, so that Abbas knew to attend closely. 'Have you seen a man who has only one leg to carry him through life? Have you seen a man who has lost a hand? Laziness is like that. It is a handicap to carry through life. The woman Naid wishes to marry is like a woman with a misfortune to bear. Better she should have a husband who knows nothing but hard work

10

than a husband who is lazy himself. Naid will always toil until the sweat falls from his face. Now he will have a wife whose beauty will enrich his life in one way at least.'

The old man was revered for the advice he gave, but strangely he found small pleasure in his reputation. And this was something that Abbas noticed, so closely did he study the old man.

'When people say you are the wisest man in the world, you always close your eyes and bow your head,' said the boy. 'It doesn't please you, I think.'

The old man smiled and took the boy's hand in his own, much older, hand.

'This is why I live in your father's house,' he said. 'To hear what you have to say.'

'Then it's true? It doesn't please you to be praised?'

'When I wake in the morning, I look at the sky and wish to return to my bed. My bones ache. But I wash and pray and eat some food and go about my work. The people who say I am as wise as a prophet don't see me wishing to sleep an hour longer. A human being cannot be a god, Abbas. He is just a man with pains in his knees and a sore back.'

'But you should be proud. People walk for a whole day to listen to you,' the boy responded.

'Abbas, every life is a life of folly,' said Esmail. 'For each intelligent decision we make, ten more are foolish. That is what it means to be a human being. I once knew a man who found a gold coin on the ground. It must have fallen from the purse of a merchant – that may be one explanation. The man found the coin and rejoiced. For a while, the gold coin made things easier for his family. Every day for the next two years, the man went back to the place where he'd found the coin to see if another one was waiting for him. But he never found a second coin. This is what we do. We think good fortune will happen again and again. But our eyes tell us that good fortune only happens now and then, not every day. I am no different. Much of my life has been devoted to folly. When people say, "Esmail, how much you know!" I think of how foolish I have been and feel ashamed.'

The old man liked to be questioned – that is what Abbas understood by the time he was twelve. And so he spoke his mind to his grandfather whenever a story seemed strange or crazy. The old man called Abbas 'the scientist' because of his habit of asking for proof. 'When a brown bear sits and talks to me, then I will believe you,' Abbas said, and the old man smiled with approval.

'But what if I tell you that the wolf is the most intelligent animal in the world? What if I prove to you that a wolf is more intelligent than a man?' said Esmail one spring evening.

'That can never happen,' replied Abbas.

'It will happen tomorrow,' said the old man. 'I will come with you when you watch the sheep. You will have your proof.'

It was Abbas' job to guard his family's sheep and goats when they were grazing on the spring grass in the hill pastures. It was not his only job, but in the spring it was the most important one. He had been a shepherd for a year when the old man told him that a wolf was the most intelligent creature in the world, but so far he had never seen a wolf come close to the flock. It could happen any day. Lambs were being born and wolves would pick up the scent of the afterbirth and come down from the mountains to hunt.

In the early morning when the sky and the land were the one dark colour, Abbas woke the old man and brought him some breakfast. While the old man was eating, Abbas took four pieces of the bread his mother baked in the *tandoor* and poured honey on each piece. Then he rolled them up and wrapped the four sandwiches in cotton cloth. He placed the parcel of sandwiches inside his jacket of sheepskin so that the warmth of his body would prevent the honey from freezing. He filled two bottles with water to drink during the day and placed them in a woven bag that he would wear over his shoulder. In the mountain pastures where the sheep were grazing, there was nothing to eat except that which you carried with you.

Abbas asked the old man, 'Are you ready?' and the old man said, 'I wish I was still in my bed.'

It was just past the time of morning prayer when Abbas and the old man started on their journey. They walked the path from the village to the mountain pastures without a lantern. Their feet knew where to place themselves. The old man was carrying both his staff and a heavy rifle of Russian make that dated from the time of the tyrant Abdur Rahman and had once belonged to one of Abdur Rahman's soldiers. It surprised Abbas that the old man should wish to carry a rifle with him. When he asked about it, the old man said, 'I am attending to your education.'

'Tell me again how the rifle came into your hands,' Abbas enquired.

'You know the story of the weapon. Why should I tell you again?' came the reply.

'For my pleasure.'

Walking through the darkness with Abbas' dog at their heels, the old man repeated the story of the rifle to the boy. He started by saying, 'This is a story that is a sorrow to tell,' which is how he began the story each time he told it. He said that twenty soldiers of the tyrant Abdur Rahman had come to the village in Hazarajat where he had lived as a boy. 'They came to shoot Hazara,' he said. 'They killed many. My mother cried out to me, "Child, run for your life!" and I ran as fast as I could. One of the soldiers chased me. I was thinking as I ran, "Where can I hide?" But there was nowhere to hide. I ran into a little valley that all of the people of the village kept away from because it was the home of snakes, both black snakes and grey snakes. When I was deep in the valley, I stopped and waited. The soldier saw me waiting and he raised his gun. I knew that his gun would fire only one bullet before it had to be reloaded. I said, "You have a choice. You can shoot me, or you can shoot the snake at your feet." He looked down and indeed, a black snake lay on a rock close to where he stood. He screamed and fired at the snake, but in his fear he missed. The soldier threw down his gun and ran back the way he had come.'

'And the snake was a black one, and not poisonous,' added Abbas.

The old man affirmed, 'As we who live here know, the black snakes are not poisonous. Only the grey ones.'

'You kept the rifle for yourself?'

'For myself,' said the old man, and Abbas knew that he was smiling in the darkness.

'And you taught yourself to fire the rifle as straight as a man can fire an arrow.'

14

'Yes,' said the old man, 'I taught myself, whenever I could find a bullet.'

Abbas was about to say something more, but the old man made a sound of displeasure in the darkness. 'Of that we don't speak,' he said.

Light had come into the sky by the time Abbas and his grandfather reached the pastures. The sheep and goats were jostling inside the fold, waiting to be freed into the fields. The fold was made up of wooden sections that joined together and had to be taken apart one section at a time. When the first section was lifted, the sheep and goats rushed through the opening to feed on the spring grass wet with dew. Abbas said to his dog, 'Hurry!' and the dog loped along with the sheep and goats, bumping them and sometimes giving a deep bark. The dog was showing the sheep and goats that he was at his post. He was well trained and he returned to Abbas and the old man once he was done.

Abbas, the old man and the dog walked up into the pastures and found a place to keep watch on the valley slope above the sheep and goats. Abbas would normally stand for most of the morning, resting on the stick that was his only weapon. But because the old man said, 'Why stand when a seat on the ground is free for the taking?' Abbas sat down and offered the old man a drink of water. Then he said, 'Would you like something to eat? I have two sandwiches for you.'

'I think I'll wait,' replied the old man.

They sat side by side, the old man Esmail and the boy Abbas. The light grew stronger in the sky above the mountains but there were no shadows yet. When at last the sun rose above the mountains the peaks changed from black to red, then to gold.

'Thank you for coming with me today,' said Abbas.

'I wish I was still in my bed. I'm too old to be on my feet before sunrise.'

'Do you still believe a wolf will come?'

'Oh yes. A wolf will come.'

'I doubt it,' said Abbas. Then he said, 'When I first came to guard the sheep, my brothers said to me, "The wolves are always watching," but I have never seen one. They said, "If you fall asleep, the wolves will seize you and eat you. They will start at your feet and finish at your head." It's nonsense.'

'Tell me about numbers. How many numbers do you know?' asked the old man.

'How many?' repeated Abbas. 'All of them.'

'You know all of the numbers in the world?'

'Numbers are not difficult,' said Abbas.

'Tell me about measuring,' said the old man. 'How is that possible?'

'It's simple,' responded Abbas. With his staff, he drew a right-angled triangle in the brown dust. 'You see this angle? It measures ninety degrees. This other angle measures forty-five degrees. In a circle there are three hundred and sixty degrees. Once you know that, you can measure anything.'

The old man shook his head, as if in wonder. He asked Abbas about the countries of the world. He said it interested him greatly to hear of the countries of the world. He knew very little about them. 'But you have read a book about countries, so tell me. Is there a country with more mountains than we have here?'

The book that the old man spoke of was an atlas. Abbas had been permitted to take home the atlas from school to study it. 'There is a country called India that has more mountains than us,' said the boy.

'Is there a country called Russia?' the old man asked. He had heard of Russia.

'Yes, and another called America. There are two Americas. One is south and the other is north. In the north, the people drive cars, everybody drives cars. I have seen pictures in a magazine.'

Abbas was speaking of a magazine kept at the school by the teacher, who let only the best students look at its pages. It was from America and was called the *Saturday Evening Post*.

The old man had some idea of what a car looked like and what it did, but he asked Abbas to tell him more. He asked him about aeroplanes, too. He was curious about everything that Abbas had learnt at school, but he kept returning to the magazine. He understood that a magazine was like a book, but with pictures, and every question he asked betrayed his interest in seeing it. Abbas pronounced the name of the magazine in English, as his teacher did. The teacher could speak some English and read even more. He had been out of Afghanistan to the city of Istanbul. He could have lived in Istanbul if he'd wished, but it was his great passion to see the Hazara educated, and so he had returned to be the schoolteacher in a poor village.

When Abbas had answered questions for almost an hour, the old man said, 'I'll eat a sandwich now.' Abbas gave him a sandwich from the fabric bag and took one for himself, also.

As they ate, they gazed across to the other side of the valley where a terrace had been constructed on the mountainside. A man named Sayed Ali grew pears on the terrace. The pears grew over a trellis made of timber. These were the prize pears of the district. Each one sold for five times the price of ordinary pears. Sayed Ali and his family looked after the orchard as if it were a goldmine. When the frosts came, Sayed Ali built a fire so that the air around the pears didn't become too cold and kill them in their infancy. In the years of the tyrant Abdur Rahman, soldiers had been sent to burn down the orchard, which was very old. But the soldiers had been turned away by Hazara with guns. Esmail had been one of those who had turned Abdur Rahman's soldiers away. He had killed two soldiers when he was only fourteen years old, but he never spoke about that time if he could avoid it.

Well into the morning, the old man lay back on the ground with his hands behind his head and his knees raised. Abbas wasn't sure if the old man was sleeping or only resting. He began to feel guilty for encouraging the old man to rise so early. Normally the old man would pray at five in the morning then go back to sleep, but this morning he had stayed awake. Abbas studied the old man's face at rest. Deep lines ran across his forehead and down his cheeks. Abbas thought sadly, 'Well, he will not live forever.'

But just as he was thinking this, the old man spoke without opening his eyes.

'A wolf has come,' he said.

Abbas was startled. He glanced quickly down at the sheep and goats. His eyesight was excellent, but he saw no wolf.

'No,' he said. 'I see nothing.'

'Look at the boulder on the north side of the little stream.' The old man's eyes were still shut.

Abbas stood slowly and scanned the banks of the little stream below. He stared hard at the boulder that loomed above the stream. He saw nothing for a minute or more, then all at once he saw the shape of a wolf in the shadow of the rock.

'Hai-wah!' he said. 'I see it!' Then he said to the old man, who was still on his back with his hands behind his head, 'How did you know?'

The old man was smiling with his eyes shut. 'The wolf has been there since we ate our sandwiches,' he said.

Abbas looked back at the boulder. Again, he couldn't see the wolf. Then he could.

'Hai-wah!' he said. 'Why does it stand there?'

Now the old man sat up and reached behind himself to brush the dust and dry grass from the back of his jacket. 'He is waiting to see if you fall asleep. See how he waits with the breeze in his face? The dog cannot catch his scent while he remains there.'

'Use your rifle, grandfather! Shoot the wolf!'

The old man was on his feet now. He was staring down to where the wolf was hidden. He was smiling. 'No, no,' he said. 'We will not shoot the wolf.'

'Why not?' said Abbas. Sometimes he couldn't follow the old man's reasoning. It made him angry. 'The wolf will take our lambs. Why not shoot him now?'

The old man said, 'No, he will not take any of your flock. He is waiting to feed on the afterbirth when the pregnant ewes drop their lambs. He is an old wolf – as old as me. We know each other.'

Abbas looked at his grandfather. The smile on his face made all the lines and furrows deeper. He seemed happy. Abbas thought, 'Maybe he is losing his wits. That would be a great shame.'

The old man looked at Abbas and kept his smile. The boy thought, 'Surely he can't read my mind?'

'Did I not tell you that the wolf is the most intelligent creature in the world?' he said. 'Now I will show you.'

He picked up the rifle, pulled the bolt lever aside then pushed it home. He gave the rifle to Abbas. 'Aim at the wolf,' he said.

Abbas had fired a rifle before, but it was a modern rifle, much lighter than the old Russian weapon. Even with a modern rifle, he was not a good shot. Perhaps average. But he did what the old man said. He planted his feet apart and with the stock of the rifle buried in his shoulder he raised the barrel and searched in the sight for the wolf. When he found the wolf in the shadow he adjusted the sight so that the gun was aimed at the wolf's head.

'Will I shoot?' he said.

'No,' said the old man. 'Tell me, Abbas, what is the wolf doing now?'

'He is standing still.'

'Where is he looking?'

'He is looking at us.'

'Now give me the rifle,' said the old man, and he planted his feet and aimed the rifle at the wolf. To Abbas' surprise, the wolf withdrew deeper into the shadows. Then the old man returned the rifle to Abbas. As soon as Abbas had hold of the rifle, the wolf re-appeared.

'Do you see?' said the old man. 'Do you understand, Abbas?'

'No,' said Abbas.

The old man took the rifle from the boy and pulled the bolt lever aside. Then he rested the rifle on the ground.

'The wolf knows that you cannot fire a rifle such as this accurately enough to endanger him. But he knows that I can.'

'How does he know?' said Abbas. He didn't feel ashamed to be seen as a poor shot. Everybody knew it.

'His brain tells him,' said the old man. Then he added, 'Do you think you could throw a stone from here and hit the wolf?'

Abbas studied the distance to the boulder and the wolf. It was twice as far as the shadow cast by a tall tree. Although Abbas was not a good shot with a rifle, he could throw a stone with great accuracy. All the boys who guarded sheep on the hills could throw a stone with great skill. It was necessary in the day to throw stones at the goats, who would climb up to rocky parts of the valley and stay there. Why the goats should wish to climb away from the grass and into the rocks was a mystery. Abbas thought they did it simply because they could and for no other reason. Simply because they could and to make his life difficult. If the dog chased down every goat that climbed into the rocks, he would tire himself out, so Abbas threw stones at the mischievous goats until they came down to escape the blows. He knew he could hit the wolf with a well-aimed stone from where he stood.

'Yes, I can hit him from here.'

'Pick up a stone,' said the old man.

Abbas searched on the ground for a good stone, one that was not too heavy and that felt good in his hand. When he'd found one, he asked the old man if he should throw the stone and hit the wolf.

'Hold the stone ready to throw,' said the old man.

When Abbas raised his arm, the wolf withdrew.

'Hai-wah!' said Abbas. 'He knows my stone would hit him!'

'Do you think I could hit the wolf from where I stand?' said the old man.

It took a lot of strength to throw a stone all the distance to the wolf. Abbas doubted the old man could throw so far at his age – well over eighty years. But to be polite, he said, 'Yes, surely.'

The old man spoke. 'At your age, yes. But not now. The wolf knows my age. Watch.'

He took Abbas' stone and drew back his arm, as if he were about to throw. The wolf had come out of the deep shadow. He remained where he was while the old man held his arm back.

Now the old man told Abbas to take the throwing stone and go back six paces. Abbas did this. The wolf was watching. When he raised his arm, the wolf didn't move.

'He knows how far you can throw,' said the old man, and he laughed. 'You see, Abbas. The most intelligent creature in the world.'

In the middle of the day, Abbas and the old man ate their second sandwich and drank a little water. The old man praised the honey, which came from the beehives of Abbas' brother Barush. Then the old man stretched out beneath a small tree that grew by itself above the pastures and fell asleep in a minute. Abbas remained awake, as was his duty. Standing on the mountainside with his staff and his dog, he worried that his grandfather would not live long enough to teach him all he knew. Thinking this, he looked down to the boulder where the wolf had waited earlier. He could no longer see the wolf. But after staring for five minutes, he saw its shape in the shadow. The wolf was lying down, perhaps asleep.

Abbas thought of waking his grandfather to tell him, but he wanted the old man to enjoy his sleep and didn't disturb him.

Late in the afternoon, Abbas and his grandfather herded the sheep back to the fold, with the help of the dog. Three of the ewes had given birth during the day. The new lambs were unsteady on their legs and had to be nudged along by their mothers. Two of the lambs were still bloody from birth and the ewes stopped to lick them on the way to the fold. The old man was pleased that the wolf would be able to feed on the afterbirth left in the pasture. 'He is too old to hunt,' said the old man. 'He doesn't have a family to care for him. He doesn't have an Abbas.'

When Abbas went to the pasture the next day, he looked for the wolf exactly where he'd seen it with his grandfather the day before. Sure enough, the wolf was there in the shadows of the boulder. It must have been the wolf's plan to stay for the whole of the lambing season and live on afterbirth, but that would only be for another month. Abbas began to worry about the wolf, in the way that he worried about the old man. Where would the old wolf find his dinner when the lambing season was over? Such a strange thing, but after living in dread of wolves ever since his brothers had warned him of their savagery, he now could not bear to think of this wolf, his grandfather's wolf, struggling through the seasons to come. That day and the next day, he called out to the wolf, 'I don't fear you and you have no need to fear me! Find what comfort you can!' The wolf gave no sign of having heard, and when the lambing season was past, it disappeared.

———

The old man remained strong through the summer and the autumn, but in the winter he began to show more signs of age. Often he would stop eating his breakfast and begin gazing into the distance. When Abbas said, 'Grandfather!' and touched his shoulder, the old man's face would take on an expression of bewilderment, as if he did not remember where he was, or who Abbas was. Abbas grew more and more concerned and took charge of the old man's affairs, as best he could. When people came to ask for his grandfather's advice, he told them that the old man was not well. There were complaints, but Abbas was firm. 'Go to the mullah,' he would say. If he felt impatient, he would say, 'Write a letter to the Ayatollah, he has a secretary.' Ali Hussein al-Sistani was a famous Shiite who lived in the holy city of Najaf, in Iraq.

When the old man's sons and daughters spoke to their father, Abbas told them to talk to him as if he would still be alive for years to come, for very often they would say, 'When you are gone, there will be many who will miss you.' They took it for granted that the old man knew he was nearing the end of his life. And in this they were right, but it wounded Abbas to hear them say so. Amongst the Hazara, people are not sentimental about old age. It is natural for a man to die when his strength is used up. When Abbas said, 'Grandfather will be with us for many Ramadans to come,' Esmail's sons and daughters said, 'Oh, surely!' but they didn't believe it.

Abbas had asked his teacher many times if he could bring home the *Saturday Evening Post* for his grandfather to see, but the teacher always refused. 'If I allow you to take it home, many others will make the same request,' he said. 'It will be damaged, and it is the only one in Afghanistan.' But Abbas persisted. He told his teacher that he would bring the wood for the furnace that gave heat to the classroom in autumn and winter, and he made sure he did. He tutored other students whose minds were not as quick as his. He brought ewes' milk for the teacher two days a week. One afternoon, the teacher said, 'Take home the magazine, Abbas. Keep it for a week. But if it is damaged, there will be a whipping.'

Abbas wrapped the magazine in cotton cloth and carried it home with the greatest care. He showed it to his grandfather, who was lying in bed. The old man looked puzzled at first, but then his eyes came to life and he smiled. He remembered what the magazine was called but had trouble pronouncing its name. Abbas sat beside his grandfather and showed him the picture on the cover, of a woman teaching a class of boys and girls combined. The picture was very skilfully painted. The date on the cover read March 17, 1956. Abbas explained to the old man that the days of Americans were different from the days of Afghans, but that the American date was the same as Sha'ban 4, 1375.

'How strange!' said the old man.

'The Hijra of our faith starts from the time of the Prophet,' said Abbas, 'but Americans have the Christian faith.'

'I met a Christian once, when I was younger,' said the old man, 'but he was not American.'

The old man enjoyed everything in the magazine. The writing was not American but English and when Abbas told him this he said again, 'How strange!' He thought the writing looked like lines of black ants marching across a field of snow. More than anything else, he enjoyed the pictures of cars. Abbas told him that

Americans place pictures of cars in such magazines as the *Saturday Evening Post* in order to sell them. Americans had thousands of cars for sale, of many different colours and shapes. Abbas was able to tell the old man the names of the cars in English, such as De Soto and Oldsmobile and Chrysler and Dodge. He said the greatest of all cars for the Americans was the one called Cadillac. The old man put the tips of his fingers on the picture of the golden Cadillac, but very cautiously.

'Americans have such a number of cars,' he said, 'and yet they speak the language of another people!'

The old man was suffering in his chest, and had to cough painfully. Nevertheless, his eyes remained bright and he thanked Abbas many times for bringing home the magazine. He was interested in all the pictures that were not of cars also, and the one that fascinated him most was of a woman in a dress of the sort that is worn in America. She was smiling as she stood beside what Abbas said was an oven powered by electricity. The oven was white and shining. Inside the oven, a huge chicken was cooking. The old man said that it was the strangest thing of all for the Americans to use ovens that were so white.

Early one morning the following spring Abbas went to the pastures after bringing the old man his breakfast. He released the sheep from the fold and saw that two ewes had lambed since the previous day. The new lambs kept close to their mothers and tried to feed even as they tottered along on their unsteady legs. The ewes would not let the lambs feed until the pastures were reached, and the lambs made small bleating sounds of protest.

When the light of sunrise reached the mountainside, Abbas

looked down towards the boulder above the little stream to see if the old wolf had returned for the lambing season. He saw nothing. Even when the sun rose higher, there was no sign that the wolf had returned.

Towards the close of the day, when the sheep were back in the fold, Abbas called to his dog and called a second time. The dog was off the path, sniffing at something amongst the rocks. Abbas walked over to the dog, calling, 'Hi! Come when I call you!' The dog turned its head and looked at Abbas but didn't come to him. Then Abbas saw that it was standing over a dead creature, a grey wolf. Abbas hurried to the carcass, suddenly sick with fear. The wolf lay with its lips drawn back from its teeth. It may have been the old wolf but it was impossible to say. Abbas put his hand on its flank. There was still a little warmth in the carcass, showing that the wolf had died only a few hours earlier.

Abbas waited no longer but began running along the path in the failing light, taking no care if he should miss his footing and fall. He ran with his chest burning at each gulp of air and kept running until he emerged from the uneven ground above his village onto the plateau. He then plunged across the creek without going further downstream to the stone bridge. He stopped to regain his breath only when he was within sight of his father's house, bent over with his hands on his knees. The dog licked his face, puzzled and pleased at the same time over this strange behaviour.

When Abbas' chest had ceased heaving, he walked slowly to the house, knowing before he reached the door that the old man had died. He could hear the sobbing of his sisters, of his mother and his aunts, and their cries of lament.

It was his father who noticed him first. He rose from the floor of the room in which the old man was laid out on a low table, his arms straight and his hands at his sides with the fingers spread. His white beard had been combed and looked much neater than it had in life. He seemed younger, too, than he had in the morning when Abbas had brought him his breakfast. He had not yet been dressed in his funeral gown but still wore the long shirt and loose trousers that kept him warm in bed.

Abbas' father said, 'Son, do not shame yourself.' He meant, 'Don't weep like a girl.' Abbas knew his responsibilities without being told. He walked to his grandfather and placed his hand on the old man's chest above the heart. Then he left the house and walked about outside for an hour and more, and longer still.

3

The Honey Thief

Ahmad Hussein was a *perwerrish dahenda,* a beekeeper, a maker of honey. This is a craft honoured amongst the Hazara since honey is the prince of foods and the process by which it is made is one of the marvels of the world. It is the bees who make the honey, not beekeepers, but to know where to place your hives, and when, is the first lesson of making the bees work for you. Ahmad Hussein knew exactly where to place his hives and a great deal more. People said, 'The bees work for Ahmad Hussein as if he were their king.' And this was true. Ahmad Hussein was not an ordinary person. Bees obeyed him. Animals obeyed him. Sheep and goats obeyed him. He was honoured by the Hazara, but even strangers who were not Hazara respected Ahmad Hussein. When they saw his eyes, they knew that he was close to God in some way, and if they had thought of doing him harm they would change their minds.

Ahmad Hussein worked alone, but once in so many years he

took on an apprentice and trained him in the craft. He had trained two of his own sons, but one had died of poliomyelitis at the age of twenty, and the other, who had shown even greater promise, had married into a family of tinsmiths and now made his living in a workshop far from the mountain pastures.

It happened that Ahmad Hussein was ready for an apprentice in the spring of Esmail Behishti's death and he chose Abbas from amongst the many boys who asked him to train them. He chose Abbas as a mark of respect for Esmail, who had been his friend and was once his master, and also because he knew that the boy was grieving. Kindness had come Ahmad Hussein's way in the person of Esmail, and because of that, he had some kindness to spare for this boy who had loved Esmail.

Ahmad Hussein's bees lived their lives in special boxes of white and blue, known as *sanduqe assal*. He had many places for the hives, some of them a great distance apart, and in each place one hundred boxes stood amongst the grass and the wildflowers. I have said that it was one of Ahmad Hussein's gifts that he knew where to place his hives. Such a skill is not uncommon, but it was rare for a beekeeper to take as much time as Ahmad Hussein in choosing a site. He did not say, 'I will place the boxes in the field,' and leave it at that, as Abbas came to know when he walked the fields with Ahmad Hussein in the first days of his apprenticeship. Ahmad Hussein strode down each side of the field and across from one corner to another. Often he would stop and think.

'Why have we stopped here, Abbas?' he once asked the boy, and Abbas said, 'Sir, I cannot guess.' It was Abbas' habit to address Ahmad Hussein as 'Sir' whenever he was asked a question.

Ahmad Hussein did not say, 'Relax, call me by my name,' for he knew that the boy would find that difficult for a time. He also knew that Abbas was concentrating more on his grandfather than on beekeeping. But that would change, too.

Ahmad Hussein looked about left and right, behind, ahead. He looked at the sky. He looked at the grass. Then he said, 'Abbas, what do you think of this field?'

Abbas said, 'It's a good field.'

'Yes, but is it the right field, little brother?'

'Yes, it is surely the right field.'

'But is this the right place in the right field?'

'Yes, it is surely the right place in the right field.'

'Should we have a look at another field?'

'No, this is the right one, Sir.'

'Why?'

'Why?'

'Why is it the right one?'

'I don't know.'

'Then will we look at other places?'

'Sir, I can't say.'

'Abbas, I have a question for you. The question is this: can a bee catch a cold?'

Abbas smiled. 'Can a bee catch a cold? No. It is impossible, Sir.'

'It is not impossible. A bee can catch a cold.'

'How do you know?'

'I have seen a bee sneezing.'

'No!' said Abbas. Then before he could stop himself, he said, 'God will punish you for telling lies!'

Ahmad Hussein laughed. He was teasing Abbas, but when a boy was as full of sorrow as this one, perhaps teasing could help.

'I have seen a bee sneezing,' said Ahmad Hussein. 'When I said, "God bless you!" the bee said to me, "You say, 'God bless you,' Ahmad Hussein, and yet look where you have placed our house! You have placed it where the cold wind comes across the field!" It was true. I had placed his house where the cold wind troubled him. So now I am more careful. Now I place the beehives away from the cold, and away from the afternoon sun. Do you see now why we must take our time when we look for the right place in the right field?'

Ahmad Hussein spent five days teaching Abbas all of the things that had to be taken into account when placing the hives. Twenty-five judgements had to be made, he said, before the hives were set down in a field, and he not only told Abbas the twenty-five judgements, he wrote them down on paper when the two of them ate their lunch on the fifth day.

When Ahmad Hussein had finished his lunch, he said, 'Do you know, Abbas, something happened in this field when I was your age that I would like to tell you about. Will you listen?'

Abbas said, 'Of course, Sir.'

'I came to this field all those years ago looking for the beehives of another man. At that time, I knew nothing of bees but I knew I liked honey. So I came here and stole the honey, just enough to satisfy my desire. It was the third time I'd stolen honey from the hives. Does that surprise you?'

Abbas was blushing. He said, 'Surely you didn't do such a thing!'

'Oh, yes,' said Ahmad Hussein. 'I had the devil in me sometimes when I was a boy. I stole the honey. But because it was my third theft, someone was hiding in the grass and waiting for me, waiting for the honey thief. Before I knew it, a man had hold of my neck. A stick came down on my behind, once, twice, twenty times, and I screamed and struggled. They were hard blows! Very hard! Then the beating stopped and I stood crying and rubbing my behind – dear God, how much it hurt! The man who had beaten me with the stick – he was watching and laughing. He said, "What did you enjoy most? The honey or the beating? Or was one better than the other?"'

'Did you apologise for what you had done?' asked Abbas. He was shocked to hear that his teacher had stolen the honey. Such a thing would never have occurred to him.

'Did I apologise?' said Ahmad Hussein. 'No, Abbas. I picked up a stone and threw it at the man. It hit him on the arm. Then he chased me all over the field, this very field in which we're sitting, down that way and over there, by the trees. He caught me, of course – he was very fast, faster than me.'

'And he beat you again?' said Abbas.

'No, he didn't beat me again. He held me by my ear and laughed. Then he said, "Now you will work for me!" and he took me home to my father and told him that I must become his apprentice. And why? Because when I had stolen the honey, I had not angered the bees. This is a rare thing, to steal honey without making the bees angry. The beekeeper saw that I had something special to bring to the craft.'

Ahmad Hussein drank some water from his bottle and passed it to Abbas.

'The beekeeper who beat me that day, his name was Esmail Behishti. You knew him well.'

Abbas' eyes opened wide. 'My grandfather!'

'Yes. That famous man, your grandfather.'

Ahmad Hussein could see that Abbas was distressed. Perhaps it was hearing that the very man he was mourning had once been capable of beating boys with a stick. Or perhaps he was upset to hear that Ahmad Hussein had thrown a stone at his grandfather, even though it was so long ago. He left the boy alone with his thoughts for a few minutes, then he said, 'We'll put the hives here, in this place.'

Together, Ahmad Hussein and Abbas walked back to the far side of the field where the horse and cart had been left, and the hives.

That day and the next and for weeks and months, Ahmad Hussein taught Abbas how to find the right places for the beehives. He taught Abbas slowly. All of Ahmad Hussein's lessons were slow lessons. He taught Abbas to respect the bees. He said that the bees knew that they would be robbed of their honey, but they made it anyway. If a bee was a creature with a mean spirit, it would make no honey and starve itself to death to spite the beekeeper. Instead, the bee made enough honey for himself and his tribe and enough for Ahmad Hussein, too.

In those weeks and months of slow teaching, Ahmad Hussein taught Abbas to respect the bees. The boxes of blue and white were the factories of the bees, Ahmad Hussein said. Inside the boxes, each bee did his work, according to a plan devised by God. He said God made his plan for the bees a very long time ago, when He first saw the need in the world for bees. Each bee had a brain. Into this brain God put the plan for making honey. The

34

home of the bees at that time was not in white and blue boxes, but in hollow trees. To hold the honey, the bees made a *khani zambure* within the hollow trees. They made it from wax. Where the bees found the wax is a mystery. The *khani zambure* is made up of many small shelves, and on each shelf the honey is stored. It was the intention of the bees to eat the honey all through the year. But one morning many years ago, a man of great intelligence, a Hazara, discovered the factory of the bees in a hollow tree, and he tasted the honey. Because of his great intelligence, the first bee-keeper of the world built hundreds of boxes of white and blue where the bees could live in greater comfort than in a hollow tree. And the bees made honey for him and for his family.

Ahmad Hussein showed Abbas the *khani zambure*, the honey-combs, inside the boxes. They were like trays that could be lifted out. They dripped with the honey of the bees. But when the trays were taken from the boxes, the bees became angry, so it was necessary for Ahmad Hussein to wear a veil and gloves and to chase the bees from the boxes with a strange device that made smoke. Bees don't like smoke. It gets in their eyes just as it gets in the eyes of people and they fly away for a time.

The anger of the bees raised a question in Abbas' mind: 'But my grandfather saw that you had a gift for stealing honey. You didn't make the bees angry.'

'That was luck. Bees are always angry when we take their honey. But maybe it was a bit more than luck.'

Something was troubling Abbas, as Ahmad Hussein could plainly see.

'What is it?' he said. He was very patient.

At first, Abbas was reluctant to say more, but finally he spoke up. 'Sir, are we not stealing the honey of the bees? Are we not stealing their food?'

'Certainly we are stealing their food,' said Ahmad Hussein. 'It would be a lie to say we are not.' Then he added, 'I make the bees work for me. They are my slaves.'

Ahmad Hussein looked at Abbas sideways with a smile. He knew that the boy would be shocked to hear him say that the bees were his slaves. In the past, many Hazaras had been made slaves by powerful people in Afghanistan.

'And the sheep, too, are our slaves,' said Ahmad Hussein. 'And the goats. And the horse here that pulls our cart. But there is a difference, isn't there, Abbas?'

'Surely!' said Abbas. Then he said, 'Is there?'

'When a man is a slave, his heart breaks,' said Ahmad Hussein. 'That is the difference. The bees are angry, but their hearts are not broken.'

The trays from the hives were taken to a wonderful machine that Ahmad Hussein carried with him on his cart. Abbas was fascinated by all machines. He saw science in their workings, science and its laws. But the machine had to be set up carefully, and Ahmad Hussein made sure that Abbas understood each step. So painstaking was Ahmad Hussein that Abbas' excitement got the better of him and he began to hop from one foot to the other.

'Abbas, what is troubling you?' said Ahmad Hussein, though he knew well. 'Do you want to relieve your bladder?'

'I want to see the machine making honey.'

'If you want to see the machine making honey you must be

patient. Can't you see that the machine has to be put together with great care?'

'Yes, yes, I can see!'

'Do you think the machine puts itself together?'

'No, it doesn't put itself together!'

'Who puts the machine together?'

'Ahmad Hussein, you know the answer!' said Abbas. It was the first time he had addressed his teacher without saying, 'Sir.' 'It is you who puts the machine together!'

'Then how can I put the machine together if I am watching you wriggling in your trousers?'

The machine came in six parts. The biggest part was a pair of large steel wheels enclosed by a metal covering. Between the two rims of the wheels, inside the covering, slots had been made. The wheels stood on a welded frame and on this frame the wheel was made to spin very fast when a handle was turned. The handle was attached to a smaller wheel with teeth on it, called a cogwheel, and this smaller wheel combined with a wheel still smaller, called a pulley wheel. The cogwheel and the pulley wheel were joined by a belt of rubber. At the bottom of the wheel a drum had been fixed, and from the drum ran a length of rubber hose.

Ahmad Hussein slid the trays into the slots of the machine. It was possible to put ten trays inside at one time. When the machine was full of trays, Ahmad Hussein sealed it shut and turned the handle. At first he turned the handle slowly, then he turned it faster. The speed of the turning made the honey fly out of the trays and gather in a reservoir at the bottom. The honey then dripped through the rubber hose into big tin buckets. After a time, instead of dripping out of the rubber hose, the honey began to flow into the tin bucket.

For Abbas, this was the first truly happy day he had known since the death of his grandfather. His delight was written all over his face. Ahmad Hussein said, 'Do you see what has happened, Abbas? The bees go to the flowers and from the flowers comes the nectar, the *assal*. Inside the factory boxes of the bees, the nectar becomes honey. And now the honey flows into the bucket. Is this not a great wonder?'

On the journey back to the village that evening in the cart, Abbas carried in his lap a large metal tin of the honey made that day. In the tray of the cart behind, a further twenty tins of honey were packed into four wooden boxes. Ahmad Hussein said, 'Tomorrow I go north to the forest hives. The honey of the forest hives tastes different. Will you come? Will your father agree?'

'I think he will agree,' said Abbas.

'And you – will you agree?'

'I will certainly agree.'

'Is this a life you might choose, Abbas, the life of a *perwerrish dahenda*?'

'Gladly, Ahmad Hussein.'

'A slave driver – will your conscience permit it, Abbas?'

'It will.'

The country they passed over was all Hazara. They didn't have to fear being robbed, something that could happen in other parts of Afghanistan. As the horse picked out its path, Abbas sat in thought. Ahmad Hussein didn't make a sound for a half hour other than to murmur snatches of songs. But when he thought it was time to interrupt the boy's thoughts, he nudged him with his shoulder.

'Are your thoughts a pleasure to you?' asked Ahmad Hussein. 'Share them with me.'

Abbas remained silent for a minute more, then he said, 'Do you believe that bears can talk?'

'Can bears talk? A strange question! No, a bear cannot talk except to another bear.'

'Have you ever seen a snow leopard?' said Abbas.

'Yes,' said Ahmad Hussein. 'In the high mountains I saw a snow leopard. It carried a dead weasel in its jaws.'

'But a snow leopard can't sing, can it? It can't sing songs, as we can?'

'No, a snow leopard cannot sing.'

'Someone told me that snow leopards could sing,' said Abbas. 'And that bears could talk. I didn't believe him, but then I began to doubt my own doubts.'

Ahmad Hussein called to the horse, 'Hi, hi! Stay awake!' To Abbas he said, 'I was told the same stories.'

'Yes?' said Abbas.

'Yes,' said Ahmad Hussein. 'By the same storyteller.'

4

The Life of

Abdul Khaliq

The life of Abdul Khaliq, destined to end in pain and sorrow, began in the second decade of the twentieth century by the Western calendar. At that time, Afghanistan was ruled by Habibullah Khan, who was of the Barakzai dynasty and known as Emir, another name for 'chief'. Habibullah enjoyed the friendship of the British – a friendship that won him gifts from time to time, some of them personal, such as English revolvers, and some designed to flatter his intelligence, such as an edition of the works of Charles Dickens. Habibullah was in fact an intelligent man, an educated man, and amongst those who ruled Afghanistan and made life a great torment for the Hazara, he was not the worst. His father Abdur Rahman Khan, who ruled before him, was more savage, and his great-grandfather Dost Mohammad Khan had not a single friend in the Hazarajat, the homeland of the Hazara. The Barakzai family for generations believed that every mountain, every stone, every river, every fish and bird in Afghanistan belonged to the Barakzai, and that those who lived within Afghanistan's borders should honour the Barakzai above all other mortals. Sometimes two Barakzai each believed at the one time that Afghanistan belonged to him. In that event, one tried to kill the other. Dost Mohammad's sons, all three of them, fought for the throne after their father's death with the fury of baboons. His youngest son, Sher Ali, ruled first, since he had been his father's favourite; then the second son, Afzal, stole the throne from Sher Ali; later still, the first son, Azam, became Emir. The Barakzai never knew whom they could trust, but they knew who they could *never* trust: their brothers, their uncles, their sons, their cousins, or anyone at all related to them by blood. It was said of the Barakzai that their sleep was plagued by nightmares. When they awoke in the morning, their first act was to check that head and shoulders were still joined at the neck.

In the mountains of their homeland, the Hazara lived in hope of a ruler in Kabul or Kandahar who took no interest in them, who did not know a Hazara from a Turk, for whenever an emir turned his gaze towards the Hazara it meant bigger taxes, or the destruction of homes, or murder, or all three. When Dost Mohammad concerned himself with the Hazara, it was only to have his soldiers drive families out of Helmand and from the plains around Kandahar so that their land could be given as a gift to his followers. Those Hazara who could, journeyed north to Hazarajat and began life again. Most made the journey on foot, with the older children holding the hands of the smaller children and the mothers and fathers burdened by heavy loads. When these refugees arrived in Hazarajat, they were taken in without complaint by those who lived there. The sight of a family struggling along the road was a familiar one for any Hazara, not just in the time of Dost Mohammad but for centuries before. The rule was always this: if there is no room, find room, and then find more, for more Hazara will come.

Over the centuries of their life in Afghanistan, the Hazara made their homes not only in the mountains of Hazarajat but in other regions too. Yet Hazarajat remained our spiritual home, our stronghold and our sanctuary. Most of the stories of the Hazara mention the mountains and the snow, for in Hazarajat the snow lies on the ground for six months of the year. We speak with knowledge and pleasure of the fleece and hides of sheep and goats that we rely on for warmth in the coldest months. We celebrate the beauty of the moon when it stands above the mountain peaks, so much bigger than the moon of the plains and valleys. We hear the voice of the wind as it rushes down the slopes and howls between boulders and we can tell when the wind is warning of bad weather to come, and when it whispers of spring rain, or sunshine. The Hazara know the weather that is on its way before anyone else in Afghanistan.

When times are bad in Hazara settlements a long way from Hazarajat, the fathers and mothers of families will begin to debate in quiet voices the possibility of taking to the mountain road that leads to the homeland. And some will say, 'But is it our homeland? We have never lived there in the past, but in Helmand.' All the same, the desire to be secure amongst other Hazara will prevail and they will put their feet to the mountain road. Hazarajat is

42

all we have and it is precious in the same way that a golden ring that has been passed down through generations of a family is precious. You don't want to lose the golden ring. It has circled the fingers of your ancestors. It has been taken from the hand at death and placed on the hands of those who survive. If you were to lose the ring, you would search the ground for days, for weeks, cursing yourself for your carelessness.

Of all the Barakzai who ruled Afghanistan, the most ambitious was Abdur Rahman, the son of Afzal Khan and grandson of Dost Mohammad. The time would come when he would send his soldiers to murder Hazara in such numbers that in some villages, blood formed in pools like the puddles that lie in the gutters after a storm. No Hazara can hear the name of Abdur Rahman spoken without spitting on the ground and putting his hand over his eyes, but the Emir's daring is freely acknowledged. It is usually the father who drives his son's ambition, encouraging him to aim high. But with Afzal Khan and Abdur Rahman, it was the son who drove the father. He led the soldiers who seized Kabul in 1866, and led them again when they defeated the army of his uncle Emir Sher Ali at Sheikhabad later that year. Abdur Rahman put his father on the throne in Kabul, then roused his army with fine speeches and travelled with it south to Kandahar in the spring of the following year, where he slaughtered more of Sher Ali's soldiers. No doubt Abdur Rahman knew how to lead an army, but when it came to advising his father about the way in which to rule Afghanistan, his imagination went no further than murder. He was like many powerful men who seize a land by force: he used the same methods to rule that he employed to take power. Abdur Rahman was the Saddam Hussein of his age; either you fell to your knees to worship him, or your throat was cut. It took no more than a year or two for Abdur Rahman and his father to rouse the disgust of the Afghan people, and Sher Ali regained the throne in 1869 when the people demanded an end to tyranny. Abdur Rahman and his father Afzal Khan made their escape to Samarkand, in Uzbekistan, to plan their return to Kabul and Kandahar.

In Samarkand, the Russians controlled everything. Their great empire, ruled by their own Emir from the city of Moscow, strove to include Afghanistan in its dominions. In Hazarajat, the words 'Russia' and 'Russians' were always spoken with a shake of the head, the same as 'Britain' and 'Englishmen.' It was not that the Hazara feared the Russians or the Englishmen, only that the ambitions of these foreigners always unfolded in such a way that Hazara were left on the roadside with their belongings on their backs while smoke rose from their houses. It was a curious thing. The Hazara didn't fight in the armies that attacked the English over the ages, or in the armies that attacked the Russians, yet the demand for money to support these wars always started with higher taxes for the Hazara. If you didn't pay the taxes because you couldn't, your house was burnt to the ground and you yourself might have the bad luck to be hanged from a tripod in front of your sorrowing family.

Foreign soldiers found it impossible to subdue the soldiers of the Afghan armies. As it was in the past, so it is now. The Russians and the British, learning nothing from their past calamities, believed that a war lasting a year, at worst five years, would settle the issue of who would rule Afghanistan. When the foreigners won a battle and advanced fifty kilometres to set up their tents, they thought that one more such victory would give them Afghanistan. What they didn't understand, then as now, is that Afghans, whatever their tribe, Pashtun, Uzbeki, Tajik, Hazara, consider a single defeat a matter of no significance. For Afghans, a war of a hundred years is an easy thing to imagine. If your enemy wins a battle today and advances fifty kilometres, then he is that much further from his home, whereas the Afghan's homeland is all around him. Between the foreigners and their final victory lie thousands of mountains, and on each mountain thousands of rocks. Afghans know to whom the mountains and rocks are loyal; they know to whom the many caves will give shelter. It is to them. If the foreigners would only listen in the right way, their ears would hear the mountains and rocks whispering a warning: 'The ground is parched. Where your blood is spilt flowers will bloom.' The foreigners – their generals, at least – could not listen and would not be instructed. They persisted. They died.

But Afghan emirs sometimes saw more profit in befriending the foreigners than in cutting their throats. Abdur Rahman believed in profit above all things on earth and embraced the Russians with a full heart. His message was simple and direct: 'My uncle rules Afghanistan today. He is aged. I am young. In a few years' time, I will rule.' The Russians needed a friend on the throne of Afghanistan to frustrate the British and were prepared to provide Abdur Rahman with a villa in Tashkent, the great city of Russian Turkestan, together with servants and bodyguards and a bag of gold on the eve of Ramadan each year. The message of the Russians to Abdur Rahman was as simple and as direct as Abdur Rahman's message to the Russians: 'Wait'. Abdur Rahman was intelligent enough to see that it would require the death of his

uncle Sher Ali before he would have the opportunity to cross the
Oxus River on Afghanistan's northern border and seize the country. If he attacked too soon, the people would rally to Sher Ali,
who hadn't the same reputation for violence as his nephew. So he
waited there in Tashkent, learning patience by growing vines in
his garden. For sport, he rode his horses at the gallop over fences.
He occupied himself with games, too; he taught the Russians how
to win at backgammon, while from the Russians he learnt more
about the game of chess than he had known before. His other
great project called for the cooperation of Tashkent's tailors, who
used their craft to provide him with new ceremonial uniforms of
endless designs and colours, some modelled on those worn by European and Russian emirs. Abdur Rahman's vanity became a
treasure trove for tailors.

Abdur Rahman waited eleven years for the death of his uncle
– long enough for the vines he'd planted to bear harvests of fruit,
long enough for his mares to have foaled many times, long enough
for the Russians to start losing to him at chess. When the news of
Sher Ali's death came through, the Russians sent an invitation to
Abdur Rahman's villa in Tashkent. 'You are to attend the mansion of His Imperial Majesty's Governor-General for Turkestan
together with such members of your household as it pleases you to
present to His Excellency.' Abdur Rahman visited the mansion in
his ceremonial uniform of green silk with his sword at his side and
swore that he would be Russia's best friend in the world once he
crossed the Oxus and seized Afghanistan with his Russian car-
bines. But when he crossed the Oxus, he met with the British, who
had thousands of troops in Afghanistan at that time, and swore
that he would be Britain's best friend in the world if those troops

were withdrawn. Lepel Griffin, the British envoy in Kabul, arranged the deal in the British fashion of mixing good manners with treachery, and Abdur Rahman became Emir of Afghanistan in 1880.

In that year of 1880, Hazarajat was divided between those in the north who had supported Sher Ali as Emir, since he'd treated them with no more than average cruelty, a tyrant they could bear, and those in the south who remembered that the new ruler in Kabul, Abdur Rahman, was a man of great violence. The Sher Ali supporters feared that Abdur Rahman would take his revenge on them, and they argued that all Hazara should stand as one against the scourge to come. I wish I could say that every Hazara stood by his brother, but such was not the case. The southern Hazarajat came out in support of Abdur Rahman for the sake of survival, and the Emir limited his vengeance to the north.

And his vengeance was terrible. His years of exile in Tashkent had acted on his ambition like a whetstone on a knife's edge. He remembered the rebellion that had cost his father the throne and regretted that he had not acted sooner and killed those who had not honoured Afzal Khan. He had made a vow that on his return to Kabul, any man who opposed him would die. He meant those who had opposed him in the present, those who might oppose him in the future, and those who had opposed him in the past. He made a blunt offer to the Hazara of the north: 'Send your leaders to Kabul to kneel at my feet, or die.' No Afghan of any ethnic group will accept an ultimatum other than in the most desperate circumstances. To even make an ultimatum is insulting; usually, the order of words is so crafted that those who are being warned can save face. Abdur Rahman knew very well that his ultimatum would be rejected, as it was. His soldiers were already advancing on Hazarajat even as the offer was being discussed.

Massacres take many forms, not only in Afghanistan but elsewhere in the world. Sometimes people are rounded up in groups of fifty or so and shot all at once. Sometimes the massacres are carried out in smaller numbers, a family at a time, so that it is only after some weeks that a final tally reaches into the thousands. The number killed depends on the organisation of the killers. The more efficient the killers, the faster the murders, and the faster the murders, the greater the final tally. Abdur Rahman's soldiers were not as efficient as the German soldiers who murdered Jews in the 1940s, but they did their job to the satisfaction of the Emir. They went from house to house, forcing the younger men into the centre of the village, where they murdered them according to the preference of individual captains and generals. In some villages, most of those killed were put to the sword, either with a single wound to the upper chest delivered with a downward stroke so that the blade struck the heart from above, or by beheading. In other villages, scaffolds were set up with long crossbeams from which five or six men could be hanged at one time. If long beams were not available, men were hanged one at a time from tall tripods. Certain commanders chose to kill their captives with gunfire, shooting Hazara on their knees. Resistance of any sort was punished by torture, conducted in the open before the gaze of those whose own turn would follow. The more savage commanders killed every Hazara they encountered, regardless of sex and regardless of age.

Garrisons were left in many villages of the north. The soldiers of the garrisons punished at will. When outbreaks of resistance were too great for the garrisons to subdue, soldiers from Kabul and Kandahar came back, sometimes twice a year, and repeated the massacres of 1880 and 1881. A further punishment was heavy taxation. The Hazarajat is a place of beauty in some regions, well watered, with abundant spring grass. But it is not a land of great wealth. Hazara families lived there hand-to-mouth, able to survive for the day but never able to set aside provision very far into the future. The heavy taxation was a death sentence for thousands. Starvation and the outbreak of diseases that develop when nutrition is limited took lives more slowly than gunfire or the blow of a sword, but they took lives just as surely.

The Hazara of the south who had escaped the wrath of Abdur Rahman had deceived themselves of the Emir's intentions. His plan was to extend his control and tribute over the whole of Hazarajat. Those Hazara who had stood aloof from their suffering brothers repented of their error when harsh taxation and reprisals were enacted everywhere in Hazarajat. In secret meetings, the Hazara of the north and south agreed on rebellion. What choice did they have? The best of their traditional lands were being confiscated and handed over as gifts to the Emir's friends and supporters, whose allegiance he would count on in the years to come. The Hazara whose lands were left in their keeping today would likely lose them tomorrow. It is a bitter thing for any man to endure, to have the lands that he has inherited from his father taken from him and given to strangers. For these Hazara who had suffered the theft of their lands, death held no terrors. Without their lands and with their hearts torn apart, they were dead anyway.

The rebellion, which began in 1888, lasted for two years and ended in defeat. Whenever he could, the Emir took the opportunity to turn Hazara against Hazara. To one tribe he would say, 'Put aside your weapons and I will return your lands.' When the tribe accepted the offer, the Emir sent messengers to tell other tribes of the bargain, and in this way sowed the seeds of hatred. Also, Abdur Rahman was shrewd enough to use for his own purpose the great division within Islam of Sunni and Shi'a. The division is the most tragic of all differences that throw Muslim against Muslim. Like divisions within Christianity, it makes no sense when so much of the faith is shared and honoured by all. But the fact is that most Afghans are Sunni, while most Hazara are Shi'a. Abdur Rahman said to the minority of Hazara who are Sunni, 'Why should we fight in this way? We uphold the true faith. Your enemies are the Shi'a who persist in their blindness and arrogance.' In this way, with promises and flattery, he persuaded Hazara to spurn Hazara, and battles were lost, and the war was lost.

Yes, the war was lost but anger was as strong as ever. Many of the Sunni Hazara who had listened to the Emir's flattery were murdered at the war's end. The promises amounted to nothing. In 1890, no more than six months after the close of the first rebellion, the Hazara rebelled again. This second rebellion was not carefully planned; it was sparked by a sudden outpouring of rage brought on by a single act of infamy.

The Hazara had come to know in what contempt they were held by the soldiers of Abdur Rahman, but even in the midst of savagery, certain rules were observed. As a rule, Muslim soldiers avoid the abhorrent crime of rape. It is a deed that destroys the spirit of the women on whom it is enacted, and destroys also the souls of the men responsible. There is no justification for rape to be found in the scriptures of Islam, not under any circumstances;

indeed it has been reviled from the age of the Prophet through the centuries. When soldiers of one of the Emir's garrisons seized the wife of a Hazara chieftain in Hazarajat and violated her, the husband of the woman led his followers to the garrison's armoury and took possession of all the weapons inside. Now armed, the chieftain slew the soldiers who had so dishonoured his wife and rallied Hazara of neighbouring villages to his cause. Within weeks, almost the whole of Hazarajat had risen against the Emir.

It was the belief of the Hazara that the Emir had instructed his garrisons in Hazarajat to provoke rebellion, so that he might have an excuse to take control of the whole region. Such a claim is impossible to prove, but is it any wonder that it was accepted as fact in Hazarajat after what the people had endured under the reign of Abdur Rahman? To me, it seems likely that the Emir had a plan of provocation in mind, for his soldiers were prepared for invasion in so short a time after the outbreak of rebellion. The Emir had called for the help of the British to instruct his army in techniques of invasion well before the second rebellion, and that help was freely given. The Emir had also foreseen the benefit of having the invasion officially declared a Jihad against all the Shi'a by his council of imams. Amongst his followers, there were those who were unhappy – perhaps I should say, 'uncomfortable' – about the massacres of women and children in the earlier rebellion. I am sorry to say, for myself and for Afghanistan, that once Jihad is declared, misgivings are swept away, for the war becomes a conflict in defence of the faith itself. It is meaningful, too, that the Jihad was declared so soon after the commencement of the rebellion. It usually took some time before a council of imams would declare a Jihad. In the modern world, such a declaration can be negotiated swiftly under certain circumstances, but protocols were far stricter in 1890. It seems likely that Abdur Rahman had gained agreement for a Jihad much earlier than the violation of the Hazara chieftain's wife.

And think of this: the Emir raised an army of 150,000 foot soldiers, cavalry and well-armed militia inside a month and was ready to invade Hazarajat in the autumn of the year. It would have been no easy task to raise a large army in such a short time – three weeks – for a great many allegiances have to be negotiated with tribal leaders. Such a task can take a year, with many jealousies to be settled before the leader of one tribe will even enter a tent in which the leader of another tribe awaits. Whether the infamy was carried out under instruction from the Emir or not will never be known, as I have said. What is known is that the Emir's soldiers faced an enemy in Hazarajat weakened by the two-year-long rebellion. The outcome of the rebellion and invasion is also known. The Hazara were crushed, and the whole of Hazarajat was dominated by Abdur Rahman's soldiers.

The reprisals against the Hazara were horrifying, even by the standards of Abdur Rahman. It had been a custom amongst the more savage rulers of Afghanistan and its neighbours since the age of the Samarkand tyrant Tamburlaine the Great to show to all what fate awaits a defeated enemy. It was Tamburlaine's custom to build hills of his enemies' heads. Abdur Rahman had chosen Tamburlaine as his hero amongst rulers. His most precious possessions were certain relics of the Samarkand tyrant that he had obtained over the years, sometimes through purchase, sometimes by stealth. Amongst these relics – a sword, a tooth, a horse's bridle – the most valued was a single long hair, said to have come from

Tamburlaine's beard. There seems no doubt that Abdur Rahman had taken to heart Tamburlaine's motto: an enemy once is an enemy forever.

After the first Hazara rebellion, beheading of captives was a common form of execution, but not the rule, for it takes much longer and requires much greater effort to behead a hundred captives than to shoot them. After the second rebellion, Abdur Rahman ordered that all captives should be beheaded, and their heads gathered in mounds standing twice the height of the tallest of the defeated enemy. Even those who had died of wounds in battle were beheaded. Hazara who were not forced to their knees to be executed were forced to their knees by the poverty and starvation that followed the reprisals. By the onset of the winter of 1892, Hazarajat was a land of mourning and despair.

And yet, early the following year, when the snows had begun to thaw, the Hazara rose again. People reduced to such misery as the Hazara have nothing to lose; death itself is preferred to humiliation. In this third rebellion, the Hazara surprised Abdur Rahman's soldiers. It was thought impossible for these defeated people to find the will to risk even further reprisals. However, in the battles that followed, the Hazara reclaimed the whole of their homeland, only to fall victim to starvation. For years, almost no provision could be made for the winter; men who would normally till the fields and guard the sheep and goats in the pastures were fighting for their survival. Weakened to the point of collapse after their victory, the Hazara were easily overrun in the counter-attacks of Abdur Rahman's army. Ultimately victorious, though shocked at the fierce resistance of the Hazara, Abdur Rahman ordered more mass executions, more public torture. But he went further, and caused the greater part of the Hazarajat population to be forced from their homeland and resettled in stony places far away. At this time, many thousands of Hazara fled to Iran, to India, to Uzbekistan, or to the far north of Afghanistan where the soldiers of the Emir were fewer.

Abdur Rahman, by God's grace, did not live forever. In 1901, his son Habibullah succeeded him on the throne. I have said that Habibullah was not the worst of the Barakzai family, and that is true. He attempted to make peace with those Hazara who remained in Afghanistan. It was his desire to be remembered as the man who built the modern nation of Afghanistan, not as a formidable warrior like his father. He granted an amnesty to any Hazara who might wish to return from his land of exile. And a number did return, perhaps with dread still in their hearts. But the legacy of the years of murder was a solemn determination of the Hazara to one day live in freedom.

In Afghanistan, memories are not made of air and light and colour; memories are made of iron and stone. A wrong committed by one man against another will stand like a statue in the wronged man's mind forever. Forgiveness is not a common virtue in my native land, no matter which tribe's blood pulses through your heart. One man may consider an insult endured by his ancestors five hundred years ago to be as fresh as a callous word spoken yesterday. The Hazara who had remained in Afghanistan and those who returned could not forget how many of their friends, how many family members had been murdered by Abdur Rahman. It was not possible. If I am a child and I put my hand in the fire, the burning and the pain will stay in my mind forever. Hazara children grew up in fear of Abdur Rahman's soldiers. Abdur Rahman was the fire that they could not forget. The son of Abdur Rahman said, 'Return! All is forgiven!' but for the Hazara, forgiveness was something that only the Hazara could grant, if they wished. To be forgiven by the son of the man who had made towers of the heads of our people? No.

The great massacres became part of who we are – we, the Hazara. I say 'part of who we are' rather than 'part of our history' because history is a thing apart; something that you can study, if you wish, and write books about. The massacres are not 'history' in that sense; they have a place in our minds and our hearts from which they can't be torn. But don't imagine that it is something we wish to have living inside us. No, it is a burden. It is like the burden of the Jews. They cannot stop being Jews – they are Jews every second of their lives, and being a Jew means carrying a burden of grief, because the Jews too had an Abdur Rahman in their past.

The reign of Habibullah the son of Abdur Rahman was not a reign of murders – no more so than the reign of any king in my part of the world. He tried to do some good, Habibullah. He didn't say, 'The Hazara poison my land, let me be rid of them.' He didn't say to his captains, 'Take a thousand soldiers and bring me back ten thousand Hazara heads,' as his father did. He had studied politics. He had studied democracy. He believed that a king has to embrace everyone in his kingdom, some more warmly than others, of course. But by murdering Hazara in such numbers, and in doing so forcing them to defend themselves, his father had succeeded in making the Hazara a people held in greater disdain than ever by more powerful tribes. Habibullah himself may have wished to bring peace to his country, but the people who kept him in power found a hundred ways to make the Hazara suffer. With their traditional lands confiscated, Hazaras were forced to look for employment in towns and cities. They were offered only the most menial of jobs and paid very little. If you needed someone to dig a ditch for you, clean your house, tend your animals, dig a well, carry water to your fields – you hired a Hazara. Living on next-to-nothing gives people a certain appearance. They look badly fed, their clothes are ragged, their eyes are dull with tiredness. And because they look tired and ragged and underfed, they are thought of as beggars, and held in contempt. A Hazara with twenty sheep is thought to have ten sheep too many for a beggar, and the ten too many are taken from him. A Hazara with money is thought to have stolen it, and so it is no crime to take the money from him.

By a process that began with mass murder, the Hazara became an underclass, the poorest people in Afghanistan, and it was thought to be their own fault. When a man has his boot on your neck, he doesn't wish to think that he is being cruel, that he is betraying God with his cruelty; no, he wishes to think that the man on whose neck his boot rests is not truly a human being, and does not have the feelings of human beings.

Habibullah Khan, as I have said, ruled Afghanistan at the time of Abdul Khaliq's birth, but he did not outlive Abdul Khaliq. No, he was murdered by close friends in the year 1919, or by people who were close friends up until the time they murdered him. He was on a hunting trip without knowing that he was the one being hunted. He had no time to be surprised because the bullets that killed him ended his life in an instant. His brother, Nasrullah, put himself on the throne of his dead brother very speedily, but lasted only a week. Habibullah's son Amanullah, who commanded the army, threw his uncle into prison and had himself named Emir. What was said of the Barakzai in Afghanistan at that time was the undeniable truth: those to whom you are related by blood *want* blood.

Amanullah was even more determined than his father Habibullah had been to turn Afghanistan into a nation that he would not be ashamed to invite his European friends to visit. Early in his reign, however, he decided to sacrifice Afghanistan's friendship with the British, judging that he could replace potential British visitors with those from Russia and France and Germany. He attacked the British in northern India with great success and made Afghanistan almost free of foreign control. This was a popular thing to do, for after killing Hazara, Amanullah's supporters most enjoyed killing Englishmen. Amanullah went about Kabul in a motor car, stopping to wave to the people who cheered him. 'We have much to do!' he said, and the people replied, 'Truly, Emir!' 'Afghanistan must become the jewel of Central Asia!' he said. The people replied, 'Truly, Emir, a jewel!'

But the Emir and the people had different ideas about the ways in which Afghanistan would be fashioned into a jewel. The people thought Amanullah was going to have more wells dug in the villages, and build a new palace of great splendour, perhaps have his engineers make a deep drain that would carry away the sewage of the city. Instead, Amanullah changed a law that compelled women all over Afghanistan to dress in accordance with the protocols of the strictest Saudis of Mecca. 'A woman may wear at any time what the women of Paris wear,' he said. Amanullah had been to Paris with his wife, Soraya Tarzi, and it was there that Soraya discovered a preference for Western garments.

'Schools will be built that both boys and girls can attend,' Amanullah said, for Soraya Tarzi had convinced him that it was only right that girls should be educated in the modern country he wished to create.

'A man may live in Afghanistan as a Christian if he so wishes, or as a Jew, or as an atheist,' Amanullah said, and he put it into the Constitution.

'And Afghanistan must fight its battles with modern weapons,' he said, and displayed a number of aeroplanes donated to Afghanistan by the Russians. The pilots of the aeroplanes were also Russians, but the day will come, said Amanullah, when Afghans will fly such machines.

'And there will be many motor cars,' he said. 'Also many libraries with books from every country in the world. What do you say to that?'

The people said no. The people had never been to Paris and what they knew of the way Western women dressed shocked them. The people believed that schools were all well and good, but sending girls to school would lead to disaster because God had not intended that girls should go to school. The people thought that any Christians or Jews who wished to live in Afghanistan should think again, and that atheists should be hanged for their own good. The people thought that libraries were madness. As for the Russian aeroplanes – okay, keep them.

The people rebelled – or many of them, not all. The Hazara had always educated their daughters and thought that people foolish enough to sit in a library all day reading books would be doing little harm. Others were a little suspicious of modernisation, but not frightened of it. But the frightened people came to Kabul in big crowds and demanded that Amanullah dress his wife in the traditional Afghan way and stop taking holidays in the strange lands of the infidels. Amanullah said that he would take all the holidays he liked, and he did, but the army deserted him and he was forced to take a holiday in Switzerland with Soraya Tarzi and his children that lasted for the rest of his life.

Amanullah's brother Inayatullah became king when Amanullah departed. It was a short reign of six days. Inayatullah spent all of the six days in fear and trembling, thinking that a rival, Habibullah Kalakani, would replace him. Inayatullah had good cause to be afraid because Habibullah Kalakani did indeed make himself king, although without murdering anyone of great importance. He spent nine months as king, fearing that each day might be his last. He especially feared Nadir Khan, a very powerful man, a descendent of Dost Mohammad, who had achieved great honour as a general. Like many powerful men in Afghanistan before him, Nadir Khan had been forced to make a choice between befriending the Russians and befriending the British. He chose the British, partly because he spoke very good English and no Russian at all. The British, who had learned to think like Afghans after years of fighting them one year and feasting them the next, arranged for Nadir Khan to win a series of battles against them in the south of Afghanistan. The agreement was that they, the British, would help Nadir Khan build a wonderful reputation as a hero of the battlefield, and then would help him become king. Once he was king, he would throw open his arms and embrace the

British. Down in the south, the British kept soldiers in forts all along the frontier with India. When Nadir mounted his horse and raised his sword as a signal to attack, the British abandoned the forts, and the legend of Nadir the Terror of Englishmen was born.

And it was the British who suggested to Nadir in October 1929 that it was time for Kalakani, who was not so friendly to the British, to go on a long holiday like the long holiday of Amanullah. On 16 October 1929, Nadir asked Kalakani for an audience at the palace in Kabul. Nadir looked happy and relaxed as he spoke with the King. He was wearing his smartest uniform and new round-lens spectacles manufactured in London. He told the King that in the near future, another man would sit on the throne of Afghanistan, and that the new king would be Mohammad Nadir. The King asked if 'the near future' meant months or years. Nadir said, 'Tomorrow.'

As good as his word, Mohammad Nadir seized the throne on 17 October. He did not know it at the time, but his reign would last only four years. He had no idea that a fifteen-year-old boy living no more than a few kilometres from the Kabul Palace would shoot him through the heart on 8 November 1933. And the boy who would shoot Mohammad Nadir through the heart did not know that he was destined to kill a king, either.

Abdul Khaliq was the eldest son of a Hazara family of Kabul. In his upbringing, there was nothing immediately obvious that would explain the mission he was to set for himself. His family was not as poor as most other Hazara families. His father Khuda Khaliq was a merchant and had not fought against Abdur Rahman's soldiers. His mother was said to have a beautiful voice for singing. His uncles, who in time to come would spend a day at prayer in a prison cell while a scaffold for their execution was constructed, were not much involved in politics. Abdul Khaliq himself was a quiet, respectful child, attentive to his school studies.

After the King's assassination, Mohammad Nadir's generals would claim that Abdul Khaliq had acted under instructions from certain illustrious enemies of the Barakzai family; that he was a paid killer. But this seems unlikely. Mohammad Nadir's enemies did not attempt to seize the throne after the assassination, and indeed, Mohammad Nadir's son, Mohammad Zahir, succeeded him without any dispute or delay. No, the assassination was the work of a boy who had never marched in the streets of Kabul on behalf of his people; a boy who had never spoken to anyone about his politics; a boy who had never taken up arms against the King's soldiers. It seems much more likely that Abdul Khaliq decided to kill the King to avenge the murder of hundreds of thousands of Hazara years earlier.

When I read the documents that tell us about the life and death of Abdul Khaliq, I imagine a boy who likes to daydream. That is how his friends think of him – as a dreamy young fellow, good-natured, harmless. But he carries a terrible pain in his heart, as do all Hazara boys of his age. He has heard the stories of Hazara chased through the streets of their villages, captured, flung against a wall and shot. They are told in every Hazara household – how could he not have heard them? He is a boy who cannot believe that such injustice, such savagery, can go unpunished. He doesn't talk about it very much, but it dwells inside him, the great injustice, and one day his daydreams and the pain he carries merge together and he imagines something he has never imagined before. 'Surely my people are waiting for a hero. Surely the pain the Hazara suffer will be relieved if a blow is struck for our freedom.' He tells no one. It isn't difficult for him to keep quiet, because he is always quiet. His mother says to him, 'Abdul, what is going on in your head? You look like a sage, like a wise man, when you are no more than a boy. You worry me, Abdul.' Abdul Khaliq makes no reply, but at least he smiles and the smile is what his mother was hoping for.

His plan is not formed. It isn't even a plan. It is just a dream. What sort of blow might he strike? He doesn't know. But the possibilities are few in number. He might kill himself in a public place as a demonstration of the agony that his people live with. But to kill himself without shedding a drop of his enemies' blood seems without purpose. He could kill one of the generals who murdered Hazaras, but generals are always surrounded by soldiers. He could kill one of the King's family, so that the King would know what it felt like to lose someone he loved – one of his sons, one of his daughters.

Or he could kill the King himself. The idea is so shocking that Abdul Khaliq draws in his breath and releases it slowly. He is amazed at his own boldness, and yet before enough time has passed for him to think of what might follow the assassination of the King, to reconsider, he has accepted that this will become his mission in life: to murder Mohammad Nadir. But it is not Mohammad Nadir he will be killing; it is a symbol of the oppression that the Barakzai family has subjected the Hazara to for fifty years.

Of course, he too will die; he, Abdul Khaliq will die. He accepts his destiny in the same dreamy way that he accepts the death of the King. He will be shot down by the King's soldiers within seconds of the assassination.

In our time, suicide missions are in the news every day. A young man, occasionally a young woman, is fitted with a vest of explosives, makes a journey to a certain target, then counts down the last two minutes, the last twenty seconds of his life, of her life. It is thought by some that these young men and women have been comforted by the belief that an eternity of bliss awaits them; that the gates of Heaven will be opened wide to admit them, and that rose petals will be strewn by angels along the path leading them to a throne of glory. But the prospect of being welcomed to Paradise is not the true solace of those who accept suicide missions. Their first comfort is that they will have stood up to injustice. Then the young men and young women think of those who will be left behind; of their families, provided for by those who have encouraged them to strap on a vest of explosives; they think of a better life for their brothers and sisters, who will be given a full education; they think of their grandparents, who will be offered an electric fan to cool them in the summer months, and an armchair, a television set, a new set of dentures, medical treatment for hypertension, a good pair of spectacles, a flushing toilet.

Perhaps their fathers and mothers will be comforted in their grief not by electric fans and dentures and armchairs, but by the praise they will hear all over their neighbourhoods for the sacrifice that has been made; for the blow that has been struck against a callous enemy. A suicide mission is a bargain struck between the young man who accepts his premature death, and his community. It is not a bargain with Heaven, although Heaven plays its part.

Abdul Khaliq's plan is not a suicide mission, in the way that we have come to understand such missions. He has chosen only one man as his victim, not some dozens of people in the midst of a crowd. He has not been granted a licence to murder by a mullah. This is simply an argument between Abdul Khaliq and a man whose family have for decades murdered Hazaras in their villages. Nor will Abdul Khaliq's family be rewarded in the way that the families of modern suicide bombers are sometimes rewarded. Just the opposite. A number of them will be hanged. Others will be thrown into prison for the remainder of their lives.

Abdul Khaliq cannot afford to think about the fate of his family. It has been announced that Mohammad Nadir will visit his school on 8 November 1933. The King will shake the hands of students who are graduating; students who might have a further opportunity to enter Kabul's university and study to become historians, doctors, lawyers. Abdul Khaliq is himself a graduate of the school. He will have the opportunity to shake the hand of the King. But he is not thinking of the honour of meeting the King. Certainly he is not thinking of a career in teaching, or medicine, or law. He is thinking of guns; of where he can acquire one; of how he can conceal it on the day of the graduation ceremony. He is thinking in a very practical way of the right part of the King to aim for. The face? No, the face is not a big enough target, and he has heard of people shot in the face who survived, although without a nose or a chin. The heart would be a better target. No one can survive a bullet through the heart. Or will the King be wearing all of his medals and decorations? Can a bullet pass through the medals, which would probably cover the whole left side of his tunic? Abdul Khaliq has to consider this problem and others over the few days remaining until 8 November.

Acquiring a handgun is not such a big problem. Guns are everywhere in Kabul. Many ordinary Afghans, then and today, are more expert in the use of firearms than soldiers in well-equipped armies. Making good use of a weapon of any sort has a long tradition in a warrior state like Afghanistan. Every Afghan, of every ethnic group, can name a dozen great warriors who honoured their people in battle. It is not the great victories of these heroes that are honoured, but their bravery. A victory might be a matter of luck, or of careful planning, or of superior numbers. But bravery has nothing to do with luck and planning and everything to do with the iron in a man's soul. It is iron that Afghans honour.

Abdul Khaliq has a friend who has a friend who knows a man with a gun, a pistol. Abdul Khaliq asks his friend to speak to the friend who knows the man with the pistol. When he is asked why he needs a pistol, he says, 'A thief may come to the house.' The friend does not believe that Abdul Khaliq needs a pistol to defend the home of his family from thieves, but he says, 'So be it,' and within a few days, he provides the pistol and a number of bullets. Abdul Khaliq hides the gun and bullets from his family, but when he finds the chance, he unwraps the pistol from the oiled cloth in which he keeps it and holds it in his hand, feeling its weight, studying its mechanism. He already knows how he will conceal the pistol when he joins the assembly of students who will meet the King. He will sew a pocket on the inside of the right-hand sleeve of his coat and the pistol will sit in this pocket securely. He is left-handed, so when the King is close, greeting the student next to him, Abdul Khaliq will retrieve the pistol from his right sleeve with his left hand and be ready to fire in an instant.

He hasn't thought of his reasons for assassinating Mohammad Nadir Shah for more than a week now. He doesn't dwell day and night on the suffering of the Hazara. He doesn't even think, 'This is a blow for freedom.' His plan is now his destiny and all feelings of hatred and enmity have vanished. There is only the deed. He will shoot the King. The pocket has been sewn into his coat. He has rehearsed the moment at which he retrieves the pistol from his right sleeve with his left hand a hundred times. He has checked the pistol's mechanism again and again. He has tested his aim. He has told himself over and over, 'Aim for the heart.' He is already dead. All that remains of Abdul Khaliq the student, the son, the brother is the power to aim a pistol and pull the trigger. He is already dead, but he is content. His dreamy smile is not a disguise hiding fear and anxiety. His dreamy smile hides nothing at all. It is almost as if the deed would be enacted all by itself even if he fell asleep before the King's visit and did not wake up until the day after. In his sleep, he would find his way to the assembly. In his sleep he would take the pistol from his right sleeve with his left hand and fire at the King's heart. The deed will be done, asleep or awake. Nothing can stop it.

On the day of the assembly, Abdul Khaliq in his coat with the secret pocket is waiting in line to be greeted by Mohammad Nadir Shah. Everything is as he'd imagined. His classmates look shy, all of them dressed in the best clothes their families can provide. The school principal, Mulavi Mohammad Ayayub, stands proudly before the assembled students, ready to bow to the King. Three of

Abdul Khaliq's teachers stand together behind Mulavi Moham-mad Ayayub, ranked in seniority from right to left.

In three weeks' time, the school principal and the three teach-ers behind him will be hanged in exactly the same order in which they now stand. But on this day, they are not to know that. Nei-ther the school principal nor any of Abdul Khaliq's teachers har-bour any designs against the life of the King, although in the interrogations that precede their hanging each will confess, after torment, that Abdul Khaliq told them that he intended to shoot the King.

Since nobody on earth knows that Abdul Khaliq is carrying a loaded pistol in a secret pocket, the young man might, if he wished, change his mind about the whole scheme and return to his family after being greeted by the King. It is a possibility. The King is greeting a student at the start of the line in which Abdul Khaliq waits. There is time to reconsider. Even when the King is about to speak to the student next to Abdul Khaliq, there is time. But Abdul Khaliq has now reached for the loaded pistol in the secret pocket, and a second later, he has fired it twice. 'Aim for the heart,' is the refrain in his head as he fires, and his aim is good. The King is dead before he has the chance to utter the words to the student on Abdul Khaliq's right, 'God grant you success with your studies.'

And so it is done. No power on earth can restore life to the King. No power on earth can save Abdul Khaliq from the torment that awaits him. The teachers and the school principal watch on in horror as Abdul Khaliq is seized by the King's soldiers and held by his arms – their lives are over. The bodyguards and ministers who carry the King's bleeding body from the courtyard are already dreading what blame may be attached to them merely for being present at this calamity. The students have retreated into a huddle, kept from leaving the courtyard by the dead King's soldiers – many of them fear that when the great axe falls, it will fall on them.

5

The Death of

Abdul Khaliq

Abdul Khaliq is a prisoner in a cell guarded by six soldiers of the new King Mohammad Zahir Shah, the son of the dead King. The prisoner is dressed in the special uniform of those detained in Kabul Prison – loose grey trousers and a black-and-white striped vest. The special uniform is the innovation of the late King, who thought the prisoners in Afghan jails should wear similar identifying garments to those worn by prisoners in British jails. For the first few days of his imprisonment, Abdul Khaliq endures beatings and interrogation. High-ranking officers of the new King's army take turns screaming at him, as if the louder the screams, the more evident their loyalty to the new King will seem. But with the passing of a few more days, it becomes clear that Abdul Khaliq was not the chosen assassin of an army of Hazara rebels. He says as much himself. The officers shriek at him, 'Carrion! Who is your master?' and Abdul Khaliq answers, 'I have no master but God.'

'And who gave you this weapon, carrion?'

'I paid for it with my own money,' says Abdul Khaliq.

The officers don't know whether to believe him or not. He seems too dreamy to be part of a clever plot. But at the same time, it is almost impossible for the officers to accept that a boy such as Abdul Khaliq could be responsible for the death of a king. It seems contrary to the law of Heaven. What? A foolish boy such as this end the life of the mighty Mohammad Nadir Shah? And yet, better that he should be a fool than a genius.

The new King's generals and ministers consult with the mullahs. The fate of the assassin will be death, of course, but by what method? He should die in a way equal in horror to the horror of his deed. And so a plan is devised.

Abdul Khaliq's classmates and teachers have been interrogated, too, including the school principal. And every member of Abdul Khaliq's family. Would this fool of a boy have dreamed up this deed without the influence of others? That would be unbelievable. His teachers and the school principal himself would have made suggestions. Perhaps they said, 'The King is just a mortal man,' or, 'Other kings have died while still on the throne; this King may go the same way.' They may have said, 'The Hazara have suffered for many decades under the rule of the Barakzai.' Perhaps someone whispered to Abdul Khaliq, 'What glory awaits the man who ends the life of this King!' It is suggested to the tormentors who serve in the prison that it would be best if those close to the prisoner – family, friends, teachers – confessed to having said such things. Such is the skill of the tormentors that a confession is signed by each of the suspects.

A mullah and a minister of the government visit Abdul Khaliq in his prison cell to inform him that the King's court, made up of experts in the laws of Afghanistan, have found him guilty of murder. They then describe the punishment he will endure. At this moment, Abdul Khaliq ceases to be a boy in chains seated on a wooden bench in a prison cell and becomes the embodiment of the Hazara people. He hears barely a word said to him. He sits with his head bowed in his striped prison shirt, his hands manacled, heavy chains looped over his shoulders, a metal collar around his neck. When he killed Mohammad Nadir Shah, he was killing a symbol. Now he himself has become a symbol. He is the Hazara of the ages, abused, attacked, imprisoned in chains, without any rights in his own country. He is the Hazara who fought back, and when he suffers on the scaffold, he will be the Hazara whose punishment for resisting is as shocking as his tormentors can devise.

A scaffold has been built in the Old City area of Kabul, known as Dehmazang. Notices have been posted around the capital stating the date and time that the king-killer, Abdul Khaliq, and his accomplices will face the wrath of the people. The notices emphasise that it is 'the people' who demand justice in this dreadful matter, not the new King, not his government. No mention is made of a death sentence, but everybody knows that a scaffold and gallows have not been erected just for show.

A great crowd has gathered in Dehmazang. Onlookers hem in the small square in which the scaffold stands, packed shoulder to shoulder. Many people have taken up positions on the tops of walls and on rooftops. Others fill windows in buildings that over-look the square. The onlookers do not include women; it is forbid-den for women to attend a public execution. Children are strongly discouraged from attending such events, but a number do, al-though none of them are girls. A small number of Europeans and Russians and Englishmen can be distinguished here and there. And many Hazaras.

Small glasses of tea are being sold by merchants moving with difficulty through the crowd. Storytellers are also taking advan-tage of the gathering, offering for a small fee to give an account of the life of the king-killer Abdul Khaliq and the role played in the murder of Nadir Shah by Abdul Khaliq's teachers and school-mates and relatives. The storytellers tell of the terrible remorse of those who are about to die on the scaffold, such 'scaffold repen-tance' stories being traditional at a public execution in Kabul. They are completely fictitious, and the public knows that they are fictitious, but a well-written repentance speech is appreciated all the same.

The scaffold is furnished with a long timber spar supported by two uprights. Three nooses are attached to the spar.

At the announced time, a call issues from the mosque, a chant that carries all over Dehmazang. The call has nothing to do with the execution; it only offers praise to God. But this call, at this time, is accepted as a signal by those present, other than the Ha-zaras, that the events about to unfold are sanctioned by Heaven.

From the gate of Kabul Prison comes a procession of soldiers and prisoners, led by a mullah in brown robes and a black turban. Behind the mullah comes the judge, dressed in black robes and a white turban. The judge is much smaller in stature than the mullah, and in fact has a lower status. Some of the soldiers carry firearms, others carry spears and swords. All of the prisoners are in chains, but no prisoner is as heavily shackled as the small figure at the rear of the procession, surrounded by six guards.

A thrill goes through the crowd. This is the king-killer, this boy, so small? Is it possible? Those at ground level push forward to see the king-killer up close, but the guards threaten them with their weapons, forcing them back. The boy himself, Abdul Khaliq, looks only at the ground, his face blank.

The platform of the scaffold is not high – only three steps up from the flagstones of the square. Already waiting on the platform are the officers of the King who have been awarded the honour of putting the king-killer to death – a shared honour.

Two other men stand waiting on the scaffold, both of them powerfully built. They are the hangmen.

A great roar erupts from the crowd as the king-killer is led up the three steps to the platform of the scaffold. Some of the cries from the crowd are curses, but many people call out humane encouragement to the king-killer.

'Have courage, poor creature!'

'Bear your death with dignity!'

The king-killer says nothing at all. The Hazaras in the crowd whisper their prayers and exhortations quietly.

The mullah, who has also mounted the scaffold accompanied by the judge, has in his hands a scroll, which he now unrolls. He steps to the front of the platform and raises his hand to quieten the crowd. When he is satisfied that the hush is reverent enough, he hands the scroll to the judge. The judge reads from his document in a high-pitched voice that disappoints many in the crowd.

The occasion calls for a deep, booming delivery. What the judge has to say is lengthy, and he reads slowly. He begins by telling the crowd that everything he reads is by order of the King, Mohammad Zahir. The King, he says, has suffered the great sorrow of losing his father, and in this period of mourning, has judged it unfitting for himself to attend the punishment of those who brought him such sorrow.

A murmur of approval issues from the crowd. It would be thought barbarous for the King to attend executions carried out in his name. It would suggest a relish of vengeance, unworthy of a monarch.

The judge now names the crime committed, the murder of Mohammad Nadir Shah, who was King by the will of God. The crime of murder against Mohammad Nadir Shah is therefore a crime against Heaven. The judge names the place at which the murder occurred, the date and hour and minute of the murder, the manner of killing, and finally, the name of the murderer himself, Abdul Khaliq of this city, who has confessed to the deed. Then the judge names the accomplices of the murderer, one by one, and the sentence passed on each. The sentence passed on Abdul Khaliq himself is simply 'Death before the people.'

When the judge lowers his scroll, he nods towards the mullah, who in turn nods towards a man with an apparatus new to some in the crowd. The apparatus is a camera, and the camera operator is in attendance to preserve an image of the king-killer in the hands of those who will put him to death – a souvenir. Abdul Khaliq is nudged by the soldiers until he takes up a position before his executioners. The camera operator in his European suit and tie adjusts his apparatus, fixed on a tripod, then calls for the king-killer to look at him directly. For the first time since his appearance before the crowd, Abdul Khaliq raises his eyes and looks straight ahead. Perhaps he is curious, or perhaps his cooperation is just one more instance of the symbolic part he is playing in the drama, permitting the onlookers one clear view of the face that stands for the face of all Hazaras.

A bright flash fixes the image of Abdul Khaliq within the apparatus.

The camera operator gathers his camera and leaves the scaffold. He will not be permitted to photograph the executions themselves, since even men who have committed great evil should be permitted to die with dignity.

The mullah has taken over from the judge, as is proper. It is the role of the judge to read sentences but not to involve himself in the carrying out of those sentences. The change suits the crowd, for the mullah's voice is deep and commanding. The squeaky voice of the judge doesn't carry the ring of authority so important when announcing the judgements of Heaven.

The mullah calls the name of Khuda Khaliq, Abdul Khaliq's father. Khuda Khaliq, nudged by a soldier, mounts with difficulty the three steps to the scaffold; his ankles are shackled and his hands lashed behind his back. He is dressed in loose trousers and a long grey shirt, as are all of the condemned men and boys, with the exception, of course, of Abdul Khaliq. Perhaps there were not enough new striped shirts to go around, or perhaps Abdul Khaliq's shirt is intended to distinguish him as the guiltiest of the guilty, the chief monster amongst lesser monsters.

Abdul Khaliq's father – not an old man by any means – does not look at his son as he shuffles past him on the scaffold. In any case, Abdul Khaliq in his heavy chains is staring fixedly at his own feet. The two soldiers guarding Khuda Khaliq hand him into the keeping of the two powerfully built hangmen.

Abdul Khaliq himself is compelled to take up a position at the fore of the platform. He shuffles there with even more difficulty than his father displayed mounting the steps. When Abdul Khaliq is in the position stipulated, one of the hangmen wraps his arms around Khuda Khaliq from behind and lifts his feet from the ground. The second hangman mounts a wooden box sitting directly below one of the dangling nooses. He slips the noose over the head of Khuda Khaliq, then manipulates the rope so that it fits firmly around the condemned man's neck. The second hangman steps down from the wooden box and pushes it aside. The first hangman releases his grip on Khuda Khaliq.

Abdul Khaliq is called on to raise his eyes and to watch the death struggle of his father. It is the mullah who makes the demand. But Abdul Khaliq refuses to watch. His gaze is fixed downward. One of the four soldiers guarding Abdul Khaliq prods him in the small of the back with the point of his spear. Abdul Khaliq keeps his eyes on his feet. The soldier prods him again. Abdul Khaliq jerks forward, but doesn't lift his gaze. Some in the crowd shout instructions to the soldiers, telling them to hold Abdul Khaliq's head upright by force. Others cry out in support of the boy, 'Leave him be! Leave him be!' All cries cease after a further minute. The body of Khuda Khaliq has ceased moving. There can be no doubt that he is now dead, or so close to death that it doesn't matter. It is only courteous to allow Khuda Khaliq's spirit to leave his body in silence.

The first hangman lifts the weight of Khuda Khaliq's body while the second hangman loosens the noose. The body is lowered to the floor of the scaffold and laid at the feet of Abdul Khaliq so that he cannot fail to see it. The mullah crouches and touches the forehead of the dead man in the sacrament of departure, rarely denied to the dead, even to alleged accomplices of a king-killer.

The body of Khuda Khaliq is then laid at the front of the platform.

Qurban Ali, Abdul Khaliq's uncle, is hanged next. Abdul Khaliq is again called on to watch, again refuses and is again prodded with the point of the soldier's spear, this time in the back of the neck.

Qurban Ali's body is laid beside that of Khuda Khaliq.

A second uncle is hanged. Then Abdul Khaliq's friend from school, Mehmood Jan, is hanged. Then three members of the council that governs Kabul are hanged, for reasons nobody can fathom. Then the three sons of a Khaliq family friend are hanged, two of them older than Abdul Khaliq and one younger. The three nooses are employed at the one time for the hanging of the three sons.

The father of the three boys is hanged next, having witnessed their death, followed by the school principal Mulavi Mohammad Ayayub and three teachers. By this time, almost an hour into the executions, the soldiers have given up prodding Abdul Khaliq with their spears. There is no point to it. He won't raise his eyes.

Qasim Khan Muheen is now made to mount the scaffold. Although a number of political enemies of the old King – enemies who have been in prison for some months and have nothing to do with the king-killer – are also rumoured to be hanged, Qasim

Khan Muheen is the last of the so-called conspirators due to die today. It is customary for the reigning monarch to grant a pardon to at least one man on a day of grand spectacles such as this, and sure enough, just as the noose is tightened around Qasim's neck, a triple drum-beat sounds and an emissary from the palace arrives with a document from Mohammad Zahir Khan. The document is handed to the mullah, who hands it to the judge without bothering to read it, who hands it back to the mullah, also without reading it. The mullah steps to the front of the scaffold platform and reads from the document. 'Mohammad Zahir Khan, by the will of God, monarch of the God-granted kingdom of Afghanistan, extends the mercy for which he is known throughout the civilised nations of the world to Qasim Khan Muheen, who will now spend the rest of his life in prison. It is also the pleasure of Mohammad Zahir Khan to declare that Abdul Khaliq's classmates Mohammad Ishaq, Abdullah Aziz Tokhi, Karim Jan, Mohammad Usman Jan Tajir, Ghulam Jan, Akhbar Jan Akhtar, Hashim Jan Akhtar, Jan Bismal Zadah and Nabi Jan will not face the penalty of death, but will remain in prison for the rest of their lives with Qasim Khan Muheen.'

The crowd is pleased that custom has been followed in the pardoning of Qasim Khan Muheen, a highly respected member of the council that administers the city of Kabul. Nobody believed that he had anything to do with the assassination of Mohammad Nadir to start with. As for the conversions of sentence for the king-killer's classmates – that was expected. None of them were amongst the prisoners brought to the scaffold. Only classmate Mehmood Jan was expected to hang. He sat next to Abdul Khaliq in class. The other classmates sat some rows in front.

The platform is now quite crowded with the living and the dead. The mullah, the judge, six soldiers, the two hangmen, the bodies of those who have been executed and Abdul Khaliq have left little room for the five honoured executioners who will shortly carry out the sentence of 'Death before the people' on the king-killer. The mullah calls on the commander of the soldiers in attendance to see to the removal of the dead bodies from the platform.

Abdul Khaliq's execution follows as soon as the dead bodies are removed from the scaffold. His death is terrible. I will not describe it here. But I will say that in Kabul today, a visitor can stand in Dehmazang on the very site of the platform that was erected to display the hatred of the King for his enemies. If that visitor were a scientist with the right equipment, he might be able to locate the last remnants of the blood that flowed from Abdul Khaliq's wounds and dripped down to the flagstones. The blood would reveal Abdul Khaliq's DNA and tell us much about him – more about him, in certain ways, than he knew about himself. This poor wretched boy, who passed so much time in dreams – it is almost as if he were chosen by fate from amongst the millions of his fellow Hazaras to show, with his pain, with his dreams, with his blood and his flesh, what it means to be Hazara. His DNA would not show that. It would only identify him as a human being, male, distantly related to the Mongols of Northern Asia. His suffering is in his story, not in his remnants.

6

The Music School

It became known as the music school, the small house outside the town on a mountain track too rocky for a horse and cart and no longer used by goatherds. The house had once been owned by Ali Hussein, the wool-dyer, but when he went mad his family took him to Mazar-e-Sharif to see a famous Uzbeki doctor and he never returned. The house was seized by Ali Hussein's creditors and finally sold to Karim Zand, a stranger to the town and according to everyone who met him, as mad as the wool-dyer.

He came to the town in the time of Shah Zahir, the son of Shah Nadir, shot by the king-killer, Abdul Khaliq. Why Karim Zand should have chosen such a small town in the Hazarajat for his home was a mystery at first. Those who saw him enter the house for the first time said that he brought no possessions with him other than a long leather case, a bag of lentils, another bag of rice and a basket of turnips. Nobody knew anything of his origins either, and he had no interest in making friends. Even stranger, he wasn't Hazara. The whole village was Hazara apart from two families of Uzbeks, known as 'the navigators', who had lost their way in a storm twenty years earlier and wandered five hundred kilometres off course.

Suspicion of strangers is as common amongst the Hazara as amongst any other people. The villagers watched the house that had once belonged to the wool-dyer to satisfy their curiosity about the new owner, and also to make sure that he was not a spy in the employment of Shah Zahir. It was thought, too, that the house of the wool-dyer might be cursed since it acted as a magnet for desperate people. Some of the older people of the town claimed that the house had been occupied by madmen even before the time of the wool-dyer. And where was Karim Zand's family? In Afghanistan, people are never judged alone but as a member of a family. If a man or a woman acts strangely, we look for the origin of such behaviour in the mother and father, or in the grandparents, or even further back. Someone might say, 'Oh, it is only to be expected that so-and-so goes about the town shooting cats, for in the time of the demon Dost Mohammad his great-great-grandfather was known to eat earthworms.' To appear out of nowhere with no family seems a type of deception.

Certainly Karim Zand looked like a madman, there was no doubt about that. He was very tall and his bones carried hardly any flesh. His beard was red but his hair that grew like the fleece of a goat in winter and fell over his eyes was grey and black. It was thought that Karim Zand must have dyed his beard with henna like the Sunni Turks, but those who'd glimpsed him from close range said no – his beard was red by nature. He never wore a hat or a turban – true madness.

The Hazara are as suspicious of strangers as any Pashtun or Tajik, as I say, but we are different in this way: we let people be, given time. It can be explained by our long history of being thought suspicious ourselves. A man like Karim Zand comes to live amongst us and we imagine that he might be desperate or dangerous. But when a month passes and two months and three months, we say, 'His beard is red, let it be red.' Or we say, 'He eats turnips, he drinks nothing, it's his insane business, surely!'

It was true that Karim Zand ate only rice, lentils and turnips, so far as anyone could see. Maybe at night he hunted hares and lizards and ate them – nobody knew. No cooking fire could be seen in front of his house. No smoke rose from his chimney. An idea was suggested by the chief of the village, Nadir Ali: 'He is a Sufi. God feeds him.' It was an idea that excited everyone until Ali Hussein Mazari (known as 'the traveller', since he had lived in Iraq) said that no Sufi would dress in the fashion of Karim Zand.

'Sufis dress in white,' he said. 'And no Sufi would grow a red beard. They pray all day and all night. Who has seen Red Beard pray?'

After Ali Hussein spoke, Karim Zand became known as Red Beard by some people, and 'the new madman' by the rest. If Karim Zand was not a Sufi, he was likely a mystic of some other sort. Some mystics were a burden to those they lived amongst, some were a blessing, and it was not yet known which Red Beard would be.

It was late in winter when Karim Zand came to the house of the mad wool-dyer and it was spring before the people of the village came to know the most important thing about him. One of the wives of the brick-maker Mohammad Barzinji had taken the track past his house to look for herbs in the four small valleys called the Claw, which took stream water from the mountains down to the Hamet River away to the west. She had her daughter Latifeh with her and an old dog whose nose had been split down the middle in a fight with a donkey. As they passed above the house of the madman on their return from the valleys of the Claw, Mohammad Barzinji's wife suddenly dropped the sack full of herbs she was carrying and threw her hands to her ears.

'Merciful God our Great Master!' she cried. 'What noise is that?'

The daughter, Latifeh, was not terrified in the way her mother was, but instead stood still with her head on one side listening closely. The dog with the split nose was listening too, his ears pricked in a manner he hardly bothered with in these days of his old age.

'It is music,' said Latifeh. 'Listen, Mama. It is the music of Karim Zand, it is coming from his house.'

But Mohammad Barzinji's wife wouldn't listen. She ordered her daughter to pick up the sack of herbs, and both mother and daughter, with the dog loping beside them, hastened down the track to the end of the village.

The wife of Mohammad Barzinji began crying out at the top of her voice as she stood in the little clearing at the end of the village. This was the clearing where farmers brought produce down from the terraced fields in the higher valleys to sell in season, and it was the place where a small monument of hard stone had been shaped by a mason to mark the site of a massacre. That was decades earlier, the massacre, when six Hazara men and one boy had been shot by the soldiers of Abdur Rahman.

On this morning early in spring the small clearing was empty. It would be another week before farmers carried down their new onions and snow peas and green beets. But it took only a minute or two for the clearing to begin filling with those who'd been startled by the loud cries of Mohammad Barzinji's wife.

'I heard it in the hills!' she was shouting. 'Latifeh was with me! It destroyed my wits!'

'Heard what?' Mohammad Barzinji's wife was asked.

'A sound not from this earth!' she wailed. But Latifeh said, 'It was music.'

The people of the town were much more inclined to listen to Latifeh, who was known for her quiet temperament, than to her mother, who had been in a strange state since a moth had died in her ear. But no more questioning was required, for the music that Latifeh spoke of could now be heard by all. Such a strange matter, for music to be heard in the village; in normal times, it would only be at weddings when musicians were hired from far off that such sounds would fill the air.

'Who can explain this?' people asked, their eyes wide with surprise.

'The new madman,' said Latifeh. 'It is coming from his house.'

Twenty people made their way up the rocky track to the house of the new madman, Red Beard as he was now called, but more properly, Karim Zand. With every step the crowd took the music became louder and sweeter. It was surely the instrument known as the *rubab* that was producing the music – that much was obvious. Everyone knew the sound of the *rubab* from weddings, and also from a strange device that played music when a small package was pushed into a machine with batteries. Such a device was once brought to the village by a scholar from England, a cheerful man with a fair beard and spectacles whose trousers were so short they showed his knees. He had been searching far and wide in Afghanistan for people who knew songs from ancient times.

I will say something more here about the *rubab*. It is an instrument that makes music with twelve strings that are plucked and stroked with the fingers. It has a belly like a lute, but not so broad and not so deep. The *rubab* is the great musical instrument of Afghanistan, although it is said to have originated in Iran at a time when Iranians called their country Persia. To master the instrument requires a long period of training, beginning with an apprenticeship that might commence at a very young age. It was no wonder that Karim Zand was thought to be mad, for the masters of the *rubab* are a strange breed to those who know only the beauty of the music the *rubab* makes, but not the way in which it is made.

On that day in spring the people of the village knew that they were listening to music made by a master. Each was glad in his heart that the new madman had turned out to be a madman of the better sort – one who did something useful. He could have revealed much more difficult tastes. When the wool-dyer went mad, he walked about the village unclothed and claimed he was a lizard. If the new madman intended to sit in his house all day and night without eating or drinking, what harm in that if he also played his *rubab*? But then something unfortunate happened. Just as people were beginning to clap their hands and sing little bits of song to go with the music, the madman himself, Karim Zand with his huge red beard, burst out the front door of his ruin of a house and roared like a bull.

'Clear out!' he shouted. Then he went back inside his house and slammed the door behind him.

The people of the village didn't take the warning seriously. Why should they? The man was mad. He had no idea what he was saying. After a few minutes had passed, Karim Zand began playing the *rubab* again, and people began to clap and sing again – not everyone, just those who wanted to show that they didn't take orders from a madman.

But mad Karim Zand again burst from his doorway and commanded everyone to clear out. Again, he was ignored. Then he appeared to give up on being granted the privacy he desired. He played for another hour and kept indoors.

Amongst those listening to the madman was a boy of fourteen by the name of Abdullah. The boy carried through life the misfortune of silence. From the moment of his birth, not a sound had come from his mouth other than croaking noises such as a frog might make. After the age of four, he ceased making the frog noises, either because he no longer could or because his father hissed at him and told him to say nothing. It was said that his silence had something to do with the colour of his eyes, a bright green like wet vine leaves, unknown amongst the Hazara. He was thought to be an idiot, although he was capable in every way other than speaking and wrote his Dari script with clarity unequalled amongst the children at the school he attended for three years. He prayed in silence and those who saw him at prayer wondered how God would know of his existence when his voice could not carry his devotion to Heaven. He lived with his uncle, Ali Reza, for as if having a child who couldn't speak was not enough of a disaster, the boy's father had died when Abdullah was only seven years old.

The man had eaten the flesh of an owl he'd found in the hill pastures – an unwise thing to do, for the owl was not native to the region and Abdullah's father should have known better. Besides, the owl was dead. Abdullah's mother remarried when he was nine years old but her new husband, who made his living as a tooth-puller and limb-setter travelling from village to village, would only take on Abdullah's two older brothers. He considered Abdullah cursed.

The music of the *rubab* came as a great revelation to Abdullah. He heard voices in the music when others heard only the sound of the strings. He sat with his legs crossed as close as he dared to the madman's house and listened with a smile on his face. It seemed to him that the *rubab* was telling a tale that had no end; a story such as Abdullah had only ever known in dreams. But the music produced yet another response in Abdullah. The people of the village who noticed him smiling to himself said aloud, 'Look! The idiot is trying to speak!' Without being aware of it himself, Abdullah's lips were moving soundlessly. 'One madman is talking to another!'

Every day for a fortnight the people of the town gathered to listen to Karim Zand playing the *rubab*, and Abdullah was always amongst them. It seemed that the madman preferred to play late in the afternoons and often his music continued well past the time of *maghrib*. Most of those listening would drift off to the *hussainia* to attend to their devotions and touch their foreheads to the *turba*, but Abdullah remained outside the madman's house for as long as the music lasted.

This time-wasting of Abdullah's could not go on. His uncle Ali Reza had work for the boy, who was really now much more than a boy; fifteen is very close to the time at which you are considered an adult amongst the Hazara – it was certainly that way for me. In spring the apple trees of Ali Reza's orchard attracted small blue beetles that climbed the trunks and if left unchecked, would lay eggs in the blossom that would later ruin the fruit. It was necessary to wrap coarse cloth soaked in a poison made from ragwort around the trunks to kill the beetles off. But some beetles would survive the poison. It was Abdullah's task at this time of the year to go from tree to tree, capturing the beetles and crushing them with his fingers. He also carried baskets of soil from the sunless valleys below the village up to the orchard. Finally, it was Abdullah's responsibility to keep the soil of the orchard fertilised by adding the ash of wood fires and the dung of sheep from the mountain meadows.

So Abdullah was forbidden to go to the madman's house in the afternoon. Ali Reza's words were law in his household, and Abdullah would not disobey. But nothing had been said about not going to the madman's house at night. Abdullah left his bed when his uncle and his uncle's two wives and the five children of the family were asleep and sat on the rocky ground close to Karim Zand's small house. It was his hope that the madman would begin playing the *rubab* late in the night, as unlikely as this seemed. Abdullah kept his vigil for two hours each night for five nights on end without ever hearing a single note of the *rubab*'s music, but on the sixth night, although no music came from the house, he at least saw Karim Zand himself step from his front door and stand gazing up at the moon. Abdullah remained still, even when the madman noticed him and took three huge strides to loom above him.

'Will you feel the force of my hand on your head?' the madman roared, and he lifted his fist as if in readiness to strike Abdullah. The boy kept his peace in a way that must have impressed the madman because he lowered his fist and accepted from Abdullah's hand a small piece of paper on which some words were written. Karim Zand turned the paper about this way and that until the light of the full moon illuminated the words: 'Teach me'.

'"Teach me"?' said Karim Zand. He looked down at Abdullah, and his long face and nose like the beak of an eagle and the great tangle of his red beard gave him the look of a monster. 'Teach you to hide in the shadows like a wolf? Is that what I should teach you? Teach you to destroy my peace?'

Abdullah climbed to his feet. He looked the madman in the eye without fear. Then he put two fingers to his lips. He made a sign with his hands, spreading them out from each other like a bird unfolding its wings. It was a sign that meant, 'I can say no more.' A man might make such a sign at a certain point in an argument when words have failed to settle an issue. But Abdullah wished Karim Zand to understand that he had no power to speak. Karim Zand frowned and put his hand to his chin, as if in doubt about the boy's meaning. Then he said suddenly, 'Will I kill you now? Will I strike you dead where you stand?' and he again lifted his fist. Abdullah didn't make a sound, nor could he. He stood his ground. Karim Zand said, 'God's grey hair!' – a strange expression, and not the sort of thing that a pious man would utter. 'You are one of the silent ones?' Karim Zand motioned for the boy to follow him into the house.

The house indoors was as poor as we might imagine. An oil lamp of the sort you might purchase in a bazaar for five hundred afghanis threw a feeble light across the floor, which was no more than the soil on which the foundations stood. In one corner of the room folded blankets formed a bed simpler than a *toichek*. Two pots and two pewter plates stood on the hearth of the fireplace in which a few embers blinked in the gloom, showing that those who said no smoke ever rose from the madman's chimney were not paying attention. On the earthen floor two rugs were spread, one of high quality, the other not so special. Four cushions rested on the rugs. On the bare mud-brick of the walls such garments as the madman possessed hung from hooks. One of two smaller rooms served as a cupboard where a number of small ornaments sat on shelves – a tortoise made of stone, coffee cups, drinking glasses with gold rims. The other room was Karim Zand's washroom.

The *rubab* that had been the cause of Abdullah's bold plan to meet the madman and make his request rested on the largest of the cushions. Beside it lay another instrument, a *tula*, a pipe made of wood with stops and a mouthpiece. Its coating of varnish shone in the light of the cheap lantern.

Karim Zand said to the boy, 'Make yourself seated.' Once Abdullah had lowered himself onto a cushion, he looked up at the towering figure of the madman. In the light of the lantern, his red beard and hooked nose and fierce gaze gave him the appearance of one who intended harm to the world. Abdullah wished to say, but could not, 'I honour you and your music.' Instead he pointed at the *rubab*, then at the place in his chest where his own heart beat.

Karim Zand spoke. 'Would that the whole world had ceased to speak! If you had uttered a word to me, I would have kicked your arse!'

Abdullah nodded. Then he pointed again at the *rubab*, and again at his heart.

The madman sat on a cushion facing the boy, and put his two hands into his beard, pulling at it in a way that seemed to help his thinking.

'"Teach me"!' he said at last. He threw back his head and let out a great roar. 'Teach me! Ha!' Then his mood appeared to change and he said, 'Perhaps I will teach you. Or perhaps I will cut your throat and cook you. But if in my generosity I agree to teach you, how would you pay me? Now, go home.'

Abdullah went home, of course – what else could he do? But he came back the next night with a new note, and this time he was brave enough to knock on the door of the madman's house. Karim Zand came out wearing a more fierce expression than ever. Abdullah thrust the note at him. The note read, in the beautiful handwriting that Abdullah had taught himself, 'I will work for you at the end of the day when I have finished my tasks for my uncle.'

Karim Zand read the new note and his anger died away. Once again, he took the boy into his house. This time, however, he made him tea. He sat before the boy, and had this to say: 'You say you would be my servant. Why would I wish for a servant? I am a man alone. Do you see a wife? Do you see any children? Go home!'

Abdullah did as he was commanded. But once again he returned, and he carried a new note for the madman. Karim Zand said to the boy, 'What, are you more of a fox than a human being? Do you stay awake all night finding ways to be a nuisance?'

But he read Abdullah's note. What the boy had written was this: 'Teach me for the sake of my soul.' The words must have found their way to the heart of the madman because he allowed

Abdullah to come inside, and he made him tea. He sat stroking his chin for some time before he placed not the *rubab* but the *tula* on the rug before the boy. He said, 'This is the instrument for you. The *rubab* must be part of your education from the age of five. The *tula* you may learn now.' Karim Zand picked up the *tula* and put it to his lips. Within seconds the dark little house with its un-plastered walls was transformed into the garden of an emperor filled with the song of nightingales. Karim Zand placed the *tula* on the cushion once more and said to Abdullah, 'Pick it up.' When Abdullah reached for the instrument with gladness, Karim Zand said, 'Wait!' Then he pointed at the top of the *tula* and said, 'Do not pick it up at this end, by any means, unless you wish to offend me.' Then he pointed to the bottom of the *tula*, from where the music emerged. 'Do not pick it up from this end, by any means, or you will certainly offend me.' Finally, he pointed to the middle of the *tula* and said, 'Do not pick it up here, by any means, or you will offend me and I will use the instrument to bruise your skull!'

Abdullah was baffled. How should he grasp the *tula* if not at either end and not in the middle? He reached out his hand once, twice, ten times, twenty times, and each time he withdrew it. Finally he climbed to his feet, brushed the tears from his eyes and went home.

All through the next day while he crushed beetles in his uncle's orchard, he thought about the *tula*, and how it could be taken up in such a way that the madman would not be offended. He could find no solution. He thought to himself, 'The master does not wish to teach me.'

All the same, his mind kept returning to the problem, but with-out reward. In the night he went to the house of the madman, driven by desire to learn the *tula*. He thought, 'I am becoming mad myself! Will that satisfy the master, when I am also a madman?'

Karim Zand sat the boy before the *tula*. 'Now, pick up the instrument. However, I am a man quickly moved to anger. If you pick it up at this end, I will beat you to within an inch of your life. If you pick it up by this end, I will tear the skin from your bones and feed you to the ants. And if you pick it up here between the two ends, I will make myself a breakfast of your entrails.'

This time, Abdullah didn't consider anything except his desire to hold the *tula*. He reached out and grasped the instrument and held it firmly. He expected a blow from the madman, or even worse, the flash of a sharp knife. Instead he saw on the face of Karim Zand a smile that stretched from his left ear to his right.

'You see?' said Karim Zand. 'It is not so difficult to pick up the *tula*.'

Abdullah's second lesson was to learn how to listen. Karim Zand played the *tula* for an hour and the boy's task after that hour was to say nothing, which was not so difficult because he could not speak. But Karim Zand questioned him when he stopped playing. 'Did I not make myself clear, beetle?' (He had begun to call Abdullah 'beetle'.) 'I said, "Say nothing."'

Abdullah lifted his hands as if to say, 'But nothing was said!'

'With your mouth, you obeyed me,' said Karim Zand. 'But with your eyes, you went chatter chatter chatter! This is what you were saying: "The most beautiful music!" But that is not what I want to hear. When you learn the *tula*, you will not want to hear those words either. It is not beauty we seek with the *tula*. It is only the truth. Do you think the truth is always beautiful? No. The truth is sometimes beautiful, but often it is ugly. In the city of Shiraz where I once made my home, I saw a man who had lost his wife to the plague. Then his children followed. He had loved his wife greatly and his children were the light of his life. When the pain was too much for him to bear, he thrust his hand into a saucepan of boiling oil and held it there. That is the truth about love. If I tell the story of this man on the *tula*, I do not wish to hear you say with your eyes, "A beautiful tune!" Do you understand now?'

So Abdullah listened with his eyes on the rug on which he sat. When Karim Zand had come to the end of the music for that night, he said, 'You, who has no voice, what did you hear?'

Abdullah couldn't answer.

'You heard voices. But not the voices of people. Come with me.'

Karim Zand took the boy outside. The night was black, with clouds hiding the stars and the moon. Karim Zand spoke. 'Listen. In the heavens the clouds are travelling from the east to the west. They have a voice. The moon that is hidden has a voice. Each star that you cannot see has a voice of its own. The mountain that stands above us has a voice, and the mountain behind it. The wind has a hundred voices. The bears in their caves have their own voice when they stir in their sleep. The fox has its voice as it searches for the eggs of the bulbul, and it has another voice when it hunts hares. The *tula* alone knows the voices of the world. Now go home!'

Before he put his foot to the track that led to his uncle's house, Abdullah reached out his hand to shake the hand of the madman.

The door of the wool-dyer's house, now that of the new mad-man, was open and the light of the cheap oil lamp fell across the threshold. As the madman accepted his hand, Abdullah noticed something he had not noticed before. The madman's left hand was badly scarred, all the way up his wrist.

It was not long before Abdullah's uncle Ali Reza discovered that the boy was leaving his bed each night. Ali Reza had a soft spot for his nephew, whose fate it had been to have a foolish owl-eating father and a hare-brained mother who ran off with a tooth-puller. And Abdullah was a boy loyal in his affections and attentive to his tasks – Ali Reza commended these qualities. But there was an-other reason for Ali Reza's fondness for Abdullah. A fortune-teller had come to the village once, a Jew who wandered the world with a donkey for transport and a rooster for company. The man had been cast out from the tribe of Jews for having stabbed a rabbi, but for what reason he'd stabbed the rabbi he wouldn't say. The Jew had also the company of a woman from the land of Syria who followed the faith of the fire-worshippers, and it was she who was thought to give the fortune-teller his information about the fu-ture. The Jew told fortunes not by reading the palm of the hand but by running his fingers through his customers' hair. He did this blindfolded, and so was able to count pious Muslim women amongst his clients. When he felt the hair of Ali Reza, who had approached him in an idle moment, he said without hesitation, 'That boy of yours will bring you honour, of that I am sure.' Ali Reza asked which boy he meant, since he had three sons. The fortune-teller responded, 'Why, the boy with jewels for eyes.'

Ali Reza asked the boy openly why he left his bed each night. Abdullah took his uncle by the hand and led him through the village and up the rocky path to the house of the new madman. He knocked on the door twice, then paused, and knocked a further three times. This manner of knocking had been taught to him by Karim Zand, who would not come to the door for anyone but Abdullah. Karim Zand showed his most fierce expression to Ali Reza, but agreed at last to talk to him. In this way, Ali Reza heard from the lips of the madman himself that Abdullah, the beetle, was learning to play the *tula*. He was amazed, of course. At first he didn't know whether the boy should be scolded for keeping secrets and beaten with a stick, or praised for his ambition. In making up his mind, Ali Reza recalled the words of the Jew with the crazy wife who followed the faith of the fire-worshippers. 'That boy with jewels for eyes will bring you honour.' Ali Reza thought to himself, 'The Jews are a strange people, certainly, but the Prophet Himself showed them respect. Perhaps they know things concealed from uneducated people such as myself.' Another consideration was the part that music had played in the traditions of the Hazara. 'Imagine a nephew who can fill the house with the music of the *tula*,' he thought. He allowed his nephew to continue with his instruction in the art of music-making.

Karim Zand was a very strict teacher. He gave this warning to Abdullah before the boy had blown a single note on the *tula*: 'This is a simple instrument, beetle. But inside it lives all that is known about the world. In forty years, I have only just begun to learn what it wishes to tell me. You will learn what I can teach you, God knows how much that will be. You have a skull and a brain within.

But how much use will that brain be to you? We will see. In four years, if you have shown you are more than the fool you seem to be, you can play in public. Not before.'

Abdullah was a good student. The madman gave him special exercises to aid his breathing. Even a clever student of the *tula* might take a year to master breathing, but Abdullah showed progress within just three months. Before a year had passed, he had learned enough of the great body of the *tula*'s music, known as the *radif*, to play three full song groups, called *dastgahs*, or forty-five *goushehs*, each *gousheh* being a complete melody from the bygone days of the madman's native Persia. It could be seen that he had a gift. And because he had no voice of his own, he had also developed the skill of listening. No one would have guessed, but the madman had a great deal to talk about. Perhaps it was because Abdullah did not interrupt him that he was willing to talk so freely. His tales were full of magic. He told Abdullah of a great master of the *tula* from the land of Iraq who could make stones rise from the ground and float in the air with his music, and of a horse who was cured of the colic by a sequence of notes that the Iraqi master alone knew. He said that there was a tree in Takht-e-Jamshid, the forest close by the city of Shiraz, that wept tears when a master of the *tula* of that city played beneath it.

The story that Abdullah thought about longest was that of the Persian king who commanded a master of the *tula* to play for his young wife, sorrowing after the death of her first child. The wife of the king had grown as pale as bones that bake in the desert and would accept no food and no water. The *tula* master, Ali Masoud Zamanzadeh, played in the morning and again in the evening for a month and then a second month, and little by little the poor woman returned to health. When Zamanzadeh tired, the wife of the king brought him dishes of walnuts and pistachios and served him with her own hand. She prepared rosewater for him, and sat dishes in a circle around him in the royal apartment – *kashk-e baadenjaan*, carefully prepared with rich whey, and *boulanee*, and *koo-koo-yeh morgh* with the flesh from chickens normally reserved for the king himself, and fresh caviar each day from the Caspian Sea packed in snow from the mountains. Zamanzadeh grew plump on the food the queen served him, and the queen too grew plump with a new baby. She said to her husband the king, 'Zamanzadeh must play the *tula* for me each day while I carry the child, his music gives me strength.' The king agreed, but with some reluctance, for the queen seemed to speak of nothing but Zamanzadeh's music, and Zamanzadeh was a handsome man with a black beard and mustachios that curled at the ends.

The queen's time came and she gave birth to a boy who announced his health with his first loud cry. The queen had never in her twenty years shown herself so full of the joy of life. It was she who fed the baby boy from her own full breasts, and it was she who washed the baby each day in a basin of polished stone. Zamanzadeh the *tula* player remained at the palace, as pampered as ever, for the queen would not hear of him going his way to make the poor living that is a musician's fate.

The king took great delight from his baby son, just as any father would. But at least once each day a voice like that of a snake with the power of speech hissed in his ear: 'King of Persia! Is the child yours? Can you say that he is?' When he could bear it no longer, the king devised a plan to test the feelings of Zamanzadeh for his wife. He called a woman of his court to him, not a woman of importance, one whose task it was to train the dancers of the court, nothing more. He told her to prepare the most beautiful of his dancers for a strategy he was devising. The woman brought to the king a girl by the name of Ashada, at fifteen already renowned for her beauty and for the grace of her dancing. The king told Ashada that she was to dance in private for the *tula* player, Zamanzadeh, and that she was to grant Zamanzadeh his every wish. The king said, 'There are ways in which a woman can please a man.'

Ashada danced for Zamanzadeh as the king had commanded. The king had concealed himself behind a screen in order to watch. And what woe this brought him! Ashada danced, Zamanzadeh watched on without smiling, Ashada drew close to him and filled his senses with the perfume that bathed the silk of her garments, Zamanzadeh shook his head. The king watching in secret took Zamanzadeh's discomfort to mean that he loved the queen, and could not bear to look at another woman, no matter how beautiful. What other explanation could there be? So desirable a woman as Ashada spurned in this way?

The king prepared one final test, this time of the queen's affections, since the punishment he had in mind for Zamanzadeh and the queen and even for the baby prince was so fierce that he would not act without certainty. He had a famous craftsman of Isfahan make him a toy of great cunning, a mechanical bird of pure gold that would lift its wings and sing when a hidden spring was released. The king called the queen to him, and the baby prince, who was now a year old, and the *tula* player. He told the queen to place the boy on the rich Hamadani rug that covered the floor, and the queen did as she was instructed. The king asked

Zamanzadeh to leave his *tula* on the rug, three paces from the baby, and Zamanzadeh did so, of course. Then the king placed the golden bird on the rug by the *tula*. When the king released the spring, the golden bird raised its wings and sang. The prince crawled across the rug with delight to where the golden bird sat beside the *tula*. Before the eyes of all – the king, the queen, Zamanzadeh – the baby reached for the *tula* in preference to the golden bird. In his grief the king with his own sword struck off the head of Zamanzadeh, and of his wife. His baby son was given to a tribe of Arabs.

This story meant more to Abdullah at his age than it would have meant some years earlier, for he had fallen in love with a girl of his own age who came to the village in summer with her mother. The girl, whose name was Leila, sold mulberries and apricots from the orchard of a landowner in Kabul, a man who had seized Hazara land in the terrible years of the Third Rebellion. The landowner was not the worst of those who had taken possession of Hazara land, for he allowed Leila's father to retain thirty per cent of the crop for himself. Many Hazara from the time of Dost Mohammad onwards were compelled to farm land that had been stolen from them for ten per cent of the crop – a bitter life to lead.

Another boy of sixteen, a boy with a voice, a boy with a mother, might have spoken to that mother of his feelings, and the mother, if she had good thoughts about the girl, would have spoken to the boy's father, and by this process, an agreement would be made that in such-and-such a time – perhaps five years – the boy and girl would wed. But a boy without a voice is no prize.

The pain of a Hazara whose love is hopeless is like that of any other person, but with this difference: the pain is to be concealed.

The Hazara in their history have not enjoyed the leisure of romance. If you are a Hazara with a broken heart, you do not tell the world. What would you say: 'I am sick with love, pity me if you will'? You would be scorned. People would say to you, 'Has the King sent soldiers to steal your land? Have you been turned out of your home with nothing but the shoes on your feet? No? Then calm yourself and go about your work.' Abdullah told no one. But a plan formed in his mind. When the remaining three years of his promise to the madman were over, he would play the *tula* for Leila, and his music would take the place of the words he couldn't speak.

The temptation to play the *tula* for Leila before the three years had passed was great. Of course it was. In the winter he barely saw her, and when spring came around again he longed to take a stool and sit at the place where she and her mother sold their fruit and play certain tunes he had mastered that would surely melt her heart. Although he rarely glanced at her, he had seen much to admire. She was modest, she was obedient to her mother, she smiled often. Once in the early days of a new spring she allowed her eyes to meet his for a fraction of a second. But that moment lived in Abdullah's memory as if he had glimpsed paradise itself.

The madman had a keen eye and it wasn't long before he noticed the melancholy that robbed Abdullah's eyes of their brightness. It was Karim Zand's custom to sit before Abdullah while he practised listening to the music of the *tula*. If the boy made a mistake, he would say, 'Don't distress yourself. Play it again.' But if Abdullah let his concentration lapse, the madman would spit on his hand and use the hand to slap Abdullah's face. Mistakes were one thing; a wandering mind was another. And it happened that the madman was compelled to slap Abdullah at least once each week in the months after Leila came into the boy's life. One night after Abdullah lost the thread of a simple *gousheh*, the madman put his hand to his chin and studied the boy in silence.

'Love has come into your life,' he said after a minute or more. 'Love, and trouble. One is the shadow of the other.'

Abdullah nodded his head. The madman, who had already shown the tender side of his nature to the boy on many occasions, reached out and took the *tula* from his pupil's hand. Then he held Abdullah's hand in his. He said, 'You live, you breathe, the time comes when you love. Is it the mulberry girl at the market?'

Abdullah was amazed. How could the master know such a thing? He, who never left his house.

Karim Zand prepared tea for the boy. Then he sat before him again.

'My wife,' he said, speaking softly, 'was of your people. She was Hazara. If you had seen my sons, you would have thought they were your brothers. The plague took them, all three. The doctor would not tend to them. I offered to pay him in gold. He said, "I do not treat Hazara." This was in Iran, where your people live as slaves, many of them. I buried my wife and my sons in one grave. I travelled for twenty years to lose my sorrow. Then I came here, to the poorest house in the poorest village of my wife's people. This is where I will die.'

Abdullah put his hand on his heart to show his sorrow.

'What can you offer the family of the girl?' said Karim Zand. 'Nothing but the *tula*. If you play for her now, she will say, "How beautiful!" But that would be a disaster, for your music is not beautiful. You would feel flattered, you would never become a master of your instrument, never. You must hope that she will remain unwed for two more years. Have courage.'

But the madman had something to add. From the hearth of his fire he picked up a smooth stone. Before Abdullah's amazed eyes, the madman split the stone in two. Within each half of the stone lay golden coins.

'When the time comes,' said Karim Zand, 'these coins will build you a house of your own at the top of the village. You will play the *tula* there for your wife, beetle. Now go home.'

Two passions ruled the life of Abdullah as he passed into his seventeenth year: his love for Leila, and his desire to master the *tula*. Each passion fought a daily battle with the other. He watched Leila grow to womanhood and closer to the time when she would become a wife, and he was powerless to reveal to her and to her mother the voice of the *tula*. Yet he had exceeded the madman's hopes for him as a student of the *tula*, and he could draw comfort from that, if possible. His fingers danced on the stops of the instrument as if all the life in his body had given itself to the *radif*. He was competent enough to play beside Karim Zand when the madman turned to the *rubab*. The master allowed the boy to lead him through changes to familiar tunes as if making a long and triumphant journey to the far side of the world and back again. The madman saw the boy concentrating with all his will; he saw pride. But he did not see happiness.

The day came, as it was certain to come, when Abdullah could keep what was in his heart to himself no more. He stopped in his labours with the baskets of soil as he passed Leila and her mother selling fruit. He lowered his basket from his shoulder and stood gazing at Leila, against all custom. Courtship amongst Hazara, as amongst all Muslims, is never open. Strong passions may fill a young man's heart but he masters them and allows his mother to carry out her duty. After months of questioning, months of thinking, the young man's mother may permit her son to drink tea with the young woman he has chosen. Most mothers would not think that a boy has the brains in his head or the experience of life in his heart to make an intelligent choice of wife for himself. But here on this day, in a village of the Hazarajat, a boy without a voice stood in the market square and without any power of speech, declared his love for Leila. It was only because he had no voice that he was spared a terrible rebuke from the girl's mother and from the people of the village. But if those same people had watched closely, they would have witnessed something rare, for a smile came to Leila's lips and she did not look away. Leila's mother called to Abdullah, 'Young man, have some manners!' She would have slapped her daughter as a mother should but Leila whispered to her, 'No harm is done.'

Abdullah went that night to the madman's house with a note written in the well-formed letters that he was known for. He sat with the madman, drank some tea, then passed him the note. It read: 'Master, permit me to play for the young woman Leila, I beg of you.' The madman read the note twice, three times.

'If you break your promise,' he said to the boy, 'you will offend me in my soul and my curse will follow you all your life.'

Abdullah carried his pain about with him for a further week before presenting his note to the madman once more. But the answer he received was the same: 'If you break your promise, my soul will be offended.' Abdullah made his request a third time after a full month had passed. But this time, he wrote more words, just as heartfelt. 'If I cannot make my life with Leila, it would be better for me if I had not been born.'

The madman gave the answer he had given before.

Late in the season of apricots, in the very midst of Abdullah's suffering, the young woman Leila called his name as he carried wood-ash for his uncle's orchard through the marketplace.

'Yes, I know your name,' said Leila. From amongst the folds of her dress she took an apricot, full of sunshine. She gave it to Abdullah. From behind her, Leila's mother called out sharply, 'What, is this a generation without shame? Come to me!'

Abdullah carried the basket of wood-ash to the orchard and emptied it beneath the apple trees. Then he sat and gazed at the apricot. Leila would return to her own small village in another day, and who could say that he would ever see her again? It was more than he could bear. 'At least,' he said to himself, 'let her hear what voice I speak with through the *tula*.'

He ran down the path from the orchard, all the way to the house of the madman. He was prepared to knock on the door, but the door was open, a strange thing. Inside the small house sat Karim Zand with his hands folded on his lap. On a cushion before him sat the *tula*. Abdullah paused for a few seconds. Karim Zand was not looking at him, but at the embers of the fire in the hearth.

'Master, please forgive me,' he wished to say, but in place of words he touched his heart. He snatched up the *tula* and ran from the house. He kept running without drawing more than three breaths until he reached the market square where Leila and her mother were packing away the rush baskets in which they offered their fruit. They looked at Abdullah in surprise.

He sat himself on the low wall that divided the little monument to the slaughtered from the market area of the square. A small number of people paused in their packing to see what strange business the boy had come on. It was a bright day, a day of high blue skies and small clouds combed into strips by the wind. Abdullah put the *tula* to his lips without any idea of what he would play, but within seconds the square was full of a music like the singing of bulbuls. Those who had lifted their heads out of curiosity now stood entranced. Hussein Anwari, the rope-maker, said to no one in particular, 'Now here's a miracle! The boy has taught himself from the birds!'

Abdullah played on and on. He followed paths through songs he had barely attempted before. So rapidly did note follow note that people began to gesture towards Heaven, as if the angels themselves had blessed the boy. Since Abdullah's songs had no beginning, he himself did not know where they would end. He saw Leila in her enchantment watching and listening as one person listens to another with a secret to tell. When at last he lowered the *tula*, an agreement between these two, Leila and Abdullah, was complete, more surely than if they had put their names to a contract before the gaze of a mullah.

Joy comes into our lives always within range of sorrow. The two are sisters. It was Abdullah's task to return the *tula* to Karim Zand once he had revealed his voice to Leila, and to the people of the town. He walked the path back to the madman's house slowly, fearing that his master would rain curses down on his head. He had betrayed Karim Zand. He could not ever ask for forgiveness.

The door to the house once owned by the wool-dyer who lost his mind stood open, as it had an hour before. His head bowed, his heart torn as if by the winds of a terrible storm, Abdullah stepped inside the house with the *tula* held before him. There he found Karim Zand, bent over a cooking pot on the fire, his back to his visitor. When the madman turned, he looked Abdullah up and down. Nothing was said for a time which may have only been one minute, but which seemed to Abdullah like an hour with his hand in a fire. At last the madman climbed to his feet.

'After all,' he said to Abdullah, 'it is not so difficult to pick up a *tula*.' Then he bent to the hearth and opened the strange stone. He took six gold coins from inside the stone and placed them in his student's free hand.

'Take the instrument home with you,' he said. 'Bring it with you tomorrow.'

Abdullah fell to his knees in relief. He attempted to take the madman's hand, that he might kiss it, but the madman scorned the gesture.

'Here,' said Karim Zand, and raised the boy up. 'Now go home.'

Abdullah took a step to the door, but the madman called him back. 'So that you know all your life, beetle, remember what I tell you now: God is patient with the obedient, but he treasures the disobedient. Go home, beetle.'

7

The Snow Leopard

He came to Hazarajat from England in the time of the communists when Afghanistan was upside-down. His true name was Abraham, like that of the patriarch in the Holy Book, but in Hazarajat he was called Dobara, short for *dobara khashisk kanid*, which means 'try again' in our language of Dari.

When he first arrived in Hazarajat on his great project he brought with him three cameras. One camera made things a great distance away appear close enough to seize with your two hands. The children of the village in which he made his home for three months were permitted to look through the camera, and they thanked God for sending the Englishman to Hazarajat. Equally as strange was another camera that took a picture and made it into a shape immediately. Every person in the village except for the most pious, who said the camera was unholy, was given a picture to keep. Some chose to stand at their own front door for their picture; some stood beside the animals they owned.

Dobara came to Hazarajat not to take pictures of people but to take pictures of snow leopards for a university in his city of London. The university paid him a salary to take such pictures, something that seemed very curious to the people of the village. Dobara explained that few pictures of the snow leopard had ever been taken and that it was important to take as many as possible. He was told, 'When you make a picture, show us,' for no one in the village had ever seen the animal. In any case, few were interested. Dobara spent nearly all of his time in Hazarajat answering questions about the machines of England and the tall buildings of his city.

On that first visit to Hazarajat, Dobara spoke only the English of his own land and a second language spoken by the Jews. He was himself of the Jews, but the Jews of England. The strangest thing of all was that he did not have his God in his heart. He said that the world made itself. People thought he must be simple, like Jawad Behsudi of another time who said that the world was a dream. Jawad Behsudi made a journey to Bamiyan and changed his faith to that of the Buddhists, which was better than nothing.

With his English and his few words of Dari and pictures in a book, Dobara went to one person and another all over the north of Hazarajat seeking the snow leopard. In the village in which he lived in his tent, the snow leopard was a mystery, as I have said. In other places, people told him that the animal lived much higher in the mountains than the Hazara. He asked to be taken to higher places where the snow stayed on the ground for nine months of the year, or higher still, where the snow covered the mountains every day of the year. No one would take him, not even for ten thousand afghanis. It was too dangerous. Those who had been there told of winds that could lift the snow from the ground and throw it with the force of stones. Also, the aeroplanes of the Russians flew over the mountains and people were frightened of them. The Russians were said to hate Afghans, those who had no war with them and those who did. Even on foot, they never left Afghans in peace. From an aeroplane, who knows? They might drop a bomb on anyone, even those watching for a snow leopard.

It was at the end of his first visit to Hazarajat that Dobara became Dobara. He said, 'I'll come in the spring and try again.' In spring, the shepherds took their animals to the mountains for the new grass. Someone had told Dobara that snow leopards came down from the high mountains in spring to eat the sheep and goats of the Hazara. Maybe the person who told him that was being kind, or maybe he was mad. A wolf might eat a sheep, or an eagle might take a lamb just born and still covered in blood. Or sometimes a ram in a bad mood will put his head down and butt the lambs away from the ewes. But Hazara who had been shepherds all their lives had no stories of snow leopards hunting their animals.

He came back in spring, as he said he would. His arrival brought two surprises for the people of the village. The first was that Dobara had taught himself many more words of Dari and the second was his beard, long and black. His beard and his Dari earned him even more respect than his cameras. He had changed his spectacles, too. He now saw through small, round spectacles, like those that Nadir Shah had worn many years before when he was shot by the king-killer Abdul Khaliq. Dobara brought presents as well – not for everyone in the village, but for the Chief,

Sayed Ali, and for Sayed Ali's three wives, and for Mohammad Majid the scholar who had read a book about the moon out of interest. Others in the village were pleased with the music he played for them on a machine, the same songs many had heard on the BBC station of Sayed Ali's radio before it was destroyed by ants. More welcome than any other gifts were Dobara's medicines, especially the aspirin for the terrible headaches of Mohammad Majid's daughter that the apothecary's medicines could not banish, and for Ali Hassan's backache that came from losing one of his legs when he stood on a landmine on the road to Kabul. (Ali Hassan was also suffering from decayed teeth; he was suing a dentist for removing his good teeth and leaving the bad ones – a waste of time, the lawsuit, for the dentist had fled to Kandahar where it was not illegal to make mistakes.)

Dobara was respected, too, for showing that he was a serious man. On his first visit, his ambition had seemed foolish. A snow leopard is not an important creature in anyone's life in Hazarajat, but if Dobara was prepared to return all the way from his city of London with his cameras, he deserved to be taken seriously. For this reason, a man who had not been in Hazarajat on Dobara's first visit came forward on the second visit. His name was Mohammad Hussein Anwari and he lived in the ancient city of Herat in the north-west. He was a man in the middle of his years and now made his living hiring out diesel generators, but as a much younger man, he had lived further north and hunted with his father. He had heard of the Englishman from a cousin in Hazarajat, a cousin he was visiting.

The first meeting of Dobara and Mohammad Hussein Anwari was a great shock to the Englishman. He asked Mohammad

Hussein if he'd seen any snow leopards with his own eyes and Mohammad Hussein said, 'Yes, I have seen many and I have shot ten.'

'Killed ten?' said Dobara.

'Yes,' said Mohammad Hussein. 'Bears, too. Ibex. Many red foxes.'

'But snow leopards!' said Dobara. It was difficult for him to master the words of Dari he needed to show his distress. 'Why the snow leopards? There are very few!'

Mohammad Hussein was not an ignorant man. He knew that people from countries such as the England of this Ibrahim-Dobara thought highly of the leopards. Indeed, he thought highly of them himself. But at the time he was hunting, the coat of a snow leopard would bring two hundred American dollars from a merchant in Iran, and there was more money, in smaller sums, for the paws, the bones and even the teeth of the animal, prized by doctors in China. It was the coat of the snow leopard that had permitted Mohammad Hussein to start his diesel-generator business in Herat.

Mohammad Hussein said to Dobara, 'I would not kill them now.'

Dobara told his story to Mohammad Hussein. He showed him the cameras he had brought with him from his university. He said that he would pay Mohammad Hussein ten English pounds each day to help him find a snow leopard. Ten English pounds was a good sum of money in afghanis, but not enough, for Mohammad Hussein would be away from his business for two weeks. He said he would have to ask for one hundred American dollars each day. This was more than Dobara could afford. He said he would talk to the people who controlled money at his university and come back in the late summer. But first he wanted to know if there was a good chance of finding a snow leopard.

By this time, Mohammad Hussein had come to like the Englishman, who knew so little about anything and next to nothing about snow leopards. He could see that Dobara was earnest, although foolish. And so he began the Englishman's education, taking care with his words so that Dobara could follow him. This is what he said:

'The snow leopard is a wild creature. He does not want to be seen by you, he does not want to be seen by me. If he could, he would kill you, because he hates you. He hates your shape, he hates your smell, he hates the sound of your voice. Nothing he sees in a whole year makes as much hate in him as you or me. But he fears you, too, and if he sees you he will hide or run. He will not attack you. Even as he runs, he is thinking, "What is this mad thing on two straight legs? Let it be struck dead by God!" Many years ago, a man came here from Turkey, where everyone is Sunni. He was a scholar, like you, but a scholar of poetry. He came for a holiday to Hazarajat because his brother-in-law was Hazara and had told him how beautiful it is in summer. He had heard of the snow leopard, too, and he hoped to see one. It was not possible, as he had only two weeks to spend amongst us. To tell you the truth, I did not want to find him a leopard at all. I could see that he wanted to show his love to the creature, and he hoped that the creature would show him love in return. No such thing is possible – not with a snow leopard, not with a bear, not with a red fox, not even with a marmot. They love freedom, Mister Ibrahim, do you understand? When they see a man like you or me, they see the opposite of freedom. That is the truth. We are not to blame – God did not give us the same freedom as the snow leopard. That is what they smell on us, the leopards, the bears, the red foxes. They smell that we are not free. It fills them with hatred and fear.'

The Englishman, Try Again, returned in late summer with the money to pay Mohammad Hussein Anwari, and with the equipment that the hunter had told him to bring with him. Once again Dobara thought to bring presents for the village, and medicines. This time the medicines included a special preparation for Mohammad Majid's daughter who suffered from headaches. This medicine was taken only once each week, and left the girl free from pain. Dobara was also successful with a new medicine for Ali Hassan's backache, and was pleased to receive a gift in return: a tin whistle, fashioned by Ali Hassan himself, on which the maker played 'God Save the Queen.' He had heard the tune on Sayed Ali's radio during the Olympic Games of 1960.

Mohammad Hussein and Dobara the Englishman climbed into the high mountains on the first day of the last month of summer. They intended to be away for as long as four weeks and had to carry their food for that time, but not water; springs ran from the mountain in many places. The Englishman had purchased a sleeping bag for Mohammad Hussein and also a two-man tent of great strength.

Mohammad Hussein carried a rifle, too, not to endanger the lives of snow leopards but to shoot such small game as he could find on the return journey – hares, above all. It was a handsome weapon, greatly valued by Mohammad Hussein, a Mosin-Nagant 7.62 sniper rifle with a special sight more powerful than the

Englishman's biggest camera. It had been in his possession for only a year. On a visit to the mechanics' market in Herat to find parts for his diesel generators, Mohammad Hussein had been approached by a Russian soldier looking for vodka, which was not for sale in Afghanistan. It happened that Mohammad Hussein knew a Kurdish Christian of the city whose brother smuggled unbottled vodka from Pakistan, and he was able to trade ten litres of the alcohol for the Mosin-Nagant. He had no use for the rifle at that time, but if the bribes he was required to pay to keep his business running should become too much for him to afford, he could join the mujaheddin of the north and earn a bounty on Russian officers above the rank of captain. The mujaheddin could fire their weapons with accuracy over short and middle distances, but long-distance sniping was beyond their skill.

'Your Russian soldier might end up being shot with his own rifle,' said the Englishman, but he did not mean it as a joke.

'No, no,' said Mohammad Hussein. 'His captain would put him in prison for losing his rifle. Or make him guard the road in the north-east. The soldiers who guard the roads in the north-east survive only for three days.'

The lower slopes of the mountains were dotted with hardy trees and bushes such as highland cedars. These did not grow to any great height but held fiercely to the soil with roots like the talons of eagles. Junipers grew amongst the rocks, fighting a battle for survival against the creatures that grazed on their foliage. Wildflowers of many types grew close to channels and rivulets, and in any place where soil still remained. Mohammad Hussein called over his shoulder the names of the wildflowers in Dari, and

Dobara, who had a knowledge of plants, replied with the names in English: oriental poppy; Rose of Jericho, a resurrection plant; Aaron's Beard; Artemisia; and small yellow blooms known both in English and my language of Dari as Prophet's Flower.

Mohammad Hussein spoke about the sky, too, and of the importance of watching it every minute. He said: 'See the small cloud by itself over to the east, Mister Ibrahim? That cloud is a spy. It looks over the mountains to see what mischief can be made. Soon it will vanish, and then we must be careful. Storms come into the mountains with no warning. Here is some more advice, Mister Ibrahim. You must stop and put your hand on a rock every half of an hour after ten o'clock in the morning. Your hand will tell you how much heat is in the sun. If the rock is too warm at midday for your hand to stay for more than one minute, you must rest in the shade. Mister Ibrahim, when you climb a mountain in Hazarajat, it is like a battle in a war. The mountain is not your friend, it is your enemy. It wants to kill you. We are going to a place that is full of jealousy. The mountain does not want you there. So many dangers!'

After two hours of climbing, the Englishman and the hunter crossed loose shale and outcrops of rock without a tree in sight. The Englishman, Dobara, was strong and lean and knew how to climb, but he marvelled at the skill of Mohammad Hussein. He said in Dari, 'You place your feet like a goat!' To which the hunter replied, 'My father was of the race of goats.'

The pack each climber carried rose high above the head. Often when he used his cameras the Englishman had to set his pack down to give himself freedom of movement. One of these times, his pack unbalanced from the boulder on which he'd left it, rolling

down the mountain further than the length of a tall tree. Mohammad Hussein said, 'Wait!' and removed his own pack and ran
down the slope to retrieve Dobara's. Running down the slope was
all very well for a man so sure-footed, but Mohammad Hussein
then ran back up the slope with the pack on his shoulders. The
Englishman, watching in amazement, realised that Mohammad
Hussein was keeping pace with him out of courtesy, and could
make much quicker progress if he wished.

Three hours of climbing took the two men into the cold zone,
where the frozen air from the snowy peaks rolled down the slopes
even if there was no wind to drive it. Whenever the Englishman
moved out of the bright sunshine to find a path between boulders,
he felt the deep chill of the air and would go from being bathed in
sweat to shivers in the space of a minute. Mohammad Hussein
said, 'When you rest at this height, go into the shade but not into
the hollows or you will freeze.'

Below them, the valley revealed its strange shape: a long, nar-
row neck, opening to a deep bowl, like the musical instrument
known as the tambur, and indeed the valley was called the Tambur. It was green all along its length with terraces climbing the
slopes of the bowl. Mohammad Hussein told Dobara that the
Hazara were compelled by cruel circumstance to use every piece
of land they could, and had become masters of living on rock.
'Hazara went into the mountains many ages ago,' he said. 'They
came here to find safety from their enemies. Now they make their
farms in every valley where soil remains. Where there is no soil,
they bring it from valleys where the sun doesn't reach and make
gardens in the sunny places. Hazara can find a way to live where
a mouse could not survive.'

At dusk, Mohammad Hussein led the way to a cave that he knew well. The two men cleared the floor of fallen rocks and spread out their sleeping bags. The cave had a high roof and ran deep into the mountain. Mohammad Hussein said that bears had lived at the back of the cave in past times, but no longer. 'The bears are gone from this mountain.'

'Why is that?' the Englishman asked.

'I shot them,' said Mohammad Hussein.

At the back of the cave, Mohammad Hussein had stored firewood many years earlier, when he was a hunter by profession, and the wood remained where he'd left it. The firewood had been chosen carefully, he explained; it burnt with great heat and it burnt slowly. He built a fire in from the entrance to the cave and made a meal of lamb and rice. He intended to use the fresh meat first before it spoilt.

The Englishman asked Mohammad Hussein, 'Are you not surprised to find the wood here after all these years?'

'No,' said Mohammad Hussein. 'It is my wood, and my family's. No one would touch it. Wood in the high mountains is like water in the desert. It always belongs to someone. I have two more caves on the mountain. In each, I will find firewood.'

They ate the rice and lamb sitting close to the fire. Night had fallen very quickly. Looking out from where he sat, Dobara could see the moon in the east, many times bigger than he'd ever known it and shining gold. He asked Mohammad Hussein, 'Do snow leopards live in caves like this?' and Mohammad Hussein shook his head and smiled.

'Where the snow leopards sleep, no one knows, Mister Ibrahim.'

'Really? No one knows?'

'It is a secret of the animals themselves. I have tracked the leopards as carefully as a fox and seen them vanish into the ground. We know they sleep, we know they make a home for their cubs, but where they do this they are too clever to reveal. This mountain on which we find ourselves, Mister Ibrahim – I know this mountain as well as anyone in this world knows the land he has crossed and recrossed all his life. If you put a hood over my head, I could lead you safely to the summit, have no doubt of that. But I am like a man who has read the Holy Book a thousand times and knows it by heart, and yet can still learn much more from a great scholar. The leopards are like great scholars, and their Holy Book is the mountain.'

Mohammad Hussein answered question after question from the Englishman as the night deepened. Finally he said, 'Now you can tell me stories of England.' Before he climbed into his sleeping bag, the hunter built a small wall of rocks a short distance from the mouth of the cave. 'This wall is to help you in the night if you wish to relieve your bowels or your bladder,' said Mohammad Hussein. 'Take a torch, of course, but remember when you come to the wall that you can only go a little way more. Or you will fall down the mountain and the bears will eat you.'

'But you said that the bears are gone!' said the Englishman.

'Then the ghosts of the bears will come and take you to a strange place. They will know you are my friend and they will keep you to punish me. Tell me a story of England.'

Dobara began a story about the tall buildings of London and of the great cathedral of St Paul's, but this wasn't what Mohammad Hussein wished to hear. So Dobara instead told a story of football and of his team called Millwall. Mohammad Hussein knew about football and it gave him pleasure to learn about Millwall, and also about Liverpool, of which he had heard.

In the night, the mountain made sounds like a living creature. At times the sounds seemed those of a musical instrument with a deep voice. As he listened, the Englishman began to believe that his mountain was talking to other mountains, because he heard more distant sounds responding. But he said to himself, 'Such a thing isn't possible!'

In the morning, Dobara left his sleeping bag to look for Mohammad Hussein, who had roused himself earlier. Outside the cave, beyond the wall that Mohammad Hussein had built, the Englishman gazed at the beauty around him. To the east, taller mountains stood against the blue sky as if in pride. On one peak, the morning sun picked out the glitter of snow, and as Dobara watched, a tall cloud passed under the sun and a shadow travelled swiftly down the mountain. Under the shadow, the snow changed colour from white to blue.

Mohammad Hussein appeared within a few minutes, carrying his prayer rug. He greeted Dobara in the language spoken in London. 'Good morning, sir! Good morning to Millwall!'

Mohammad Hussein worked patiently to bring the embers of the fire to life. Once he had a flame, he added tiny fragments of dry grass, then splinters, then fragments of wood no bigger than a man's finger, and at last lengths of wood as thick as a child's wrist. In the centre of the fire sat a round stone, a bread-making stone. Mohammad Hussein mixed flour and water and salt and white pepper into dough. Before flattening the dough on the hot stone, he added a small amount of brown powder from a cloth bag.

'Herbs?' asked the Englishman.

Mohammad Hussein said, 'Smell.'

Dobara put his nose to the opening of the cloth bag. Blood came rushing to his brain.

'Bloody hell!' he said. 'What is it?'

'Something for climbing the mountain,' said Mohammad Hussein.

The climbing on this second day was not straight up the mountain, but a slow circling well below the peak that made the Englishman think they were losing ground. Mohammad Hussein saw him looking puzzled and explained to him that if they made a direct climb at this point, the eagles in the sky would reveal to the leopards the presence of danger. 'When the eagles see humans, they climb higher, out of range of a rifle. The leopards understand this. If a leopard is out hunting, he will find his den and stay inside for three days, four days. He cannot find our scent because the wind takes it away down to the valley. But he watches the birds and he listens to the rocks. If he becomes suspicious, we will never see him, even if he is no further away than your shadow.'

In the middle of the afternoon, Mohammad Hussein found a great boulder on the mountainside and climbed to its top. He sat with his eyes closed for a long time, perhaps as long as thirty minutes. The Englishman did not interrupt him, but he felt worried. After all, it was a big task to find a snow leopard on such a huge mountain. He gazed away to the east at the snow peaks, wishing that his wife in London was with him to see the beauty of the land. He was away from her too much.

When Mohammad Hussein came down from the boulder, he did so in a hurry. He said, 'Be quick. Follow me.' The Englishman, full of worry even more than before, pulled on his pack and followed the hunter who was climbing more swiftly than ever, too swiftly for him to keep pace.

'Mohammad Hussein!' he called. 'I haven't the strength!'

The hunter threw off his pack and climbed down to Dobara. He pulled off the Englishman's pack, unstrapped it and began filling a smaller pack he'd brought with him. When the smaller pack was full, he said, 'Hurry!' Mohammad Hussein now carried two packs, one on his back and one hanging from his neck. Without any knowledge of the emergency, the Englishman's thoughts tortured him, but with his lighter pack, he found the strength to keep up with Mohammad Hussein, his breath whistling from his mouth. The speed at which Mohammad Hussein moved was frightening. Even more than to rest, the Englishman was desperate to know the cause of such haste because he could see nothing that might make Mohammad Hussein race up the mountain in the way he did. When he found a scrap of breath to cry out, 'What is it, for God's sake?' the hunter shouted, 'Don't talk!'

And then Dobara had no need to guess at the cause of Mohammad Hussein's great haste, for the answer came down on him in the form of a shadow. Overhead, the blue sky was being devoured by a rolling black cloud that stretched across the horizon. The storm came unlike any storm the Englishman had ever seen, not even in the lands of South America where he had taken his cameras in years past. The first gust of wind pushed him forward onto his hands and knees, and in the few seconds it took him to find his feet again, a darkness as deep as evening had overtaken the mountain. The rain came down like the waters of a cataract. Before Dobara's eyes, the path on which he was walking became a rapidly flowing stream. The wind seized hold of him and tumbled him first one way then another. With the burden of his pack, he no sooner won the struggle to be upright than he was thrown down again.

'Mohammad Hussein!' he cried out. 'Mohammad Hussein!'

His voice was overwhelmed by the roar of the wind. As heavy as the rain had been, it became much heavier still. He heard rocks crashing around him, picked up by the force of the torrent and rolled down the mountain. He thought, 'Dear God, I'll be crushed!' His fear almost became his fate, for he felt a rock strike his knee like the blow of a hammer. He fell and tumbled, reaching blindly with his hands. He screamed in his fear, 'Mohammad Hussein! Please! Mohammad Hussein!' He raised his hand to shield himself from a shape above him, and found his hand grasped, found himself lifted to his feet. Mohammad Hussein shouted into his ear, 'Put your weight against me! Even if I fall, keep hold!'

Dobara, poor man, could not make sense of what he was told, but he held with all his strength to Mohammad Hussein's arm. Pebbles and grit carried by the wind struck his face whenever he looked up. He was certain that both he and Mohammad Hussein would die on the mountain and he wished to surrender, but the hunter wrenched him forward into the face of the storm.

Mohammad Hussein was not striving in this way without pur-pose. He found the opening to the cave he was seeking and pushed the Englishman through it. Dobara knew only that he was drenched and bruised, but safe at last. In the darkness, the two men drew their breath and listened to the tumult outside. Mohammad Hussein lit four candles from his pack and the flames shone in the curtain of water that covered the entrance.

For some minutes, neither man said a word but watched in wonder the patterns of light dancing over the roof and walls of the cave. Then Mohammad Hussein, sitting with his legs crossed, be-gan to sing, and not softly but with the full force of his voice.

'Sing!' he roared. 'Sing to thank God!'

Only one song came to Dobara. It was the song of his team, the Lions of Millwall, called 'Let 'Em Come'. He sang it as loudly as Mohammad Hussein, or even louder. The words of the song were all to do with the victories of his football team, but in his mind he was praising all the gods of the world.

The storm lasted for two hours. In this time, Mohammad Hussein and Dobara removed their wet clothes and wrapped their sleeping bags around themselves. They ate food from tins since it was only the afternoon and Mohammad Hussein hadn't yet lit a fire. Dobara asked Mohammad Hussein, 'Do you have such storms every year?'

'No,' said Mohammad Hussein. 'Only twice before have I seen a storm like this. The last time was in the years of Shah Zahir.'

'Last night when we slept in the cave, I thought one mountain was talking to another, as if they were angry. Is that possible?'

Mohammad Hussein laughed and clapped his hands together. 'You heard the mountains talking, Mister Ibrahim?'

Now Dobara felt embarrassed. 'It was like they were talking.'

Mohammad Hussein laughed again. 'Mister Ibrahim, the mountain is made of rock. It cannot talk.'

'No, of course not,' said Dobara. 'It was my imagination.' He was blushing.

Mohammad Hussein must have thought the talking mountain a very great joke, because he laughed again and again and shook his head and said, 'A talking mountain! No, no, Mister Ibrahim!'

Late in the afternoon when the storm had moved far away and the water had stopped showering over the mouth of the cave, Mohammad Hussein and the Englishman put on dry clothes and stepped outside. The sky was blue once more and the sun blazed on its journey to the west. Water still ran over the ground beneath the feet of the two men, but not in torrents. High above, two eagles flew in circles.

'Will the storm frighten the snow leopards?' asked the Englishman. 'Will they stay in their dens for a long time?'

'No,' said Mohammad Hussein. 'The sun has returned. They will hunt.'

Enough wood was stored at the back of the cave for a big fire. Mohammad Hussein held his wet clothes and those of the Englishman above the flames to dry them. The Englishman offered to help but Mohammad Hussein refused, saying, 'Take some pictures outside. Take a picture of the talking mountain.' Dobara stepped outside the cave with his camera into the cool air of late afternoon. No sooner had he lifted the camera to his eye than a great roar sounded overhead – the sound of jet engines. Moham-mad Hussein came out of the cave and looked up at the sky to the east. Trouble was written on his face. He aimed his rifle at the jet planes, now almost overhead.

'Are you going to shoot at the planes?' asked Dobara. He could see that the aircraft were fighter-bombers. 'Is that sensible?'

'Russians!' cried Mohammad Hussein, shouting above the roar.

'Yes, but why shoot at them?'

When the jet planes had disappeared from the sky and the roar had died away, Mohammad Hussein said, 'Did you think I would shoot the aeroplanes? No, I was looking through my sight. These aeroplanes drop bombs.'

'Here? Why? The Russians don't fight in the Hazarajat.'

'No, not here,' said Mohammad Hussein. 'They are going to Herat. My friend, a catastrophe has overtaken our search for the leopards. I must go home to Herat.'

Even as he spoke, Mohammad Hussein had begun to pack. The Englishman's heart turned over in his chest, such was his disappointment. 'But we are so close!'

'Pack!' said Mohammad Hussein. 'I will take you down the mountain.'

'But why? I don't understand.'

'I will tell you as we return. Be quick, Mister Ibrahim!'

'I will stay.'

'No, that is not possible. It is a disgrace if I leave you on the mountain alone. You saw the storm. The mountain has many more tricks like that.'

'You said the mountain is made of stone. How can a pile of stones have tricks?'

But Mohammad Hussein was not listening. He made Dobara pack, leaving the fire smouldering. The Englishman's heart was broken.

They descended the mountain at twice the speed at which they'd climbed it. The Englishman was always behind. He cried out many times, 'Mohammad Hussein! I have to rest!' but Mohammad Hussein wouldn't stop. Finally Dobara burst into tears and sat down with his head in his hands, and this time Mohammad Hussein put down his pack and walked back to the Englishman. He said, 'Mister Ibrahim, I am sorry. We will rest.'

He found cool water in a spring and filled a cup for the Englishman. Then he opened a tin of peaches and told Dobara to eat them. This kindness did not stop Dobara's tears.

Mohammad Hussein tried to explain. 'Mister Ibrahim, my family is in danger, do you understand? The Russian aeroplanes, they were going to Herat to drop bombs. When I left Herat, Ismail Khan ruled the city. He took it away from the Russians. But now the Russians are returning. They will drop bombs everywhere – I know what they are like. My wife, my children – I fear for them, I fear for all the people of Herat. Listen to me. I will come back to this mountain with you. I will come back in winter if you wish. I will find the leopards for you. Do you believe me?'

Dobara did not believe him, but he said, 'Yes.' He did not believe he would ever see a snow leopard outside of a zoo. He understood the need to come down from the mountain, and yet his disappointment was so great that he found it hard to think of the people of Herat and their danger. He felt ashamed to confess such a thing to himself. When Mohammad Hussein started the journey down again, the Englishman stayed with him. He thought, 'I only want a picture. That's nothing. May this good man's family be safe.'

He went back to his own country, the Englishman, and reported to people at his university that he had failed to photograph the snow leopard. He was told, 'Your friend was right. The Russians have invaded Herat.' He waited with great anxiety to hear from Mohammad Hussein, who had promised to send him a letter. But even if a letter had come, the Englishman's wife had forbidden him to return to Afghanistan, such was the danger now that civil war was raging.

Even if he could not return to Hazarajat, just to hear of Mohammad Hussein's safety and that of his family would have been a blessing. But Abraham's wait for the letter from Mohammad Hussein was a long one of four years. In that time, he sent many letters of his own to the address Mohammad Hussein had given him, and spent many hours at the Afghan Embassy in South Kensington trying to find information about the situation in Herat.

In those four years, snow leopards had been photographed by others in India and Nepal. Abraham had missed his chance, but his disappointment did not last forever. His wife gave birth to a boy and then to a girl. Instead of travelling with his cameras Abraham stayed all year long at his university and taught students about the endangered creatures of the world.

The letter that arrived from Afghanistan after those four years was not from Mohammad Hussein but from his son, Rousal Ali. The letter was written in English and it told of sorrowful news. Mohammad Hussein had been dead almost from the time of his return to Herat. 'Dear Mister Ibrahim, has my father Mohammad Hussein

Anwari spoken of me to you? I am Rousal Ali Anwari, the second son of my father after Kamil Ali Anwari who taught children in the Hazara school of Herat not far from the tomb of the poet Jami. My father Mohammad Hussein Anwari was killed by hanging, it is my sadness to tell you. I have not been able to write this letter to you before this day because I have been hiding with the soldiers of Ismail Khan. The Russian soldiers have gone from Herat now and I am safe. I will tell you, with your permission, of my father's death by the Russian soldiers. It happened that the Russians came to our house in Sheikh Ismail two days after my father returned from Hazarajat. The soldiers went to many houses and at each house they did painful things to people. One man in Sheikh Ismail said, "Mohammad Hussein has a gun." It was not his fault to say this because the soldiers made him say it. The soldiers found my father's gun in our house, and it was a Russian gun. The captain of the soldiers said that my father had killed a Russian soldier and stolen his gun. For punishment my father was hanged by the soldiers in the doorway of our house and my brother Kamil Ali was hanged too. The soldiers would like to hang me but I escaped and hid myself with the soldiers of Ismail Khan. Mister Ibrahim, when my father came back to Herat from Hazarajat he was very sad that he did not find a leopard animal for you in the mountains for your pictures. Mister Ibrahim, if you are still looking for a leopard animal for your pictures, I will take you to Hazarajat. This will be my honour.'

Abraham shook his head in sorrow at the news of his friend's death. He had thought that a man like Mohammad Hussein, so strong, would live into old age. It seemed a disgrace to the nation of Russia and a disgrace to the world itself that a man like his friend should be hanged in his own doorway.

Abraham showed the letter to his wife, remembering, 'We walked on the mountain and I told him the names of the wild-flowers in English. He called me "Mister Ibrahim". He wanted me to teach him the Millwall song, you know. I wish I had.'

'You want to meet this Rousal Ali, don't you? You want to go back to Afghanistan,' replied Abraham's wife Sophie. 'Very much.'

Abraham's wife was silent for a minute or more. Then she said, 'The war is over. Go, if it's safe.'

Letters were written; arrangements were made. Abraham's university gave him leave of absence for six weeks.

In summer of the year 1990, Abraham returned to Hazarajat and met Rousal Ali Anwari in the village of Chakar near Darreh-ye Awd. Rousal Ali was taller than his father, but he did not look as powerful. Indeed, Rousal Ali was more of a scholar than a hunter as his father had been. He taught at the same school as his brother Kamil Ali had before Kamil's death. He said, 'My father did not want us to hunt or fight. He said in Afghanistan, if you pick up a gun you will never put it down. When I hid with Ismail Khan's soldiers, I dressed wounds and cooked rice.' He also confessed that he had never seen a snow leopard alive and did not know the secrets of the mountain. He wanted to keep his father's promise to Abraham for the sake of honour.

So when Abraham and Rousal Ali set off up the mountain in the summer to find a snow leopard, it was Abraham who led the way, and it was Abraham who said, 'Watch the sky,' and 'Put your hand on a rock to test the heat of the sun.' It was Abraham who told the story of the cloud that spied for the storm to come. And it was Rousal Ali who said, 'You walk so fast!'

At the end of the second day, Abraham searched for the cave that had saved him and Rousal Ali's father when the storm came from the east. He found it only when he glimpsed an empty tin left behind five years ago. In the cave that night, he lit a fire on the ashes of Mohammad Hussein's fire and told the story of the storm. When he had finished, Rousal Ali told his own story of his father. 'He stayed home in winter if he could, but in summer and spring he went to the north. In autumn he travelled to Kurdistan for bears. Once, in Kurdistan someone asked him to shoot a bandit, a very cruel man who had killed many people for money. My father said no. I asked him if it was worse to kill a man than a bear or a leopard. He said that it was not worse but he would not kill any man or any animal if it gave him pleasure. To shoot the bandit would have pleased him too much. He carried with him a piece of the tomb of a Sufi who had gone to Heaven on golden wings one hundred years after he was buried. When he killed an animal, he would take the piece of stone from its bag and kiss it, to show that the killing had given him no pleasure. Do you know, Mister Ibrahim, my father shot a Russian captain in Herat who was beating a mullah with a chain in Badmurghan near the mosque? This was before he met you in Hazarajat. But he was sorrowful. He said, "I will pay one day." And he did.'

Rousal Ali showed the piece of stone from the tomb of the Sufi. It was marble, with a red vein running through it. Abraham held it in his palm. He asked Rousal Ali if he might kiss it, to honour Mohammad Hussein. Rousal Ali said, 'Of course.'

After four days the Englishman and Rousal Ali were as high on the mountain as they dared to go. Patches of snow lay on the ground in places where the sun could not reach.

Up until this fourth day, the two men had followed a path upwards and around, or not so much a path as a way forward that could not be mistaken. But now the mountain became a place of ridges and ravines, impossible to scale or cross without climbing equipment. It became clear to the Englishman that his quest was foolish. Rousal Ali had no experience of the mountain and no knowledge of snow leopards; he had come to honour his father's promise, but it was Mohammad Hussein himself who was needed.

Abraham, the leader against his will, found the only place at this height where a tent could be safely raised. With no cave to shelter them, the two men prepared for the night ahead. The tent was held firmly to the ground with steel pegs hammered in to a depth of fifteen centimetres, but even so, the strength of the wind in the night was enough to make the two men fear that they would be hurled down the mountain in the darkness.

Rousal Ali said to Abraham, 'If we live through this night, I will pray at the mosque in Herat for ten days and keep a pebble in my shoe for six months.'

'Yes, and if we live through this night I will walk to Herat beside you in my bare feet.'

'No, no! You must do something for your God, for the God of the Jews!'

Abraham thought for a minute then said, 'I will attend my brother-in-law's Seder two nights in a row at Passover. Believe me, that's doing a lot for God.'

The morning was so bright and the sky so blue that the two men reconsidered their fears and decided to stay another night. After Rousal Ali's prayers, and then breakfast, they climbed a little higher, leaving the tent and their packs where they were.

They reached a place where they could look east, north and south, with only the western view hidden from them. The sun stood in the sky so fresh in its beauty that it may have been the first day of its life amongst the planets. To the east, a chain of mountain peaks each higher than the other gleamed with the snows that remained for the whole of summer, and the whole of the year. On all the earth, no greater wonder could be imagined. It seemed as if the world itself was saying to the Englishman and the Hazara, to Abraham and Rousal Ali, 'Remember this.'

But when the day had passed and the two men huddled in their tent once more, the wind howled as if in anger and Rousal Ali and Abraham swore again that they would hurry down the mountain the next day.

'I have three children and a wife who is dear to me, I think I must return to them,' said Rousal Ali.

'Sophie will worry every day I am gone, yes, we must go back tomorrow,' agreed the Englishman.

Then Rousal Ali spoke clearly. 'I do not believe we will ever find a leopard.'

Abraham responded, 'If your father were here, maybe. But neither you nor I have the skill.'

And yet they stayed one more day, and then one more still, and another and another. It was not the beauty of the mornings alone that kept them on the mountain. Each man spoke of a feeling that the journey down the mountain was not yet right, not ready *for him*. At one point Abraham said to Rousal Ali, 'If a storm such as the one that came down on your father and me blew in from the east now, we would die. We must promise each other to go tomorrow, no matter what we feel.'

The next day dawned, but the reluctance to leave was still strong, and so the two men remained. They didn't search for a snow leopard but only spoke of their children and their wives and of how much each wife, Sophie and Fatima, would worry. Rousal Ali told Abraham of the Russians in Herat; Abraham told Rousal Ali of his adventures in South America when he was photographing tapirs.

Of the Russians, Rousal Ali had this to say: 'The soldiers are very young. They hate Afghanistan and wish to go home to their own country. The first thing they think of is killing – it is their answer to every problem. They drink alcohol all the time and put needles in their arms. Mister Ibrahim, they killed my father but I feel sorry for them truly in my heart. Ismail Shah's soldiers killed many of the Russian soldiers and many of the soldiers of the communists in Kabul. Mister Ibrahim, I am sorry to say that they make them die in painful ways, in cruel ways. I was excused from watching because I only dressed wounds and cooked rice. Now the Russians have gone and they accomplished nothing. Many thousands of Herati died, as well as many thousands of communist army soldiers and many thousands of Russians. Like water poured on the ground in the desert. The water is a waste and in two minutes it has disappeared into the sand. The Herati disappeared, the Russian soldiers disappeared, the Afghan soldiers of the communist army, they disappeared too, all into the sand. It was a waste and a tragedy.'

The morning of the tenth day on the mountain began with the sound of a human voice outside the tent. Rousal Ali lifted his head out of his sleeping bag in alarm, and his alarm was greater when he saw Abraham looking back at him. The Englishman had put on his spectacles.

'What in the Prophet's holy name is that?' said Rousal Ali.

The voice seemed that of a man speaking as if in confidence to another; a low voice, and gentle. Rousal Ali, listening closely, could not make out a single word yet he was sure the voice was speaking Dari. Then the voice broke into laughter.

Rousal Ali scrambled to the opening of the tent, drew down the zipper and thrust his head outside. In the grey light of morning before the sun had appeared over the mountains he saw nothing but the sky and the rocks. Both men crawled outside the tent and stood in the dawn light looking this way and that.

'Who's there?' Abraham called, not loudly. He called again, this time in Dari. No answer came, and there was no one to be seen who could have answered. Each man held the hand of the other, as if amazement had made them into frightened children for the moment.

Abraham said at last, 'It was the wind.'

'Can the wind laugh?' said Rousal Ali.

They remained silent for some time, as long as ten minutes, and in that time they barely moved. Then Abraham became aware that he was clasping Rousal Ali's hand and in embarrassment he released it. The sun had lifted its face above the mountains of the east and the snow peaks glittered as if each mountain were capped with gems. It was a windless dawn and indeed the night itself had been still and calm. Giant shadows lay on the slopes of the eastern mountains below the radiance of the peaks. As the Englishman and Rousal Ali watched, the shadows were overtaken by the golden glow of the rising sun.

Abraham went to the tent for his camera for the sake of some final pictures of the mountain peaks. Neither man had said so, but each knew that this tenth day was surely the day of return. After the pictures of the eastern peaks, Abraham photographed Rousal Ali standing beside the tent. Then he placed his camera on a stand with three legs and turned a dial that would permit him eight seconds to take his position beside Rousal Ali before the camera came to life. The two men stood smiling with arms around each other's shoulders while the camera, as if in the hands of a ghost, opened its eye for an instant and made a picture of all that it saw.

The journey down the mountain was made in only three days. At the village of Chakar, Abraham and Rousal Ali stayed the night in the house of the headman, Najaf Husseini, who bred each year the finest goats of Hazarajat and who did not believe in such an animal as a snow leopard. The next day, Abraham and Rousal Ali travelled by horse and cart to a place known only as Taxi, two houses on the track that led to the Great Highway. The town of Taxi was occupied by one family, that of a man who owned an ancient Cadillac automobile that carried passengers to the bus stop on the Great Highway. This man was also called Taxi, although his true name was Abbas Dai Choupan. All around the two houses of the town lay the ruins of the many vehicles that Taxi had collected over the years – trucks and limousines, the shells of armoured vehicles, even the skeleton of a helicopter. All of these vehicles had been damaged in the long civil war and abandoned in the wilderness.

On the way to the Great Highway, Rousal Ali and Abraham agreed that the true reward of the expedition to find the snow leopard had been the friendship they had found. Rousal Ali made a gift of his father's Sufi stone with its red vein. The most valuable thing that Abraham had to offer was the gold badge that commemorated a famous victory of the Lions of Millwall. He gave the gold badge to Rousal Ali, and taught him the song of Millwall, 'Let 'Em Come', translated into Dari.

At the Great Highway, Rousal Ali took the bus to Herat, while Abraham, after a wait of ten hours, took another bus to Kabul.

The house in which Abraham Lew lived with his wife and children was in the suburb of Bermondsey. He and Sophie had lived there before the time of their children. In those years, Abraham had a room set aside for the making of photographs, but when the first baby was expected the room became a nursery. If Abraham wished to make pictures he instead went to the laboratory of his university. It was there that he made pictures from those he had taken in Hazarajat – three hundred altogether. It was all done by a machine.

Abraham took the pictures home after no more than a glance, intending to share them with his wife. When the two children had been put to bed that evening, he sat at the table in his kitchen with Sophie and passed one picture after another to her. He said, 'That's Chakar, you can see the market, you can see the figs,' and, 'The sunsets were the most beautiful I have seen.' Finally, he said, 'This is Rousal Ali praying on the mountain. He didn't mind me taking pictures. The water bottle is for *wu'du*.' When he came to the pictures of the tenth morning on the mountain he explained: 'Me and Rousal Ali outside our tent. I took it with the timer.'

Sophie looked at the picture with her head to one side, musing, 'But you told me you never found a snow leopard.'

'It's true, we didn't. Why do you ask?'

Sophie passed him the picture. At first he could see only himself and Rousal Ali smiling in front of their red tent, each dressed in jeans and yellow waterproof jackets from a shop in Oxford Street. With his dark beard, he and Rousal Ali could almost have been taken for brothers. The picture captured some of that morning's blue sky and also the steep wall of clay-coloured sedimentary rock behind the tent in which fragments of marble could be found.

'Look,' said Sophie, tapping the photograph with her finger.

On a ledge of the steep wall, high above the tent, a snow leopard lay at ease in the morning sun, head raised, thick tail curled. So closely did the coat of the leopard blend with the rock that the animal could easily be overlooked. But snow leopards, as Abraham knew, were the most cautious beasts in all the cat family, the most secretive. It seemed impossible that this snow leopard could lie in the sun in such a relaxed way while humans walked and talked twenty metres below.

'That could never happen!' he said. He walked over to the window and held the picture to the light, since there was still colour in the summer sky even at seven o'clock. But how could daylight change the picture, change what was true?

It was a snow leopard, and it gazed down at the scene below – at Abraham and Rousal Ali, at the camera itself – as if it were as close a friend of the two men as they were to each other.

'I have never seen you so amazed!' smiled Sophie.

Abraham shook his head, but now he too was smiling. A snow leopard! What sort of morning was that in Hazarajat? A morning of laughter outside the tent. A morning of jewels sparkling on mountain-tops.

'Darling, a picture can't lie,' said Sophie.

8

The Behsudi Dowry

The house of Ahmed Behsudi in the valley of Masjed-e Negar west of Chaghcharan was surely blessed by fortune, as Ahmed himself would never deny. His six orchards flourished; his two wives, Fatima and Rabaab, were each as intelligent as the other; his mare remained strong into her eighteenth year, and his first four children honoured him with their obedience. In the last years of the reign of Shah Zahir, Ahmed Behsudi was prosperous enough to install a glass window in his house that permitted him to look west and study the nearest of his orchards while still inside. He also owned a sugar bowl made of crystal, purchased from a Baluchi merchant, a *kytigar* in our language of Dari, who travelled Hazarajat selling such oddities.

I have said that Ahmed Behsudi was the father of four obedient children, and so he was, but he was also the father of a fifth child, another boy, who was not obedient. It was this son, Hameed, who became the burden to his father that God asks all fathers to bear, in one way or another.

Hameed was not disobedient by choice. He wished with all his heart to make his father proud of him. But it was the sad truth that all the common sense that Ahmed Behsudi could pass on to his children had been divided among Hameed's brothers and sisters, leaving none for him. As a small child, he felt the force of his mother's hand, as many children do, but it was always with a heavy heart that his mother punished him because it often seemed that the trouble was just bad luck. When he was six, he climbed onto the roof of the house while trying to see a hoopoe bird up close – no harm in that – but he fell from the roof and landed on top of the family's rooster, killing the poor bird. In the same way, he fed the mare in summer on some grass he'd pulled from beneath the water tank – a good deed, for the mare's yard was all dust. But hidden in the fresh grass was a small toad, and when the toad startled the mare she kicked Hameed's brother Mohammad Ali in the chest and broke five ribs. Hameed's father said, 'Do you not know that toads gather in the grass under the water tank? Why didn't you think?'

'Father, I will know next time,' replied Hameed.

Other disasters had less to do with bad luck. One cold morning in autumn when it was his task to chase ravens from the apple orchard, Hameed lit a fire to warm himself and by mistake set a tree ablaze. The tree would normally produce seven hundred apples, but the damage to the trunk kept most of the tree's fruit from ripening that autumn. His father said to him, 'Did you not have the sense to light your fire far from the tree?' Hameed replied, 'Father, I'll know next time.'

But next time was worse, for a book came into Hameed's hands in a peculiar way, and what Hameed read in the book made him blind to his duties.

To the misfortune of being witless, Hameed had to add the misfortune of not knowing what made it possible for the Hazara to survive. Every Hazara boy and every Hazara girl is taught the answers to the survival of our people from a young age. The teaching takes the form of an almost-song of questions, to which the child responds. The mother asks her daughter, the father asks his son:

'Where do our enemies live?'

'To the east and west, to the north and south.'

'Where is our safety?'

'Our safety is in our Shi'a faith, in our family, in our village, in our people.'

'How do we greet an enemy?'

'We say, "Peace, brother!"'

'And if our enemy is obstinate?'

'By God's will, we prevail.'

'What is the best use we have for our hands?'

'To make them strong.'

'What is the best use we have for our ears?'

'To hear what our mother tells us, to hear what our father tells us, to hear what God whispers to us when our way is lost.'

'And what use do we make of the hours of a day?'

'First we give our thanks to God, next we strive.'

There is nothing in these teachings about the reading of books, and if the reading of a book is spoken of, it concerns the Holy Book. There is nothing about sitting under a tree in the shade of the apricot orchard and giving hours of each day to words on a page. The Hazara wish to see their sons and daughters educated, even in strange ways, such as reading books that tell stories and do nothing else, but in a family such as that of Ahmed Behsudi reading strange books came after chasing ravens from the fruit trees and keeping the water channels clear of rubbish. It was because the boy Hameed was witless that he didn't understand why the Hazara have survived this many ages.

I must explain how Hameed came by the strange book in the first place.

The Baluchi merchant who sold the crystal sugar bowl to Ahmed Behsudi was a very shrewd man. From a distance so far that a man's face could not be seen in its features – the colour of his eyes, the length of his nose, how many teeth remained to him – the merchant could tell the number and value of the coins that man kept in his purse. And from the thousands of things he carried in his two carts, all of them for sale, the merchant knew exactly which item, which two items or three, would appeal to any man or woman he came across. Yet even a man as clever as the Baluchi merchant can make a mistake, as he did when he met the old man who sold chestnuts outside the gate of the embassy of America in Kabul.

But I see that I must explain how the chestnut seller came by the book that ended up first in the hands of the Baluchi merchant, then in the hands of Hameed, a story in itself.

The chestnut seller was sitting on his four-legged stool one afternoon in winter waiting for the hour at which the Americans went home. At that hour, as the Americans passed through the gate, he was bound to sell most of his chestnuts. He had taught himself certain American words, such as 'Beautiful day!' and 'Okay!' and so had become a favourite of those who worked in the embassy.

It happened this day that no Americans came to the embassy even though it was not a Sunday, the holy day of the Americans, and the chestnut seller was left a puzzled man. He tried with his few words of American to ask the soldier at the gate the reason for this sudden holiday. The soldier made no reply but only stood with his head bowed and his rifle held upside down. Within a few minutes the day grew stranger still, for soldiers came to the embassy gates in a truck and stood with their weapons ready outside the gate. Then came a black car carrying the King of Afghanistan, Zahir Shah, in a green tunic decorated with a big medal in the shape of a star and many others. The chestnut seller in his amazement called out, 'Aiee! God's blessings on you, sir!' Zahir Shah and his sons and many people of importance walked past the chestnut seller without seeing him and continued on their way into the embassy.

The chestnut seller approached one of the soldiers who had remained outside the gate.

'Brother,' he said, 'what matter has brought Zahir Shah to see the Americans?'

The soldier, a young man, explained, 'The King of the Americans is dead.'

'Aiee! An evil day in the world! Was he old, the American King?'

'No. Too young to be my father.'

'Aiee! A disaster!'

In Afghanistan, the most common way for a king to lose his

life is to be shot. The father of Zahir Shah had been shot by the king-killer, Abdul Khaliq. And so the chestnut seller asked the soldier, 'Was he shot by one who hated him?'

'Yes,' said the soldier. 'He was shot in his car.'

The chestnut seller was greatly saddened to hear this news. He felt ashamed that he had whispered to himself earlier in the afternoon ignorant things about the laziness of the Americans in taking holidays without warning. The metal drum that kept his chestnuts hot was mounted on wheels and capable of being moved to another place, a busier place, but he remained where he was outside the gate as a mark of respect for the dead King of the Americans.

After the space of an hour, Zahir Shah and all the important people with him came out of the embassy and returned to their black cars. The American who was known as the ambassador walked to the biggest of the black cars with Zahir Shah and shook his hand before the King departed. As the ambassador and an Uzbeki assistant who helped him with the Dari language walked back to the gate, the chestnut seller asked the American to accept a gift of chestnuts, a very large portion wrapped in fig leaves that had to be stolen each evening from an orchard on the outskirts of Kabul.

'What does he say?' the American asked the assistant.

'Sir, he wishes to give you chestnuts as a mourning gift. It is our custom to give such gifts.'

'Is that a fact? Well, I can't refuse such a gift, can I? Thank him for me.'

The assistant thanked the chestnut seller, who added some further words of condolence for the ambassador.

'Sir, he says that he weeps for your grief and for the sad day that has come to America. He says it is a tragedy for the American King to die so young. He means "president", not king.'

Tears sprang into the eyes of the ambassador, for the murder of the President had come as a terrible blow to him. 'Tell this good fellow that Mrs Kennedy and her children would be comforted to hear of his sympathy,' he replied. Then he added, 'Find a gift for him.'

The assistant said that he would of course find a gift for the chestnut seller, but what gift that could be was a puzzle. All that he could find was a set of four famous American books in Dari, each book with the English version at the back. The embassy kept several sets of these books to give to schools in Kabul. Embassies in other countries kept such sets in the language of that country. The assistant walked down to the gate and handed the set of books to the chestnut seller, with the thanks of the embassy and the special thanks of Mrs Kennedy and her children and Mr Lyndon B. Johnson, the new American President.

The chestnut seller was honoured to be given such a gift as the strange books. Although he could not read Dari and certainly could not read English, the books were kept safe in the house he shared with his brother and brother-in-law, with his wife and three children, with the wife of his brother-in-law – his sister – and with their three children, and with the wife of his brother and their two children. The set was wrapped in a cloth and tied with string and placed at the bottom of a tin chest that held bedding reserved for guests. Only once in two years did the chestnut seller take the books from the chest, when he showed them to a mullah. His wife had told him that the books might be considered impious

and should be approved by someone who knew about such matters. The mullah kept the books for a week and looked at every
page and at the pictures on the covers. He said that the books
were foolish, but not impious.

It was a season of feasting ordered by Zahir Shah that led to
the strange books coming into the hands of the Baluchi merchant.
Zahir Shah had paid many visits to the nations of Europe and it
was well known that he wished Afghanistan could become a
modern country with its own tall buildings and steel bridges and
aeroplanes. Two years after the chestnut seller became the owner
of the strange books, Zahir Shah invited important people from
Europe to Kabul to talk with them about the future of his country.
The important people stayed for weeks, and when they left, more
arrived, and then even more. Each day for three months, all of the
chestnuts in the market were purchased by the cooks of Zahir
Shah's palace to make a special meal for the King's guests. The
chestnut seller in his despair went a long way out of the city to
find chestnuts, but without success. Finally he asked the Baluchi
merchant, who was making one of his visits to Kabul, to come to
his house and choose amongst his possessions those he wished to
purchase.

The Baluchi merchant was a clever man but he was not a greedy
man. He paid the chestnut seller a fair price for his saucepans and
bedsheets and rugs. The strange books delighted him and he paid
the chestnut seller twice their value, although in truth he didn't
know what they were worth. 'Where did they come from?' he
asked the chestnut seller, and he was told, 'When the American
King was shot in his car, they came to me as a gift.'

In the year that followed the Baluchi merchant's purchase of the strange books, he suffered such ill fortune that he began to feel that a curse had been fixed on him by an enemy. First, his wife went mad and jumped into a well, then the older of his two horses choked on a pomegranate. Worst of all, the merchant grew a mole above his right eye where no mole had existed before, and this was a sure sign of a deep curse. He went to see a woman in the west of Hazarajat who understood curses and she searched through everything in his two wagons until she came upon the strange books.

'Little wonder your wife went mad!' said the woman. 'Have you lost your senses? Get rid of them!'

But it is no simple matter to rid yourself of a possession that attracts ill fortune. The owner cannot simply throw it away – that would only double the bad luck. He must pass it on to someone else, and the person it is offered to must accept it freely. A saucepan or an oil lamp or a birdcage would quickly find a new owner ignorant of what he was accepting, but a book was of no use to anyone; besides, it aroused suspicion. And so it was only when the merchant came upon the unfortunate Hameed that he was able to end his year of bad luck.

The merchant spied Hameed in the apricot orchard of his father just to the side of the track that passed between the trees on one side and a building on the other side that had been the church of a Christian from Germany many years past. The German was shot by soldiers of Nadir Shah for hiding Hazara children in the time of massacres. When the merchant first saw Hameed, the young man was talking to the dog he had with him in the manner of a man who expected answers from the animal. The merchant thought, 'I have found the simpleton I have been seeking!' He called out to Hameed, 'Friend, good morning to you and the blessings of God forever!'

Hameed walked over to the merchant's cart, stumbling twice on the way, and the merchant was even more convinced that God had given him a chance to cast away the curse of the strange books.

'What name do you go by?' asked the merchant.

'Hameed Behsudi of my father's house on the hillside by the big orchard,' said the young man.

'Ah, I know him well! Ahmed Behsudi, a most honoured man! I sold him a sugar bowl. Friend, would it be within your power to pick me a few apricots on this morning? I am tormented by hunger.'

'Well, I will,' said Hameed. 'But for my father's sake, I must ask you to pay.'

'Would I take fruit without payment? Never in life!'

Hameed picked twenty of the finest apricots he could find on the nearest tree and brought them to the merchant.

'If these do not satisfy you,' he said, 'then God has given you no taste for fruit.'

'Would I complain of apricots such as these?' said the merchant. 'Never in life, I tell you from my heart. But friend, do you know, I have searched in my purse and have never felt it lighter. Not a coin to be found. Would you accept a trade?'

'What do you suggest?' replied Hameed, on his guard.

'What do I suggest? Not a second sugar bowl, since your father's house already boasts the finest sugar bowl in our land of Afghanistan. A new pestle for your wife – would that please you?'

'Alas, I am yet to find a wife.'

'Is that so? You surprise me, a handsome chap like you. Hmm, let me see. Well, I have something here that came to me from the King of the Americans who made a visit to our city of Kabul and asked me to accept it. Have you ever seen books like this, friend?'

Hameed's interest was pricked as soon as he saw the books. Slow as he was at the tasks that are favoured amongst the Hazara, he was a good student at the school he had attended in years past. He could read our language of Dari, and he could write at the speed of five words per minute.

On the cover of the first book, in both Dari and English, the words 'The Adventures of Huckleberry Finn' were written in gold. The word 'adventures' appealed to Hameed, and the picture on the cover was a wonder. It showed a boy with hair of a strange colour and a tall man coloured black. The boy and the man were standing on a craft of wood and the craft itself was floating in a river. Hameed had never seen a boat – this was not to be wondered at for very few in Hazarajat had seen one – but he had heard of them. He had never seen a stream like that which was shown in the picture either, and the boat, the boy with strange hair, the tall man coloured black and the great stream excited him.

'Will these books pay for my apricots?' asked the merchant, who was just as excited as Hameed, although for a different reason.

'Oh, yes!' said Hameed. 'I thank you, sir, with all my heart!'

'Just so we understand each other,' said the merchant. 'You are accepting these books freely? That is true, surely?'

'Yes, the books are accepted freely, and I thank you again.'

'You are quite sure?'

'Very sure!' said Hameed.

With no further words between them, the Baluchi merchant shook the reins of his cart and urged his horse to move along. Hameed waved to the merchant before he disappeared from sight around a bend, but the merchant, who seemed in haste, did not look back.

Hameed began reading without delay. Each of the four books he had to choose from had a different name. The first, of course, was named 'The Adventures of Huckleberry Finn Mark Twain.' The second was named 'The Adventures of Tom Sawyer Mark Twain.' The third was named 'Little Women Louisa May Alcott.' The fourth was named 'Uncle Tom's Cabin Harriet Beecher Stowe.' He sat beneath an apricot tree, shaded from the sun by the leaves, sipped some water from his clay jar made to stay cool in the heat, and turned to a page in the Dari part of 'The Adventures of Huckleberry Finn Mark Twain' headed 'Here Begin'.

I must explain to the reader that the type of books called 'novels' in English hardly exist in Hazara culture. Such books come from the imagination of a writer, which is to say, the stories are not true, or not true in the way that a book about caring for fig trees is true, or a book about the moon, such as that read by the scholar Mohammad Majid. For this reason, Hameed was at first baffled as his eyes and brain struggled with the sentences. He believed the story of Huckleberry Finn to be true, but he could not understand why a boy from a poor family would tell his story in a book. The boy Huck was not a prophet, he was not a mullah, he was not a king. Then Hameed thought, 'Ah, but the boy will become a king after many troubles,' and was able to keep reading without feeling puzzled.

Hameed had the sense to keep the books to himself. He knew

that it would be difficult to explain to his father that he had traded twenty choice apricots for strange books that had no value. He wrapped the books in cloth, just as the chestnut seller had kept them, then hid them under a rock in a place where any rain that came to Hazarajat would not reach them.

It was Hameed's task the next day to walk all about the fig orchard and make sure that the fruit was not stolen. While he did this, his brothers harvested the apricot orchard, where the fruit was already ripe. Not only did Hameed remain in the orchard during the day but also at night, with his bedding under a tarpaulin held up by a pole. His father thought that even Hameed could not come to grief with such a simple task, so long as he didn't again set fire to a tree. The truth was that few people in Hazarajat would ever steal the fruit from an orchard, but thefts had happened and it was wise to be cautious. Sadly, Hameed did not walk about the orchard but instead slowly read his way through the story of Huckleberry Finn by sunlight and candlelight. Sadly, some of the people known as nomads in Hazarajat – not Hazara, but not anything else either, a mystery people – happened to be in the valley of Masjed-e Negar at that time. Without kinship to the Hazara, they felt no guilt in taking the fruit from unguarded trees they came upon. But not all at once. They took a few from the trees nearest to the track each night. Hameed read the book of Huckleberry Finn slowly. It took him a month to finish the part with the heading 'Here Begin'. In that month, two fig trees were stripped of all their fruit.

Hameed discovered the theft before anyone else noticed. He struck himself on the head as punishment for his stupidity. He knew that his father, if he found out about the theft, would fetch him a much stronger blow. But a clever scheme came to him out of the blue sky. He went to the far side of the orchard, the most hidden part, and picked all the figs from two trees. The figs were still four weeks from full ripeness, but that could not be helped. He brought the freshly picked figs home and said to his father, 'I became bored, so I began the harvest. These are from the trees closest to the track.'

Ahmed Behsudi frowned at his son. 'No harm is done, but in future wait until the figs ripen.'

Hameed returned to the orchard full of good intentions. He would put the book of Huckleberry Finn aside and walk about in the orchard all day. He would sleep at night thirty minutes at a time, and keep his eye out even in the darkness for the fig thieves. But the spell of the story had its way. Hameed looked up from the book every now and again, saying to himself, 'I will go now and walk about the orchard.' And so he did, but as he walked he read the book of Huckleberry Finn. A brown bear could have blocked his path and he wouldn't have noticed.

The fig thieves by now had no fear of Hameed. They considered him insane, wandering about with a book under his nose. Soon they had stripped four more trees of fruit.

Hameed could not help but see that the entire six trees on the roadside were bare of fruit. He had no other choice than to take the fruit from four more trees at the very back of the orchard.

'The ravens came,' he said to his father, 'so I began the harvest.'

Ahmed Behsudi danced with rage on the place where he stood. 'Did I not tell you to wait for the fruit to ripen? Were your ears full of beeswax?'

Every son fears his father's wrath. Certainly Hameed feared his father. Certainly he wished to honour him in every way he could. And yet he was powerless to put the book of Huckleberry Finn aside and give his mind to his task. Not only had he been forced to lie to his father, he was forced to lie to his mother when she asked him if he knew where the candles had gone. Hameed's mother kept twenty candles in a wooden box at all times, replacing each one when it was taken. She now had five candles.

'I took them to the orchard,' he said, 'but on the way I misplaced them.'

Hameed's mother said to her husband, 'If it were not against God's law, I would tie him to a tree for the wolves to enjoy.'

Ahmed Behsudi thought to send his eldest son Abdul Ali to the orchard to discover the reason for Hameed's madness. But Abdul Ali was married and had many other tasks to fill his day. Ahmed Behsudi's other sons, Mohammad Ali and Hussein Ali, were also married men with no time to spare. So Ahmed Behsudi himself walked to the fig orchard in the heat of the sun to see what Hameed was up to. He didn't call out his son's name when he reached the orchard but instead crept about quietly until he spied this most difficult of his children sitting under a fig tree with the book of Huckleberry Finn in his hands. Ahmed Behsudi was amazed. He kept his temper and stepped closer to his son, and closer still, and finally he stood no more than the length of his arm from Hameed. So deep in the book was Hameed that he did not see his father until Ahmed Behsudi roared at the top of his voice: 'What madness is this! Will I put my hands to your neck and choke you now or first whip you raw?'

Hameed leapt to his feet in dread, but he kept a tight hold on his book.

'Give this object to me!' cried Ahmed Behsudi. He meant the book of Huckleberry Finn, of course.

Hameed, so much younger than his father, was able to spring away in time to avoid capture.

'Father, no.'

'Do you defy me? Has such a day come in my family?'

'Father, no.'

'I tell you, boy, give me that object!'

'Father, no.'

Disobedience of this sort is never found amongst the Hazara. A father is honoured. To insult your own father with disobedience is asking for trouble. And yet, Ahmed Behsudi found the strength to seize back control of his passions. This boy of his had made a habit of angering him, but never through spite. Whatever the vile object Hameed was guarding, it must be precious to him. And so Ahmed Behsudi raised his hands with his palms out, a signal that he was calling for peace. He gestured towards the mossy ground and sat down. Hameed, after some hesitation, sat before his father, but he kept the book safe.

'What is it, this thing?' Ahmed Behsudi asked calmly. 'Tell me.'

'A book of America, a book of a boy Huckleberry and Jim, a book of Mississippi.'

'In God's name, talk sense.'

'I swear to you!'

'How came it into your hands?'

'The merchant gave it to me.'

'Ah, he gave it to you! For his pleasure? Strange, I have always known him to ask something in exchange.'

'I gave him twenty apricots.'

'Twenty apricots! For *that*!'

'For this and three more.'

'Ah! Four worthless objects instead of one for twenty good apricots! My happiness is restored!'

'Father, it was a *chana*.'

Chana in our language of Dari means a great bargain, but not a bargain won through trickery. A *chana* is a bargain that grows out of the goodwill of those who are making the trade.

'Ah!' said Ahmed Behsudi. 'A *chana*, is it? Well, my heart is at peace. It was a *chana*. Twenty apricots that took a year to grow for some such rubbish as "Mispee", but it is a *chana*. Thank God for that!'

Ahmed Behsudi, calling on all of his ancestors who had found their way to Paradise for patience, looked his son in the eye. This boy – was he indeed Hazara? Yes, he was Hazara, it must be admitted, but what sort of Hazara? Ahmed Behsudi had known a man many, many years in the past, who found a stone of astonishing beauty, redder than a ruby, a stone that caught the sun and sent shafts of rose-coloured light about the room. And the man had contemplated the beauty of this stone each day, this rare gem, until one day, with a smile on his face, he swallowed it. Those who witnessed him swallowing the stone leapt back in amazement. 'What have you done, and why?' they cried out. And the man said this – Ahmed Behsudi remembered exactly: 'I had no words left, so I ate it.' The stone was not lost forever. It emerged from its owner's regions before long. But the man said he was not sorry for what he'd done – no, he was glad of it. Such passions can take a hold of any man, it was well to remember.

Ahmed Behsudi only discovered in that moment that he loved the boy Hameed. He loved him because he was difficult to love.

'Keep the books,' he said. 'What else must you tell me?'

He meant that he wanted to hear the truth about the figs that had been brought home with a story of ravens. Hameed told him the truth. Ahmed Behsudi said nothing at all for some minutes, then he spoke. 'Hameed, a man might have four brothers, five brothers. He might have many sisters. He might have four wives, if he can afford them. He might have fifty friends, in his good fortune. But he can have only one father. In all the world, no man will grieve for another as a father grieves for his son. Keep me in your heart, as I keep you in mine.' Then he added, 'Leave the book at home until the figs are in their baskets.'

The fig harvest was over within the week and Hameed was free to enjoy the book of Huckleberry Finn. His father found the time to hear the boy read the book aloud, against his better judgement, and discovered an enjoyment in hearing the story. He thought to himself, 'Such a river, Mississippi! Would that we had a river like Mississippi in Hazarajat!' When he began to understand the story of the black slave Jim, he thought of the many Hazara who had become slaves during the years of massacres. But at the same time, he worried about Hameed. No Hazara can make a life for himself by reading the books of America. And was it not possible that Hameed would take it into his head to travel the country, like the boy Huck? In America with so many cars and bridges and tall buildings, a boy might travel on a road or a river and find his fortune. Not in Hazarajat, not in Afghanistan.

He told his worries to his second wife Zainab, Hameed's mother, and she listened with the attention for which she was known. She said, 'He must marry.'

'Do you think so?' said Ahmed Behsudi. 'Yes, perhaps you are right. With a wife and children, he will cease reading books, he will find some sense. But who would marry him?'

Ahmed Behsudi's second wife said, 'Najaf Khalaj has a daughter of twenty years. Her father wants her to marry.'

Ahmed Behsudi threw back his head and laughed until tears ran down his cheeks. 'Najaf Khalaj's daughter? Proud Nadia? That one? What, do you hate the boy so much? Better to marry him to a brown bear!'

It was true that Najaf Khalaj wanted a husband for his daughter and would probably accept Hameed with all his faults, but the daughter, Nadia, was no blessing. As beautiful as she was, with fine eyebrows, no man in the whole of Hazarajat would take her for his wife. Many had courted her through her mother and father but the girl's temper had ruined every match. To one young man she had said, 'If your nose did not resemble that of an anteater, it would be better for you.' Another who came a great distance to drink tea with her was asked to turn sideways. When he did so, Nadia stared at the side of his head. 'Yes, I thought so,' she said. 'I can see in this ear and out the other. Nothing between.' Her mother said to her, 'Do you think we will feed you forever? Your pride will go with you to your grave!' But Nadia felt no caution: 'If I am turned out into the world to live on crumbs like a sparrow, so much the worse for me. The men you bring are fools.' Some may have been fools, but even those with wits revealed some flaw to Nadia. 'He is too short. I would spend my life looking down at the top of his head…He is too tall. Am I to destroy my neck by looking up all day?…He smells like a stoat…He has a wart on his chin bigger than a chestnut…'

What hope, then, for an awkward young man such as Hameed? Ahmed Behsudi put his mind to the problem and came up with a solution. 'I will sweeten her thoughts with a gift. If she will marry Hameed, the small fig orchard will come with him.'

Zainab said, 'You will give a dowry to the bride? And for how many years will our neighbours laugh? More than a hundred!'

Ahmed Behsudi persisted in his plan. He visited Nadia's father, who himself owned an orchard, much smaller than any of Ahmed Behsudi's, however. Najaf Khalaj listened to Ahmed Behsudi, and smiled as he listened, and laughed as he listened, and sighed as he listened.

Finally, he spoke. 'The girl has an imp in her heart. Think of my shame when I say that I have no influence with her. And her mother? She listens to her mother even less than me. Some grave sin of mine must be known to God that I am burdened with such a child as Nadia and her pride. Send Hameed, by all means! But prepare for disappointment.'

It was arranged for Hameed to walk the road to the village where Nadia's family kept their orchard to greet the girl's unfortunate mother and father, and to drink tea with the dreadful girl herself. The road to the village was a long one and would take the whole of the morning, and since this was a journey that Hameed had no taste for, ending as it would in meeting a girl he had no interest in, he carried with him his book of Huckleberry Finn, and read it as he walked. He had finished the book once already and had considered reading *Uncle Tom's Cabin*, but his love of the Huckleberry book had grown so strong that he began it again, and this second reading thrilled him even more than the first.

Hameed arrived in the village well after midday. It happened that Najaf Khalaj's house was the first in the town. Nadia and her mother and father were waiting at the door and saw Hameed with the book under his nose walk straight past and into an old gundy tree allowed to grow where it stood for the sake of its shade.

Nadia's mother put her hand to her face and shook her head. Najaf Khalaj sighed deeply. But Nadia laughed aloud. 'Well, this is a gift,' she said. 'The biggest fool in the world has come to my doorstep.'

'Child, build treasure in Heaven,' pleaded Najaf Khalaj. 'Be kind to the boy.'

Hameed with a bump on his forehead allowed himself to be helped to his feet by Najaf Khalaj. He picked up his book, cleaned the dust from its cover and made an apology to Najaf, to his wife and to the daughter, Nadia. Hameed was shown indoors, according to our custom, for a young man who is courting will wish to see a clean and tidy household. 'Study the mother, know the daughter,' as we say, and in the case of Iram Khalaj's first two daughters, now married, the advice was good. The third daughter, Nadia – alas!

It was Nadia's habit to first show great courtesy to the young men who came to her father's house. This suited her well, for the shock to come, when she abandoned her manners, would be that much greater. She asked Hameed if he would be pleased to take a glass of tea. She asked if he enjoyed sugar. She handed him the glass of tea on a saucer with two sugar cubes. She asked him – and here her mother moaned to herself – if the book he was reading had any words in it.

'Of course,' said Hameed, who wished for nothing more than to return to his own village and never leave it again.

'And did the words tell you to walk into the gundy tree?' said Nadia, her smile as sweet as the sugar she had given Hameed. 'Is it perhaps a book of instruction in being a fool? You are wasting your time. You need no instruction.'

Hameed scratched his head, not sure what Nadia was saying. He took up his tea, sipped it loudly, wiped his mouth with the back of his hand. 'It is a book about the boy Huckleberry, and Jim the black man. On the river of Mississippi in America. The woman Douglas is a widow and must take the place of Huckleberry's mother. A raft is made, a word for a boat, not such a boat as we have in Hazarajat. Bigger than a raft is a paddle-boat, which I will explain.'

Hameed gave the best description of a paddle-boat that he could. Then he remembered that the cover of the book showed a paddle-boat behind Huck and Jim. He showed the cover of the book to Nadia, who, for the first time in her life, was lost for words. She held the book as if it might suddenly reveal itself to be alive, and dangerous.

'What *is* this?' she asked.

Hameed took the book and showed her the English words in the front. Then he showed the Dari words in the back. He read to her from the page he had reached:

I started across to the town from a little below the ferry-landing, and the drift of the current fetched me in at the bottom of the town. I tied up and started along the bank. There was a light burning in a little shanty that hadn't been lived in for a long time...

Nadia's eyes, thought so beautiful, were now as big as the saucer on which she had served Hameed his tea. Hameed gave the book back to Nadia. She held it at the page from which Hameed had been reading. By the movement of her eyes it could be seen that she was herself reading the words on the page.

'The boy Huckleberry is telling the story to us,' said Hameed. 'These are his words. Do you understand?'

Nadia, baffled, murmured, 'What?'

Hameed turned the book to the page that read 'Here Begin'.

'This is where the story starts,' he said. 'I will read it to you.'

And so he did. Every time he stopped, Nadia cried out, 'What are you doing? Read!' Iram Khalaj and Najaf Khalaj listened with great attention for as long as they could remain. When she was compelled to leave to attend to her tasks, Iram Khalaj told her daughter to come with her. This was necessary, for Nadia could not be left alone with Hameed or with any young man courting her. But Nadia would not move. She sat on her four-legged stool, overpowered by the spell of the story. Finally her mother threw up her hands and left Nadia where she was.

It was evening before Hameed was permitted to depart. Najaf Khalaj begged him to stay the night in his house, and his pleas were exceeded in strength by those of the daughter, Nadia.

'Bandits will attack you!' she said. 'For all mercy, remain here and read the story!' But Hameed, strangely, recalled that his father would need him the next day when the roof of the house was to be thatched again. That he should have recalled this obligation was itself a miracle, and that he was prepared to make a long journey in darkness to assist in the work a second miracle. 'Return when the roof is made,' instructed Nadia. Then she said, more courteously, 'If it pleases you.' Next she said, 'Bring the book of Huckleberry.' Then she added, more courteously, 'If it pleases you.' Finally she said, 'I will have melon ready for your refreshment, and tea.'

Hameed returned within the week. He might have chosen to forget the pleas of Proud Nadia, but the plain fact was that he had taken a liking to the girl. She had asked questions about the black man Jim and Widow Douglas and the two big rivers that joined together – questions that Hameed was able to answer. And Nadia had thanked him for his answers. In his life, no one but Nadia had thanked him for his answer to a question.

When he arrived at Najaf Khalaj's house, the melon that had been promised was prepared for him by Nadia herself, and it was Nadia who brewed the tea that followed, and it was Nadia who offered the small cakes that followed the tea. It was Nadia who said to Hameed, 'Now read the book.' And it was Nadia who added, more courteously, 'If it pleases you, sir.'

At the end of this second visit, Iram Khalaj kissed his hand. She said, 'Sir, come again.' Najaf Khalaj kissed Hameed on both cheeks, adding, 'Tell your father that Najaf Khalaj wishes him a hundred years of life,' to which Nadia added, 'Sir, bring the book of Huckleberry when next you visit.'

Hameed not only brought the book of Huckleberry, but also the book of Little Women and that of Uncle Tom's Cabin and that of Tom Sawyer. This was the first Nadia had heard of the other books. She had been sitting on a four-legged stool when Hameed revealed them, but at the sight of them she jumped to her feet.

'You have more? Why did you not tell me?' she cried. Then she remembered her manners. 'Surely you had your reasons.'

Nadia served her guest and her parents *dogh* and *boulanee* and *naan*. Then she placed before Hameed a big white plate of *kishmish panir*, the cheese freshly made and the raisins sweet and plump. Red grapes followed in one of the bowls from Kandahar kept for special guests. Nadia had carefully removed the seed from each grape. Finally she offered Hameed apricots in halves, and melon juice.

With her guest satisfied, Nadia asked Hameed's leave to study the books he had brought. Her excitement was so great that she began to cry, startling her mother and father and of course her guest, Hameed.

'But daughter,' said Iram Khalaj, 'is there no pleasing you? You were happy to see one of the books of America, and now you have three more!'

Nadia gave no explanation but instead asked her mother if she would come with her to the well. Along the way she said, 'I will marry him.'

'Is it true?' asked Iram Khalaj.

'I will marry him,' said Nadia. And she added, 'There. It is done!'

Two days after, Najaf Khalaj and Iram Khalaj took the road to the village of Ahmed Behsudi. Uppermost in the mind of Najaf Khalaj was the small fig orchard that was promised. Uppermost in the mind of Iram Khalaj were the books of America, for her daughter had told her that she cared nothing for the fig orchard but craved only the books. If the books came with Hameed Behsudi, certainly her father must accept his proposal.

Najaf Khalaj and Iram Khalaj were received at Ahmed Behsudi's house as honoured guests. After a fine evening meal of *shorwa* and *bichak* – the *bichak* served with *badenjan* – and last of all (a specialty of Hameed's mother's) *she'er berinji* sweetened with raisins soaked in honey, Ahmed Behsudi walked in the evening air with Najaf Khalaj, while Zainab Behsudi sat with Iram Khalaj beneath the eucalyptus tree that the bulbuls favoured.

Najaf Khalaj said to his host, 'A fig orchard was spoken of, if I remember truly.'

Ahmed Behsudi replied, 'Will you see the orchard for yourself in the morning, brother? The mature trees number thirty-five, while ten trees on the eastern side have yet to reach full age. And yet even these young trees produce four-and-a-half bushels each in the season. A spring from the mountains feeds the channels drought or no drought, and you will recall that we were stricken with drought on this side of the big mountain three seasons past. What does your wife say to this match?'

'It pleases her, brother.'

'And your daughter?'

'So long as your gift of the small fig orchard comes with the boy, she will be content.'

Under the eucalyptus tree, Zainab Behsudi asked, 'Your daughter will accept my son?'

To which Iram Khalaj responded, 'Her liking for the boy has grown. His books please her, so it seems. So long as the boy comes with the books, she is content.'

There remained one last difficulty with the match. Hameed, although he had come to like Proud Nadia well enough, did not show any interest in marriage. When his mother told him that Nadia would marry him, he said, 'Who asked her?'

'But why do you think these visits to the village of the good man were arranged?'

'Oh,' said Hameed, 'I thought my father was going to purchase Najaf Khalaj's orchard, that was all.'

'But the girl has treated you with courtesy,' said Zainab Behsudi. 'You told me you liked her. She offered you *boulanee* and *kishmish panir*. She made the cheese with her own hands. And the beauty of the girl! Only think, she has spurned twenty young men, some of them from as far away as Kariz and Jarghan! Further! From Mazar-e-Sharif! She sent a silversmith away who would have adorned her with his metal!'

'Well, let her call the silversmith back, and great joy may she find with him.'

The news was conveyed to Nadia that Hameed of the books had shown some reluctance to marry her. Nadia flew into a rage. 'He? That fool? Let him marry a block of stone, for no living thing will bear him! What, because he has four books he can give himself such airs and graces? Let him take his books for a wife if I have failed to please him!'

But an hour later, the desire to hear the stories in the books gnawed at Nadia's insides like the pain of eating rice that has grown mould. She went to her mother in a more tender mood: 'What does he require of me? In what way have I failed to please him?'

Iram Khalaj was washing bedsheets at the trough near the well. She first sighed, then she stood and dried her hands. 'Daughter,' she said. 'When did you mention to the boy the joy that would come into your life and into his life with the birth of children? Did you say, as I said to your father before our marriage, "Five children is my desire, do you agree?" Did you say, "A clean house is my desire, do you agree?" Did you say, "Let us always eat well, if God provides the means, do you agree?" Did you say, "Our household will honour God, above all things, do you agree?"'

'What, is it my task to court him? Is it my task to ask every question that needs to be asked? Is it not enough that I made him *kishmish panir* with my own hands?' asked Nadia.

Iram Khalaj shook her head, thinking, 'I thought this annoying girl was off my hands, now look!' To Nadia, she said, 'You are charmed by this boy's books of America. Good. But when you are a wife, a day comes when you are too tired to stand up and care for your children, and a day comes when your husband snores loud enough to make the plates rattle on the shelves. What will you do? Lock the children outdoors while you read yourself a story? The stories are one thing. Marriage is a thousand things. Better that you should love your husband in a thousand ways.'

Proud Nadia thought on what her mother had said for a full day. 'So, I am to love this blockhead, am I? Well, I will.'

Hameed of the books was invited to the house of Najaf Khalaj one more time, and agreed to make the journey at the urging of his mother. He thought, 'I will read to the girl but nothing more.' When he arrived at Najaf Khalaj's house, the daughter Nadia greeted him modestly. Her two sisters were guests for the day, too, and their husbands, and their six children. Nadia served him *ashak* first, then *palao* with lamb. On the best plate in the house, the last unbroken one of three patterned all over with nightingales, she served *badenjan*, offering the dish first to Hameed. Although a meal at midday would normally be simple, Nadia provided *gosh feil*, as crisp as any hungry man could crave.

All through the meal, Nadia's sisters taunted her with reminders of what she was known for.

'Sister, the children are present – when your temper returns, spare them for our sake!'

'Sister, in this light you remind me of Nadia. But I don't hear Nadia's voice!'

'What, Nadia and not her temper? Is this possible on earth?'

The tormenting did not cease even when Nadia had cleared away the dishes and served tea.

'Such a sad day in Hazarajat – the sweet voice of our sister is nowhere to be heard!'

'Mama, is the vinegar all gone? Has our sister not taken her cup of vinegar as she does each morning?'

The tormenting finally brought tears – just two, which Nadia quickly brushed away, trying to hide the damage with a smile. But Hameed noticed. He understood that the girl was struggling against her nature, yet until that moment her struggle had meant little to him. He had liked her for the enjoyment she found in the story of Huckleberry Finn and for her questions – otherwise, she had meant little. Now he asked himself why she was struggling in this way and he found the answer: to please him. From that moment, he looked at her in a different way. He thought, 'If I were a king, she could do no more to make me content.' And later, when he was preparing to read to her, thinking more on the matter, he said to himself, 'Indeed, she would scorn a king if he came with nothing but his name and his rank. It is the book that compels her to struggle.' And finally, this thought came to him: 'Be worthy of her.'

He read to Nadia for an hour. During that time, her sisters and their husbands and the children gradually drifted away, for the enjoyment of the story soon waned. But Nadia remained. Of course she did.

Before the time came for Hameed to return to his own home, he said to Nadia: 'Will I leave the book of Uncle Tom's Cabin, and the book of Little Women for you to enjoy by yourself? Will I leave the book of Tom Sawyer?'

Nadia asked her mother who was close by if she might reply to Hameed. Her mother said, 'If I were you, I would say something.'

'Sir, are we to have a life together?'

'If it pleases you, yes. If it pleases your father and your mother, if it pleases my father, if it pleases my mother, yes,' said Hameed.

Nadia smiled. Iram Khalaj had not seen such a smile on this daughter's face since she was a small child.

Nadia had more to say. 'Do you think of the joy that will come into our lives with the birth of children?' followed by 'Six children is my desire. Sir, do you agree?' Then she said, 'A clean house is best for us, do you agree?' and 'Our house will honour God above all things, surely.' And finally, Nadia, Proud Nadia, said this to Hameed: 'Take the books with you. We will read them together, that would be best.'

Iram Khalaj, who had heard everything, blessed God for the love that had come into her daughter's heart. And thinking of the smile on her daughter's face, she said to herself, 'Love is not the smile. Love is the struggle before the smile.'

9

The Beekeeper's Journey

In the years that had passed since Abbas Behishti took on the trade of *perwerrish dahenda*, or beekeeper, the throne of Zahir Khan had been stolen by his cousin Sardar Dawood Khan and then taken over by the communists. Many Afghans regretted the loss to the country of its king, and many more were glad of it. The people of Kabul, watching to see what the communists would make of the country, at first were heartened when three more cinemas opened in the capital. But disappointment soon followed. Zahir Khan had allowed cinemas to show films from Hollywood, but the communists showed only films from Russia.

Abbas Behishti went to the cinema in Kabul when he visited the city to buy parts for a new honey-making machine, one he had designed himself and that employed ball-bearings. The film he saw told the story of a boy in the snowy parts of Russia who made friends with a black bear. He enjoyed the film, mostly because the boy who made friends with the bear had a smile like that of his own son, Esmail. But he was almost alone in liking the story. Others in the cinema cried out, '*Balay fier qoneit!*' which in Dari means 'Shoot the bear!'

Strangely enough, when the Russians themselves came to Afghanistan two years after Abbas Behishti's visit, the cinemas again began to show films from Hollywood. The Russian soldiers did not wish to see films about black bears in the snowy parts of Russia. They wished to see James Bond.

Abbas did not get the opportunity to visit the Kabul region again until the reign of the Russians in Afghanistan was five years old. Even then, he went unwillingly. The great leader of the Hazara people, Abdul Ali Mazari, who lived in a village south of Mazar-e-Sharif, had asked him to take a message to a man in the city of Charikar, a long journey to the east.

The summons came as a surprise to Abbas. Abdul Ali Mazari was known to him and to all Hazara as Baba Mazari, Father Mazari, even though he was not yet in his middle years, not even forty at the time of the summons. Abbas' grandfather, Esmail, had in his lifetime known Abdul Ali well. He had predicted for him the life and honour of a hero, even when Abdul Ali was still a boy. He had told Abbas, 'Men such as Abdul Ali come one time in a thousand years. He is picked out by God for greatness. But he is not picked out by God for happiness.' Esmail was right in this prediction as he was in so many other matters. Baba Mazari had fought the soldiers of Zahir Khan when they attacked the Hazara in Hazarajat. He had fought the communists when Zahir Shah lost his throne to them. And he had fought the Russians when they came with their trucks and tanks and cannons and aeroplanes. In the time of fighting he had seen his brother, Mohammad Sultan, younger than he, killed in battle against the communists. Then he lost his beloved sister in the fighting, then his father, his uncle, another uncle. Esmail did not live to see Baba Mazari's sorrow, but he knew it would come.

It was Ahmad Hussein, once Abbas' master in the trade of bee-keeping, now his honoured friend, who brought the summons to him. He came on a day when the sky was dark with clouds above the Sangan Hills, and a day only a week from the tenth birthday celebrations of Abbas' son, a boy who had brought joy to his life since the hour of his birth. Abbas had two other children, two daughters, but he kept the boy Esmail in the dearest place in his heart on account of his smile.

Ahmad Hussein had kept to the trade of beekeeping, even with a beard now more white than black. His hives were still placed in the fields that Abbas remembered from his time of learning the trade. Abbas himself had moved to fields further south, where he yielded ten per cent of the honey harvest to the landowners, or seven per cent in a season of drought. Abbas' honey was flavoured by the wildflowers of the Sangan region that the bees craved – briars, Persian roses and a bright red tulip with blooms that lasted no more than two days.

Ahmad Hussein's arrival was a great surprise. In his fields to the north this was a busy time. The rains of late spring on his side of the hills caused blooms to crowd the fields. His bees filled the honeycomb so quickly that honey would drip in waste to the ground unless Ahmad Hussein drained the trays once every three days. Yet here he was, two days by horse and cart from where he should be.

It is an honoured custom of the Hazara tribes that Abbas and Ahmad Hussein were born into – that is, the Daizangi and the Jaghori, only two of more than twenty Hazara tribes – not to show any great surprise when good news arrives, at least as adults. To remain calm, no matter how welcome the news, is thought to be a sign of maturity. If a Daizangi or a Jaghori becomes excited by good news, like a child receiving a present, people might say, 'Such a shame!' or 'He has a beard but does he deserve it?' It is also thought to be a good sign if a man remains calm when the news is bad, but people are much more forgiving in the case of bad news. When Abbas recognised with joy his old master from a distance, he stood still in the field with a smile on his face and waited until Ahmad Hussein in his horse-drawn cart was beside him before raising his voice.

'My master,' said Abbas. 'God has brought you safely into my sight. You are very welcome on this ground.'

'God keep you in health for a hundred years, and all of your family,' replied Ahmad Hussein.

The master climbed down from his cart and the two men embraced. Nothing more was said for five minutes while Ahmad Hussein held a big bowl made from the hide of a goat and filled with water for his mare to drink. Even when the mare had satisfied her thirst, the two friends, master and pupil, remained silent. Except for the warmth of their smiles, a person not familiar with the ways of the Hazara might have thought that the two men had no voices at all. Ahmad Hussein tapped the mare lightly on the nose just above her nostrils, meaning, 'We will be staying here for a time, crop the grass.' He pulled out the burrs that had become trapped in her tail, and with a rag, dried the sweat inside her ears

174

because it annoyed the mare to feel damp there. Then he asked Abbas, 'The bees remain your friends?'

'Surely.'

'Your children?'

'They are well, I thank you. And your sons and your daughters?'

'I thank you, they are well. And your wife?'

'She is well, I thank you. And your wife who is living?'

The first wife of Ahmad Hussein had died ten years earlier, leaving him with a grief that still bowed his head.

'My wife who is living is well, I thank you. Your father?'

'My father is well, except for his ears. He hears little. And your father, master?'

The last Abbas had heard, Ahmad Hussein's father, at the age of ninety-three years, had expressed a wish to marry again, since he was a widower.

'He is well, I thank you, but his mind wanders in these late years of his life. God sends us trials.'

Something difficult was about to be said. Abbas understood this from the pauses between Ahmad Hussein's questions and replies. The very fact that Ahmad Hussein had come across the hills to the bee-field made this seem more likely.

Abbas had only water to offer his old teacher, but Ahmad Hussein had brought tea with him in a vacuum flask. The tea was still hot. This was the first vacuum flask Abbas had seen and it filled him with the desire to own such a device himself. Partly in order to postpone the difficult news, out of respect for Ahmad Hussein, who would not want to see anxiety in his eyes, and partly to satisfy his curiosity, he studied the vacuum flask closely.

'What is the inside made of, master?'

'I think it is glass. It can be broken, and then you must purchase a new inside.'

'The tea remains hot inside the device?'

'It remains hot if it is filled with hot tea. If it is filled with cold water, the water remains cold.'

'A marvel. And it is called a "vacuum flask", as you say?'

'A vacuum flask, as I say. I don't know why.'

'A vacuum,' said Abbas, 'is nothing. I must think about it.'

'Truly. Think about it while you work. I have been to see our master.'

'Our master?'

'Baba Mazari asked for me.'

'An honour.'

'A great honour.'

'He is well, by God's grace, our great master?'

'He is well by God's grace. But he has his sorrows.'

'God has asked much of him.'

'God has asked much of him, as you say. He hopes to see you.'

'To see me?'

'He hopes to see you not this day or the next or the next, but the day that follows.'

'Then I must go.'

'You must go, Abbas.'

'Do you know the reason?'

'I do. But you must hear it from Baba Mazari himself.'

Abbas Behishti had listened when his grandfather Esmail Behishti told him all that he knew of war. It was not a long speech. Esmail

had said, 'I fought with a gun and a blade because it was necessary. I put my knife to the throats of young men of my own age. I
washed their blood from my hands afterwards and cleaned my
blade. Now I weep for my folly.' For the sake of what his grandfather Esmail had told him of war, or for some other reason, something perhaps that was born in him, Abbas kept as far from the
fighting in Afghanistan as he could. Three friends of his child-
hood had fought in the service of Baba Mazari; fought to protect
Hazara land and Hazara lives. Two had died, one remained. Of
the two who had died, one had been killed by communist soldiers,
and one had been killed by Russian soldiers. The friend still living
had returned to his village at Ramadan, but only for a month. He
had greeted Abbas with all the warmth of their friendship and had
asked if he would not come and fight the Russians.

Abbas said, 'I won't fight the Russians.'

To which his friend replied, 'If the Russian soldiers came to
your house to kill your wife and your son and your two daughters, would you kill them?'

'Surely.'

'Then join us. For one day the Russians may come to your
house.'

'On my doorstep I will kill them. Nowhere else.'

On his journey to the north, Abbas carried only the food he
would need for three days: dried figs, raisins, bread, some cold
rice with parsley and peppers. He did not know with certainty
what would be asked of him, but if Baba Mazari instructed, 'You
must take up your gun and your blade,' Abbas would have to
obey, and since this command was what he expected, he would
need food only for the three days of the journey.

He chose the simplest garments in his possession, and as few as possible. Those fighting the Russians – the Hazara of Baba Mazari and the soldiers of the mujaheddin – wore more garments than were necessary into battle: scarves that tied three times around their necks, fabric belts that circled their waists three times, more than one shirt, turbans padded with more fabric beneath. They had to act as their own doctors, and would use what they wore as bandages. A man lightly dressed would not be thought a soldier, even by the Russians. In the country he would pass by snipers who sat behind rocks in the hills and shot anyone resembling a soldier. The Russians were said to have special rifles that could kill a man from a very great distance. There were few Russians in Hazarajat, but there were snipers employed by the Russians and armed by the Russians.

If Baba Mazari told him that he must become a soldier, Abbas was sure he would die on the battlefield. He could not fire a rifle with accuracy, he could not use a blade with any skill, and he knew nothing about fighting. So he would die, that seemed certain. His wife, Sabah, had put her head into a corner of the kitchen and wept when he'd told her of the summons. He could not keep from Sabah the danger he faced. How would that have been possible when he must explain to her how to manage the sale of the beehives if he didn't return? Not only the sale of the hives, but of the honey-making machine with ball-bearings that made it turn faster and smoother. And Abbas had a special letter for her to give to his eldest son Esmail when the boy became twelve years of age. The letter was for the future. For now, he'd kept from the children the danger he might face. He said he was going for a holiday. But the boy Esmail knew better and would not smile.

A Hazara has two walking paces: slow and fast, nothing in between. Abbas covered the rocky land with ease, keeping off the roads. As I say, few Russians ever came to Hazarajat but those who did had been known to shoot from their moving trucks at travellers on foot. They shot for no reason, for amusement, or because of their hatred for their mission. It was known that the Russian soldiers did not wish to be in Afghanistan. Amongst the mujaheddin forces of the north there were those who took pleasure in cutting captured Russian soldiers into pieces and leaving the debris on the road to be found by the victims' comrades. The Russians' hatred for their mission was mixed with a dread of capture, and that dread made them cruel.

It was Abbas' habit to pray twice each day; once in the morning, once at dusk. His wife Sabah, more pious than he, prayed four times. As the sun set on this first day of his journey northward, he found a place amongst the rocks, washed himself in the ritual of the faith and laid out his prayer rug, really a shawl, a *patoh*. In the midst of his prayers he sensed that he was not alone and opened his eyes. No further from him than the distance of two strides a black snake lay at the full length of its beauty with its head raised. The snake was not preparing for attack, as Abbas knew, for the black snakes of Hazarajat flee rather than strike if flight is possible. No, this snake had been attracted by the smell of the water for *wu'du* in the small bowl. A snake will rarely drink still water unless from a pond, but this region of Hazarajat was without natural springs and at this time of year no rain fell to gather amongst the rocks.

'Brother, you are welcome to drink,' said Abbas.

The snake moved its head from side to side. The smell of a man

179

is a horror to every wild creature, yet the snake set aside its fear and drew itself slowly to the water bowl. As it drank, its head dipped and lifted, dipped and lifted. Abbas on his knees remained still for the whole length of time the snake required to satisfy its thirst – long enough for the sun to sink further behind the hood of the mountains and for darkness to deepen. The snake raised its head one final time, before it departed without haste towards the stones.

In the Holy Book, tales are told of Satan, who is said to be like a snake in his stealth and cunning and danger. But Abbas had always seen the great beauty of the creatures more than their menace, and when he had completed his prayers and eaten some figs and wrapped himself in his blanket for sleep, he said to himself, 'It is the snake who should fear the man.'

The house of Baba Mazari was no different to the other houses in the village. It was the house of a farmer. But the path that led to the door of the house was more worn than other paths. Visitors arrived every day of the year to ask Baba Mazari's advice on one matter or another, often simple matters, such as the digging of a new well or the best way to deal with an ant plague. The dwelling of Baba Mazari was special in only one other way: the well-worn path to the front door was guarded by two men with Kalashnikov automatic rifles.

When Abbas Behishti approached the home of Baba Mazari after his journey of three days, one of the men called to him, 'Say if you carry a weapon!'

'No, brother, I have no weapon,' Abbas replied.

'Hazara of which people?'

'Of the Daizangi, brother.'

The man walked down from the verandah of the house with a smile on his face. He said, 'My sister has a husband of the Daizangi. An honest man who plays the *rubab* on feast days.'

Then he explained, 'Our master told me to expect a Daizangi of Garmab by the name of Abbas Behishti.'

'I am Abbas Behishti of my father's house at Garmab, but I have a house of my own now past the Sangan Hills,' Abbas responded.

The guard led Abbas to the verandah of the house and asked him to wait. He returned within the space of a minute and now led Abbas to the back of the house and then into the courtyard. A vine of sultana grapes coming into fruit gave shade to a fountain that dribbled water from a brass spigot in the shape of a horse's head onto a flat stone of grey shale. The vine and the fountain were common features of the small gardens that farmers kept in the Sar-e Pol region, more like an Iranian garden than an Afghan one.

Baba Mazari stood beneath the vine, ready to receive Abbas. Two things about Baba struck Abbas immediately: that he was a handsome man, and that behind the shrewdness of his gaze dwelt a deep sorrow. He thought, 'This is my grandfather Esmail as he would have looked in his fortieth year.' Even Baba's beard grew as Esmail's had: pure white on the chin and a darker colour along the jaw line and cheeks.

Baba Mazari opened his arms to Abbas and kissed him on each cheek. 'God has granted you a safe journey to my home,' he said.

'God has given you good health, Baba,' replied Abbas.

'We will enjoy our tea before we talk.'

It was not Baba Mazari's wife who brought in the tea and small sweets on a tray, but the guard who had shown Abbas in.

'My family,' said Baba, 'those that remain to me, by God's grace, I have sent into Mazar-e-Sharif to pray at the mosque. They will return tomorrow. Until then, my meals are prepared by those who are strangers to the kitchen. The tea is tepid.'

They sipped their tepid tea seated on four-legged stools under the shade of the vine. The shadows cast by the leaves moved across the stones of the courtyard in the faint breeze that always came at this late hour of the afternoon. Abbas noticed that Baba placed his hand on his cheek every so often. 'A toothache,' Baba explained. He called to the guard for oil of cloves. When it came, he poured a small amount onto a strip of cloth and dabbed the afflicted tooth. The strong smell of the clove oil filled the air.

'Ahmad Hussein did not tell you why I asked you to come?'

'No, Baba,' said Abbas. 'Has the oil relieved the toothache?'

'I thank you, the oil has done its job.'

'Baba, before we talk, may I offer you something for your kitchen?'

Abbas took from his cloth bag a tin with a press-lid. 'This is honey from my bees, saved from the spring harvest. Its sweetness will not harm your tooth.'

Baba received the honey with a bow of his head. He placed it on a small table beside the tea tray and touched Abbas' hand in a gesture of gratitude. Then he said: 'Did you think I would ask you to fight the Russians, Abbas?'

'Baba, I did. I am ready.'

'Things go so badly for us that I must call a man from his bees on the far side of the Sangan Hills? No, no, Abbas. I have a million Hazara who can fire a gun. How many can make honey? But tell me this: your grandfather Esmail Behishti, an honoured man, by me and by everyone blessed to know him, did you ever notice on the top of his wrist, here, running up to his elbow – the right hand, the right wrist – a scar of raised flesh, still livid?'

'Baba, I saw it many times. A wound from battle.'

'So he would say. I will tell you the true story of that scar. When Esmail was at my age of forty years, a captain of Zahir Khan and two hundred soldiers were sent into Hazarajat to make an example of Khalid Naseri and his followers, who would not pay the Khan's taxes. Khalid was taken. On a day of great shame to himself and his family, he told the captain that Esmail Behishti was the true leader – a falsehood. The captain knew well that Khalid Naseri had told him a lie but he tormented your grandfather for the pleasure of it. A length of rope soaked in oil was wired to your grandfather's arm from the hand to the elbow. When an end was lit, it burned slowly, like a fuse, and left the honoured man scarred. But he said nothing while the rope burned. Khalid Naseri lived beyond that day but he lived in shame. He travelled first to Iran to put his shame behind him, and then to India, and finally to America where he lived in the great city of Brooklyn. Brother, Khalid Naseri became something rare amongst the Hazara – he became a man of great wealth. Do you know how his wealth came to him? I will tell you. He sold orange juice. Have you heard of anything stranger than that? A fortune came to him from orange juice! In his great factory, a thousand men put orange juice into boxes and he sold it in the American markets, in every city. His orange juice was called "nectar". In America, a man may find wealth in orange juice, so hard to believe! But in all his wealth – such wealth that he drove two cars, not one but two – in all that wealth, his shame endured. He paid his penance in money, in American dollars. Each year for twenty-five years he has paid to have schools built for our Hazara children, he has paid for children to be given a medicine that turns away the scourge of the dysentery disease and the hepatitis disease. He has paid his money for Hazara children to travel to the great hospitals of Germany and England – children with growths in their bodies. He has paid his money for a mosque to be built in Mazar-e-Sharif – a mosque in which a *muezzin* calls us to prayer with an electrical device, the most wonderful thing for the ears you can imagine! So much for penance. Now hear what I will tell you.'

Baba Mazari poured more tea for Abbas and again cursed the incompetence of soldiers who attempted to make up for an absent wife.

'Abbas, a bad conscience will drive a man to punish himself tenfold for the sin that brought him shame. On his deathbed his final thoughts will be of the wrong he did. Brother, you have been to Kabul – Ahmad Hussein told me this. But have you ever travelled to Charikar?'

'Baba, I have not.'

'The plains start at Charikar. And at the back of the city are the hills that lead you up to the mountains. It is a city of the Tajiks. You can walk the road to Charikar from Kabul in two days. In my heart is a wish for you to go to Charikar.'

'Baba, I will go.'

'But not with a gun. Not with one of those.'

Baba nodded towards a rifle that leaned against a post.

'In Charikar,' he said, 'you will go to a house in the north part of the city. I will tell you how to find it. Inside that house you will meet Khalid Naseri. He has come to Charikar from his city of Brooklyn. In Kabul he has enemies who would kill him if they knew where he was. He will not rise from his bed to greet you, alas. He is dying, brother. It is the wish of my heart for you to greet him in Charikar, and it is the wish of Khalid Naseri's heart that you will speak some words of forgiveness.'

'Baba, I will go. But why me?'

'Why you, brother? Because you loved Esmail Behishti. Forgiveness must come from a man who loved the one abused. But brother, can you forgive Khalid Naseri, who betrayed the honoured man?'

Abbas lowered his head and closed his eyes. He was silent for a minute, and for another. 'Baba, I will know when I see him.'

People came to visit Baba one after another, and more still. Abbas watched and listened, as he had watched and listened when Esmail gave his advice to the many who came to him. In Baba's face he saw the strength and wisdom of the man, but he saw more than that. He saw intelligence, he saw anger kept under stern control, and especially he saw tenderness when Baba spoke to a mother who had come with her three young sons.

Abbas stayed that night in the house of Baba Mazari and ate his evening meal with Baba and the guards. A very old woman of the village came to the house to prepare the meal, trusted by Baba's wife not to bring a demon into the kitchen, as could happen. Such demons caused pots to disappear and salt to lose its savour. The old woman provided *shorma* to begin the meal, then *qorma* to eat with the *chalow* and the *lavash*, followed by melon and plums from Mazar-e-Sharif. When the meal was eaten Baba called the old woman in from the kitchen and thanked her for her trouble and told her that the food was excellent. The old lady, who had a temper, listened to the praise but at the end she said, 'You would eat straw boiled in ditch water and still think it excellent.'

At the evening meal Baba would not talk of the politics that occupied him all day. Instead he spoke of fruit and of honey. 'In Charikar the sweetest grapes in all of our country hang from vines a century old. The Tajiks are masters of the vine. Do you know, Abbas, when our ancestors came to this land they knew nothing of growing fruit, nothing of growing grain. They knew only battle. Do you know who taught them to grow figs and grapes and pears? It was the Tajiks. When we had learned how to grow fruit, we went into the mountains of Hazarajat and found soil where there was none, we found water where no water flowed, we made the stones themselves bloom into gardens. Of honey, I know only what I taste. But there was a man from the country of Denmark who came to our country to teach about irrigation. You know what I mean by irrigation? Good. Yes, he came to teach our farmers about irrigation, of which he knew much. In my house, where we sit now, he tasted the honey of Hazarajat. He said that in the world it has no equal. Irrigation and honey were his passions. No equal in the world of the Hazara honey. Do you believe him, brother – you, who commands a million bees?'

'I hope it is true,' said Abbas.

In the morning after prayer, a man on a motorcycle came to the house with a great noise like the roar of a Russian jet aeroplane flying low overhead. Abbas had seen motorcycles before this day and he feared them. Now Baba Mazari was telling him that the boy on the motorcycle, a boy of seventeen or eighteen years by the name of Konrad, this boy would take him on the motorcycle to Charikar. Dread and confusion gripped Abbas, but Baba said, 'His mother is Hazara, his father is German, of the Red Cross. Do you know the Red Cross, brother? It is for Christians but in past times Red Cross came to Afghanistan with medicines for those of our faith. He lives in a city with a name I cannot pronounce. What is your city, child?'

The boy Konrad said, 'Wilhelmshaven.'

'Yes, such a city as the one he named. But he has come here to be with his uncle and fight the Russians. I will send him back to his mother in one month more. You will be safe in his hands, brother. He is a genius of his machine.'

Abbas was given a sturdy bag of goat hide in place of the smaller fabric bag he'd brought with him. The bag was filled with foods from Baba Mazari's kitchen and with water in plastic bottles. Baba Mazari said, 'Once you reach Barfak do not drink water from streams. The Russians throw our dead into them.' And finally, he said this: 'Brother, fighting the Russians is not what God gave us our lives for. War is not what God gave us our lives for. God gave us our lives to grow the fruits for which we are famous, and to make the honey of Hazarajat known everywhere as the best in the world. I think God gave us our lives to see our children grow strong and intelligent, do you not agree?'

'Baba,' said Abbas, 'with all my heart.'

'But in war, when we can, we must take what chances we are

offered to show God the better side of ourselves. This man in Charikar has lived with the shame of a bad deed. In a short time, he will answer to God. But while he lives, he will answer to you.'

The motorcycle was heavily laden with its driver and its passenger, with the goat-hide bag of food and water, with bedding rolls and spare clothing and with flat-sided metal containers of petrol. But the boy Konrad drove the machine as if he were racing Satan to the gates of hell. Abbas barely passed a minute without prayer as the machine flew over rocks and ditches and plunged along dry creek beds in place of roads. Holding firmly with his arms around the boy, Abbas promised God that he would become a better servant than ever he had been if only Konrad should stop the machine and allow him to walk to Charikar. A hopeless prayer, for Abbas could hear below the unholy shriek of the machine the laughter of the boy as he drove. The reckless passage of the motorbike over the land was to Konrad sheer joy.

The regions through which Abbas and the boy raced were not the most unpopulated in Afghanistan, such as might be found in the mountains of the north-west below the peak of Nowshak, a cousin to Everest in its towering height. But my country of Afghanistan makes a trial of any journey, except in the fertile plains of the north and north-west where the deepest rivers flow. It is a land of mountains, and most of these mountains begrudge the space a single tree would occupy. They are mountains that turn their face from the companionship of people, offering a home only to the hardiest of animals – those who can live on weeds and brambles. And in their unfriendliness, the mountains are matched with the climate. I have stood under a sun that would have made my skin bubble like tar in a cauldron if I had remained motionless for fifteen minutes, and I have stood in the same place hours later in cold so fierce that my heart would have frozen solid had I persisted. Such a fate befell the soldiers of Ahmad Shah's army in the year 1770 of the Western calendar. Eighteen thousand of them were found frozen like ice sculptures in the valley where they sought shelter from a blizzard that came from nowhere, some kneeling in prayer. And yet in this land that will not forgive a small mistake, let alone folly, my people the Hazara and our neighbours the Tajiks and Uzbeks and Pashtuns have fashioned small Edens in sheltered valleys, places of greenery and afternoon shade where fruit trees hang with pears and apples and figs and apricots unrivalled in sweetness anywhere on earth. It is as if God had said, 'It suits my purpose to raise treeless mountains in this place, and deserts that every living thing must shun. But if I must be harsh, let me also remind you of Heaven here in the north by the Oxus.'

They drove east through the province of Samangan, hour after hour with no more than a pause for each to relieve his bladder or for Konrad to fill the petrol tank of his machine from the flat-sided containers. Even when motionless, Abbas endured the shudder of the machine in his bones and heard the roar of the engine in his ears. Konrad avoided all traffic, all habitations, so that in the space of five hours Abbas saw only a handful of people, nearly always Tajiks, one with his family in a wooden cart pulled by a donkey. The Tajik waved Konrad down to ask for water.

'Brother,' said the man, addressing Abbas as the older, 'the mujaheddin took our water, shame on them. You stand between this family of mine and death.'

'Not the Russians?' asked Abbas.

'No, mujaheddin from the north. Tajiks of my own tribe. War makes them cruel.'

By nightfall Abbas and Konrad had passed into Baghlan Province. They camped in the hills above the A76 highway south of Pol-e-Khomri and less than fifty kilometres from the city of Baghlan itself, which had to be avoided to keep clear of the Russians. At this time of year the snows had melted other than on the heights but the nights remained cold enough to kill a man not aware of the chill that came down near midnight. Konrad had little experience of the Afghan climate, but Abbas knew well what to expect. He searched amongst the boulders until he found a cave – it is always possible to find a cave in the Hindu Kush – and in its shelter he and Konrad ate dried apricots and salted beef and spread their bedding. Konrad sang songs of Germany, although not so much of Germany as America and England, but popular in Germany, as he explained. The songs were as strange to Abbas as if they were sounds from the mouths of wild animals. Yet he enjoyed them, especially the sight of Konrad dancing as he sang with the golden moon behind him. Konrad sang a song called 'Billie Jean', and another called 'Bette Davis Eyes'.

It was strange, also, to hear Dari from the mouth of this boy who did not look like an Afghan, with his light hair and blue eyes. Abbas asked him about his mother, how she had come to marry a German of the Red Cross.

'My mother was a nurse in Herat when the Red Cross came. Really she was a doctor but was permitted to work only as a nurse at that time. She was employed by the Red Cross where she met my father, whose name is Richard. From the first moment, they loved each other. My grandfather said that my father could marry my mother if he became of our faith, and so he did. He took my mother to Frankfurt am Main, a very great city of West Germany, and then to Wilhelmshaven. My father is not in the Red Cross now. He has a surgery, and my mother also has a surgery. My mother spoke to my sisters and me of the Hazara, so that we would know our heritage. I came to Afghanistan to see my uncle Mohammad Ali and all of my cousins in Herat. But I came also to fight the Russians.'

'Does your father know that you fight the Russians? Does your mother know that you fight the Russians?'

'Oh, no! If they knew, they would come to Afghanistan and take me back to Wilhelmshaven!'

'Your uncle does not tell your secret?'

'My uncle made me a servant of Baba, for my safety. He keeps my secret. I am not permitted to use a gun. I take Baba sometimes on my Yamaha to Mazar-e-Sharif. Of all motorcycles, Yamaha is the best for Afghanistan.'

Abbas listened to Konrad's story with great interest. He liked the boy, who laughed so much, and danced and sang. War was an adventure for him. Abbas said, 'Your mother and father are of the faith, but I have not seen you pray.'

'I am an atheist.'

'An atheist? What is an atheist?'

'I do not believe in God.'

'But that is impossible!' said Abbas. Nothing Konrad had said until then so amazed him. People might believe in gods of all faiths, Abbas understood that, but to believe in no god at all seemed madness.

'How then did the world begin?' said Abbas.

'Oh,' said Konrad, 'a big explosion.'

Now Abbas knew that the boy was teasing him. He resolved to keep silent on the matter of faith.

Konrad drove all through the next day into Parvan Province. They camped in the heights above the Salang Tunnel where the A76 Highway dived beneath the mountains. Abbas made sure that they were well sheltered from the sky, for the Russians would fly overhead in helicopters looking for mujaheddin. From his covered position he could still gaze down at the highway and at the many vehicles that disappeared into the mouth of the tunnel. In one minute, he saw more cars and trucks than he had seen in all the years of his life in Hazarajat.

Before he slept, Abbas thought again about the vacuum flask. It kept things cold, it kept things hot. 'Konrad, do you know what is meant by a vacuum flask?'

'Yes,' said the boy.

'It can keep hot tea hot, it can keep cold fruit juice cold. How?'

The boy was silent for a time. Then he said, 'It's a mystery.' And he fell asleep.

The journey of the following day would bring Abbas and Konrad to Charikar and suddenly the war was all around them. Three helicopters with red stars on their undersides came up from behind a range of hills and flew fast overhead. They were close enough for Abbas to read numerals on the underside of each craft. From the south came the thud of artillery shells exploding, and then plumes of smoke. A force of mujaheddin appeared from nowhere on Yamaha motorcycles like Konrad's and raced past them, two to a cycle, the man at the back with an automatic rifle or a grenade launcher held upright. Then in a shallow valley no more than thirty kilometres from Charikar, Abbas and Konrad came upon a sight of such horror that they were compelled to bow their heads with their hands over their eyes. A bus that had left the highway to find a path around a checkpoint lay on its roof burned and blackened. Scattered on the ground and hanging from windows more than fifty bodies could be counted. All were charred, like sticks from a fire. It appeared that none had survived. 'Rockets,' said Konrad. 'From helicopters.' The explosions that had killed all of these people could not have been very recent. Sand had begun to bank up around the wreck of the bus.

Abbas said, 'They must be buried.'

For the rest of the day the two men dug graves with strips of metal from the bus. It would have been easier and quicker to bury all the bodies together in one great hole in the earth, but Abbas wished each body, or such parts of a body as could be found, to occupy a single grave. The soil was pebble and clay beneath the sand and the digging was arduous. But by evening, five rows of graves had been filled, fifty-six bodies buried, amongst them twenty children. Those of our Shi'a faith, such as Abbas, would normally show full respect to the dead at burial, and the bodies would be washed in the ritual of *wu'du*, the hands bathed up to the wrists, the face washed, the mouth and nostrils cleansed with strips of cotton, the head itself gently wiped with a damp cloth, then the entire body washed three times over and rubbed with camphor and sandalwood. A white cotton shift would be fitted over the body of a man, two white cotton burial garments fitted over the body of a woman. Such washing, such careful cleansing prepares those who have ended their life on earth for their reception into Heaven. Prayers would be spoken by a mullah and the mourners, four *takbirs*; all those who had come to honour the one who had died would stand in rows as they prayed, the rows always of an uneven number.

Abbas did not have the leisure or the equipment for such a burial. The charred remains of the bodies could not be properly washed in the ceremony of *wu'du* even if water and white cotton had been on hand. But at least Abbas could pray. In our faith, whether Shi'a or Sunni, any man of sound belief can speak the prayers for the dead, Janaza Salah, confident that his words will reach the ears of God. And so Abbas spoke reverent words over each body before closing the grave with the soil of clay and pebble. He said, 'Glory be to thee, O God, and Thine is the praise, and blessed is Thy name, and great is Thy majesty, and none is to be served besides Thee.' These words are the first of the Holy Book, known to every Muslim except those who profess to be atheists, such as Konrad.

Over each grave, Abbas also spoke the words of the third *takbir*. 'O God! Grant this Thy servant protection, and keep this servant close, and pardon this servant, and make this servant's entertainment honourable, and wash this Thy servant with water and snow and hail and cleanse this Thy servant as a white cloth is cleansed of soil and blemish.'

It was usually possible to distinguish children from adults amongst the bodies, and when it was a child who lay below him in a grave, Abbas said these words: 'O God! Make this child a cause of recompense for us and make the child a treasure for us on the day of resurrection.'

Konrad worked all through the heat of the day without complaint, so admirable in the eyes of Abbas. He stood in silence when Abbas prayed over each body. Since the prayers were spoken in Arabic and Konrad could not know what was being said, Abbas took the opportunity to do something for the boy's soul. At the end of each recital of the third *takbir*, he added these words for consideration in Paradise: 'Oh God, lead this boy Konrad to the faith and away from foolish talk of explosions.'

It was well past sunset when Abbas and Konrad entered Charikar, a city more ancient than our faith. The house of Khalid Naseri was easily located in the north of the city. Once Abbas had shown a guard armed with a rifle and two pistols in holsters a letter from Baba Mazari, he was permitted to enter the house with Konrad and shown to a room where a man of some age with a deeply lined grey face lay raised on cushions in a bed. Abbas saw in an instant that the man was Hazara of a tribe that lived near Herat. Sure enough, when the man greeted him he spoke in the dialect of his tribe.

'I thank God for His kindness in sending you, Abbas Behishti. Will you, too, accept my gratitude?'

'A small thing,' said Abbas. 'God be with you.'

Abbas then introduced Konrad, and in few words explained his presence and his history. Konrad smiled.

While tea and biscuits and melon were being prepared, Abbas, seated on a low stool close to the bed, gazed about the room with curiosity. On one wall a number of flags were displayed bearing words that Abbas knew to be English. Each of the flags said, 'METS', followed by a year in the numerals used by Americans.

Photographs of young men in caps were also displayed on the wall. Abbas was surprised to recognise a black man of America who had appeared in the *Saturday Evening Post* of his teacher many years ago. The black man's name was Willie Mays. The story in the *Saturday Evening Post* was about a famous catch in the game played by Americans called baseball.

Khalid Naseri said, 'It is my love, baseball. I went many times. This is the team of my heart, the Mets of New York. It is a team from Queens and I live in Brooklyn, but Brooklyn lost its team to the Americans of California. See this picture, this is Tom Seaver. This picture is Gary Carter. This one is Mr Met, the mascot. And this one is Gil Hodges. I carried these pictures with me from my home in Brooklyn. I carried the pennants with me. This one is my best. Do you see these words? They say, "World Series 1969". The Mets became champions of America. I think they will be champions of America this year, too. But I will not see it.'

Konrad asked to be excused, since the matters to be discussed were private. Abbas nodded. Khalid Naseri raised a hand from the bed covers.

A woman Abbas had not seen when he entered the house now served the tea and biscuits and melons. She was not Hazara, not Afghan. She kept part of her hair covered with a scarf in our custom, but the part of her hair that showed was very fair. Most startling to Abbas were the trousers that the woman wore – blue jeans, in fact, such as he had seen two or three times in his life on Afghan men in Kabul. The blue jeans showed the shape of the woman's legs and hips. Abbas felt a blush spreading rapidly over his face and up into the flesh of his scalp below his turban.

'My wife, Barbara,' said Khalid Naseri.

Barbara, the wife of Khalid Naseri, smiled at him with teeth so white that Abbas thought he was being tricked in some way. Amazed and confused as he already was, Abbas had yet more wonder to behold, for the wife of Khalid Naseri addressed him in perfect Dari – the Dari that is used by the most educated Afghans, very like the Old Persian spoken by mullahs from wealthy families.

'A pleasure to meet you,' said the woman Barbara. 'Your great kindness in coming to my husband's sickbed touches me deeply.'

'It is as God wills,' replied Abbas.

He noticed that there were tears in the woman's eyes, and this caused him to blush a second time.

'I will leave you then,' said Barbara. And still speaking Dari, she said to her husband, 'Honey, don't exhaust yourself.'

When she had left the room, Khalid Naseri said, 'Americans call those they love "honey". It took me a long time to understand. We have been married for thirty years. Our sons are grown.' Then he added, 'Abbas, you know why I have come here, to Charikar. You know the shame I have carried for so many years. A man like you, Abbas Behishti, you will never know the burden of shame.'

Abbas met Khalid Naseri's gaze, but he said nothing.

'Let me say this,' said Khalid Naseri. 'I have lived a life of comfort from my thirty-fourth year. I have a house in Brooklyn that would seem a palace to all but a small number of Hazara. I have a second house in the state of Massachusetts in the town of New Bedford. That town of New Bedford stands by the ocean – such an ocean is never seen by the people of our land of Afghanistan. Very beautiful, Abbas, I promise you. I have a special boat that I sail on the ocean, a special boat with sails that catch the wind, can you imagine? It has been my pleasure to sail this boat with Barbara and my sons for the past so-many years. I have a third house where I can live outside of America at Grand Bahama, a distance into the ocean. Such beauty there cannot be described, but I can promise you that it would astonish any Hazara who saw it. My sons have attended fine schools, each of them, Abbas, three sons in all. And to enjoy this comfort, what did I do? I listened to a man who told me that Americans would buy fruit juice in small cardboard boxes. Nothing more. All the blessings I have described followed, and not least the blessing of my wife. Some people think to themselves – I have seen it in their eyes – "A woman so beautiful as she has been paid for with the Naseri fortune." But I met Barbara when I still slept on the floor of a friend's house in the Bronx. To make some money I taught Americans how to cook food in the Hazara fashion – *qabil palao*, *qorma*, *mantu*, *khameerbob*. Barbara visited one of my classes with a friend of hers, a woman who was interested in the food of other lands. Who can say why, but we liked each other from the moment we met. So strange! I prospered at everything I turned my hand to, Abbas! At everything! Even at love. With shame in my heart, I prospered. But year after year as my fortune mounted, the weight on my heart grew heavier. Barbara said to me, "You seem so sad!" In my life in America, so many times I could never count them, people say to me, "Khalid, you are the most fortunate man ever to come from your country, why do you never laugh?" How could I answer? How could I say, "God gave me good fortune to sharpen my pain"?'

Abbas listened closely. He still did not understand why Khalid

Naseri should have come to Afghanistan all the way from America to tell a story to a stranger.

'May I speak to you of Esmail?' said Khalid Naseri. 'Of your grandfather? Will you permit it?'

'Please. As you will.'

'You and I in our lives have seen wounds of the flesh. Who in this land has not? Abbas, a day came in my life when I saw a wound made in the flesh of Esmail Behishti. A rope burned along his arm from his wrist to his elbow. I stood no further from him than you are from me at this moment. I stood and watched and prayed that he would not betray me, as I had betrayed him. He did not betray me. While the rope burned, he turned his face from me and stared at the wall of the room where he was being tormented. He said nothing. Nor did he cry out. The captain of the soldiers who had done this thing to Esmail allowed him to live, as he allowed me to live. Do you know why, brother? Where is there a man who does not know sin when he sees it for once in his life? The captain watched the rope burning and heard not a sound from your grandfather. Was this the one time in that captain's life when he saw sin and knew that he was the sinner? He released your grandfather out of respect for a great man, and he released me out of disgust. Out of disgust, Abbas, as if my life was so vile to him that he could not bring himself to notice me. The rope burned into your grandfather's arm for a long time, brother. The rope that torments my flesh has been burning for many, many years.'

Khalid Naseri closed his eyes. When he opened them again, pain had dulled their colour.

'I did not ask you to come here to forgive me,' he said. 'That is not possible. I asked you to come because you loved Esmail Behishti. Do you see?'

'Yes, I see, of course I do.'

'Tomorrow, I have something I will ask of you. For now, if you will excuse me, I must sleep.' And he added, 'My illness kills me by degrees, so God wills.'

Abbas and Konrad were guests for the night. They ate well from dishes prepared by Barbara Naseri, *kofta* and *osh pyozee* and *dampukht*, with *sher berinj* to follow and then Charikari grapes. Barbara asked Abbas and Konrad if they would like to try English tea, and with their consent, served them something called 'Prince of Wales'. Konrad was well used to English tea and preferred it to Afghan tea, but to Abbas it had the odour of something he might smell while working with animals that had passed urine, and he declined to taste it, with many apologies.

It was difficult for Barbara Naseri to keep her scarf in place, although she persisted. Konrad said, 'Mrs Naseri, please feel free to remove your headwear. It will not offend Abbas and it will not offend me. My mother dresses in the Western fashion.' Barbara Naseri accepted this offer with relief, but it was not a relief to Abbas, who was suddenly faced with golden tresses that fell down Barbara Naseri's back to her waist. No longer young, although younger by many years than her husband, Barbara Naseri remained a woman of great beauty, as Abbas recognised. It was impossible for him to look at her directly, and seeing this, Barbara Naseri said, 'And yet, I should practise for the times when I am outdoors,' and replaced her blue scarf.

But Abbas became more relaxed with this American woman as the evening wore on and the shock of her blue jeans and smiling manner wore off. He had never heard a woman speak in Barbara Naseri's way, with no allowance made for the fact that he and Konrad were men, while she was a woman.

'Khalid was not my first husband,' she said. 'Before Khalid I was married to an inebriate – a very wealthy inebriate, but an inebriate nonetheless.'

Abbas had asked, and now he asked again, 'What is an inebriate?' The Dari words that Barbara Naseri had used were closer in meaning to 'incontinent taker of beverages' than the word employed here.

'Abbas, he drank too much alcohol. You know?'

'Ah, I see.'

'We were only married for two years. I walked out.'

'Walked out?'

'I left him. I got tired of ducking.'

'I am sorry, madam. "Ducking"?'

'He hit me with his fists.'

'He hit you?' said Abbas. 'An infamy!'

'And then I met Khalid. He treated me like a lady. You know? Such beautiful manners. Khalid asked me if I would become a Muslim. It's not so complicated.'

'You are of the faith?'

'Well, as best I can, Abbas. Maybe I'm not such a good Muslim. I wasn't such a good Catholic, either!'

Abbas was so moved to hear that Barbara Naseri had embraced the beliefs of the Shi'a that he clapped his hands as if applauding. He didn't know how else to show his joy.

'You must keep your faith,' he said. 'Even after your...'

He had intended to say, 'Even after your husband dies,' but realised that such a remark would be in bad taste.

Barbara Naseri saw the distress the mistake had caused Abbas. 'It's okay,' she said quietly. She looked away for a few moments. When she looked back, she was composed. 'I will keep our faith, Abbas.'

Khalid Naseri was too ill to see Abbas the next day. It was necessary for him to breathe the gas from a special iron bottle. A young doctor who had come with him from Brooklyn – an American Hazara – provided the relief of morphine. Abbas took Khalid Naseri to the toilet – that was one way in which he could help.

But the sick man also asked if Abbas would speak for him in his prayers. This was difficult for Abbas, because speaking for Khalid Naseri in his prayers was the same as offering him forgiveness, and Abbas did not forgive the man who had betrayed his grandfather. He did not despise Khalid Naseri, but he was a long way from commending him to God. Konrad saw the trouble in his eyes and asked him the cause. 'If you had lived in the time of my grandfather, you would know what troubles me,' Abbas replied.

Then Abbas remembered the Sufi apothecary who had come to the fields in the valley of Farah many years ago. These fields Abbas visited only once in every seven years when a rare flower bloomed with crimson petals and a golden stamen. The honey that the bees made from the nectar of these flowers would heal ailments of the skin when used as a balm, especially the scaling illness that would madden the victim and cause him to scratch his flesh until his body was bleeding. The Sufi said, 'I came here when Esmail Behishti harvested the honey balm. Now you.' Over his white robes he wore a brown apron to keep his garments clean when not at prayer. In the hem of the apron, tied with a knot, he kept a stone the size and shape of an almond that was as clear as glass except for a blue vein at its heart. With permission, he held the stone against the flesh over Abbas' heart. Within a few seconds, the blue vein had disappeared. He tied the stone into the hem of his apron once more.

The Sufi said, 'You intend me no harm.'

'Did the stone tell you that?'

'The stone told me that.'

'I could have said as much.'

'I must leave my body here for six days. It is well to know that it will be safe.'

'Are you ill? Are you in danger of dying?'

'No,' said the Sufi. 'I will leave my body while I am with God. Then I will return.'

Abbas was doubtful. Perhaps the Sufi was mad. Some were. 'Why does God not keep your body safe while you are with Him?'

The Sufi said these words, remembered by Abbas: 'God has no interest in my body, or in yours. Our bodies are in our own care. But the soul – that is another matter.'

The Sufi found a place to sit in the open field and closed his eyes and did not open them again for six days. When he did, he said, 'Good morning!' and went to relieve his bladder.

So Abbas spoke to God on behalf of Khalid Naseri. He did not ask for Khalid Naseri's body to be healed nor for his pain to be relieved, but for his soul to be judged with charity. He added to his prayer a poem he'd learnt from the old Sufi who came in search of honey balm: 'A pail is lowered into a well. On its journey of descent, the pail may believe the worst. But it comes to the top of the well overflowing with water. Your mouth closes here in the grimace of death, but opens again with a shout of joy.'

Khalid Naseri asked to see Abbas the following morning. He was resting in his bed on pillows – such a bed as an American would own, raised above the floor. He looked as ill as he was. He asked the doctor to leave the room. Barbara Naseri remained, but he said, 'Sweetheart, may we have this time alone?' Barbara Naseri kissed his forehead and departed.

Then Khalid Naseri spoke to Abbas. 'I did not ask you for forgiveness because forgiveness is a hard journey to make. You must think to yourself, "Why did this sinner not return to Hazarajat in the lifetime of Esmail and ask forgiveness himself?" And you must think of me, "He has made his fortune in America, and now when death is near he dares to ask for my love?" So I don't ask you to say, "Khalid, you old sinner, you have my forgiveness." Why should I ask for words like that when I can see in your eyes that you do not forgive me?'

Khalid Naseri began to struggle for breath. He waved in a distressed way at the iron bottle. Abbas gave him the plastic mask that covered his mouth and nose. Khalid Naseri held up two fingers, and Abbas understood that he should turn the dial on the machine to the numeral '2' above the red mark. He knew Western numerals. Khalid Naseri breathed from the iron bottle for some minutes, then took the mask from his face. Abbas turned the dial back to the red mark.

'In America, the doctors could keep me alive for another three months,' said Khalid Naseri. 'Such machines for hospitals in America that you could not imagine, Abbas! But I wanted to die in Afghanistan. I had hoped to die in Hazarajat, I had hoped my sons would join me there and sit beside me with their mother while I waited for death. But I could go no further than Charikar. My sons still believe that I have three months of life left to me. Barbara knows the truth. How many fingers would a man need to show the days left to me, Abbas? I will tell you. One finger would be enough. Perhaps two.'

Khalid Naseri again gestured at the iron bottle. Abbas turned the dial to '2' above the red mark. When his breathing had eased, Khalid asked Abbas to take a small calico bag with a green draw-string from the table beside the bed. He then asked Abbas to open the bag and look at what was inside. Abbas found a ball that had once been white but was now discoloured from use. It was also covered in handwriting, some blue, some black. He also found a triangular flag like those displayed on the wall. Like the ball, the flag of orange and blue was covered in handwriting.

Khalid Naseri spoke again. 'The ball was pitched in the famous victory of the Mets in the 1969 World Series. It is signed by five of the players. The pennant is signed by seven of the players. After my ring of marriage to Barbara, I value the ball and the pennant above all else. This is what I would like you to do for me, brother. I want you to take the ball and the pennant with you back to Hazarajat. Go to the grave of Esmail Behishti and beside his headstone dig a hole to twice the depth of your hand. Place the ball and the pennant in the hole and pack the earth tight above them. Say these words to the honoured man: "The sinner Khalid Naseri offers these to you." Will you do that, my brother?'

Abbas said nothing at first. He studied the handwriting on the ball, and the stitching. Then he said, 'As you will.'

Tears came to the eyes of Khalid Naseri. With difficulty, he raised his hands and turned them palm outwards towards Abbas. It is a gesture amongst our people, the Hazara, that means: Peace between us, surely.

Khalid Naseri closed his eyes late in the afternoon of that day and did not open them again on this earth. In the evening after prayer, Abbas and Konrad sat in the cool of the courtyard discussing the mystery of vacuum flasks. Abbas had become more beguiled with vacuum flasks with each day of thought that passed. Konrad spoke of atoms, and of molecules, which were patterns of atoms. The talk of atoms and molecules thrilled Abbas. As a boy in school, he had listened to his teacher who owned a copy of the *Saturday Evening Post* speak of atoms.

Barbara Naseri came into the courtyard at a time in the evening when the moon had made its shape in the eastern sky. Her face was wet. She said, 'Well, it is done.' She sat with Abbas and Konrad and wept into her hands. Abbas was too shy to comfort a woman with touching or embracing, but Konrad had no such fears. He put his arms around Barbara Naseri and spoke words of comfort to her. Abbas wished that he could do the same, but it was not possible. When the chance came, he said to Barbara Naseri, 'May your husband find his way to God.' Barbara Naseri dried her eyes with her hands, and found a way to compose herself. 'Oh, I do hope so! May he find his way to God, Abbas,' she responded.

10

The Russian

Abbas and Konrad remained in Charikar for the funeral rites of Khalid Naseri, who would be buried with further ceremony in Hazarajat once Abbas gave his approval in person to Baba Mazari.

For the journey back to Baba Mazari's village, Konrad filled the flat-sided cans with petrol from a depot in Charikar. The goat-hide bag was packed with food and bottled water. Barbara Naseri said, 'God protect you on the long road.' And then she asked Abbas, 'May I hope that my husband will lie in his native soil once you have spoken with Abdul Ali Mazari?' Abbas said that he would not deny Khalid Naseri his final wish. But he did not say that he forgave Khalid Naseri.

Abbas feared the role of passenger on Konrad's motorcycle no less than on the journey to Charikar. He fixed in his mind a vision of his wife and children awaiting him and hoped that concentrating on what he desired with all his heart would make him see beyond what he dreaded with all his heart. And he attempted to solve the problem of the vacuum flask while the motorcycle's engine roared in his ears, thinking of atoms and molecules in their invisible combinations.

He thought, too, of the great part of a man's life that was taken up with tasks he would avoid if he could. In his own occupation, many hours were spent carrying beehives from one location to another. There was no pleasure in it, but it was necessary. He said to himself, 'Most of life is what is necessary.' But then too much of what was easeful would cheapen the pleasures of life when they came. And so he must make no complaint.

Even as he was thinking of life and its trials, catastrophe was awaiting him and Konrad over the next rise. South of Pol-e-Khomri in a region of broken ground far above the highway, Konrad was ordered to stop by two mujaheddin in a Toyota truck. Guns were trained on him, and on Abbas. The two mujaheddin shouted at the one time, demanding things that were impossible. One said, 'Plague, flatten yourself on the ground!' The other said, 'Run, Plague!' The angry instructions of the two men made no sense. Abbas called out, 'Brothers, what are we to do? You contradict each other!'

One of the men ran at him and held the muzzle of his rifle to his throat.

'Are you tired of wearing a head?' said the man. He had strange eyes that did not focus and a torn lower lip. He seemed the madder of the two, and perhaps he was also the commander. Abbas knew enough about the war to obey whatever orders a mujaheddin gave. In our country at that time, a thousand bands of mujaheddin roamed the north-east, some of them disciplined, some a law unto themselves, and it was never easy to see which were mad and which were not.

Abbas said, 'Pardon me.'

Konrad had been forced to his knees. 'The boy fights the Russians in your cause, brother,' he said.

The commander barked, 'He is a Russian himself, like that cur.'

A boy not much older than Konrad lay in the back of the truck. He wore a Russian summer uniform; his hands were bound. Even in his crumpled position, it had to be said that he resembled Konrad. Abbas did not wish to think of what fate lay in store for the boy, the prisoner. He was now certain that the two men were not mujaheddin, but bandits. They would sell the Russian boy to the real mujaheddin.

Now the bandit with the strange eyes forced Konrad into the back of the truck with the Russian boy. The second bandit untied the two flat-sided containers of petrol from the motorcycle and the goat-hide bag.

'Plague, will I shoot you?' said the bandit with the strange eyes.

Abbas didn't reply. The second bandit poured petrol from one of the flat-sided containers into the tank of the Toyota.

The bandit with the strange eyes said again, 'Plague, will I shoot you?'

This time Abbas responded, saying, 'As you will.'

At that moment, the second bandit suddenly stopped pouring petrol and stared in alarm at the eastern hills. 'Aiee!' he cried, and threw the petrol container to the ground. The bandit who was threatening to shoot Abbas ran to the truck and climbed into the cabin.

As the engine struggled to start, Abbas now realised the danger that had startled the two bandits. A helicopter came over the eastern hills, filling the air with its thrum.

The Toyota swerved first one way then another as the shadow of the helicopter raced over the red sand and broken rock. As a boy, Abbas had seen a falcon swoop down on a hare. The hare knew it had become the falcon's prey and had tried to save its life by swerving and baulking in the same manner as the Toyota. But the falcon had prevailed, folding its wings and descending at a speed that changed its shape to a blur. Now as Abbas watched and prayed, the helicopter fired a rocket and in an instant the Toyota leapt into the air, turning end over end. He shouted, 'Aiee!' just as the bandit had, and for a moment he shielded his eyes with his hands. When he looked again, the Toyota was burning on the sand. The helicopter made a wide arc in the sky and sped away westward.

Abbas ran to the burning Toyota, but even before he reached the wreckage he could see that his prayers for Konrad's survival had been futile. The boy was surely dead. Abbas flailed at him with his hands to put out the flames, then knelt over the body, weeping without restraint.

The bandits – the false mujaheddin – they were also dead, and the Russian boy was dead, too, thrown a distance from the truck.

Abbas sat back on his heels, offering the prayers of our faith for those who have died in innocence. The term in Dari for one who has perished in this way – *shahid* – has no cousin in the

English language. It means a hundred English words: one who has died without having contributed to his own death, but at the same time, one who has placed himself in danger for a greater good; not exactly a martyr, but one who will find a home in Paradise.

Staring down at the broken body, Abbas recalled holding tightly to this same body on the motorcycle for hours, for days. He had felt the life of the boy surging in him, his joy in mechanical things, his love of speed. The life that God had given him in his mother's womb was now taken back and could not be restored.

Abbas washed the boy's face and feet with the bottled water from the goat-hide bag left on the sand when the bandits fled.

As he had at the site of the destroyed bus, Abbas wrenched a strip of metal from the wreckage of the vehicle and began to dig graves. The earth was hard under the red sand and the digging slow. He buried Konrad first, then the two bandits. He dragged the body of the Russian to a separate place, since the boy was probably a Christian and may have wished to be put under the earth away from those of another faith. Abbas worried that he had no Christian prayers to offer the boy's God. He thought he would ask our God to commend the boy's soul to the God of the Christians.

And Abbas did not know if it was the custom of Christians to wash the body of one about to be buried. But it could do no harm, surely. He tore fresh fabric from one of his shirts and wet it fully. He wiped the pale cheeks of the Russian boy, whispering fragments of prayers and lines of poetry, and words came from the mouth of the corpse, words of the boy's own language.

Abbas cried out, 'Does he live?'

He parted the boy's lips and poured water into his mouth. The muscles of the boy's throat moved.

'Does he live?' he cried again, and the boy's eyes opened.

The wounds on the Russian's legs and arms and neck and right shoulder were of the sort that bled freely but were easily staunched. A doctor would insist on closing the wounds with many stitches, but all Abbas could do was to clean them with boiled water and pick fragments of cloth from the flesh with the tip of his knife.

The boy screamed, of course.

Abbas was admired for his healing hands in his village of the Hazarajat. It was believed that he had amassed treasure in Heaven as the grandson of Esmail Behishti and God had given him the power to call the dying back to the light of life. Abbas did not believe that he had any such power. He kept wounds clean, he set bones straight, he knew the benefit of many herbs – that was all.

The herbs he needed for the Russian boy were not to be found in the sand and rock of the mountains between Pol-e-Khomri and Sar-e Pol – not this late in spring. But he found the plant known as *khora-kema*, and by God's good grace it was still in flower. He took leaves from the plant and the long stalk that held the flower. When the stalk was stripped, it would yield a green fruit like a cucumber, full of a milky liquid. The liquid would ease the Russian boy's pain and help him to sleep. The leaves would serve as bandages for the wounds. Abbas also found honeysuckle, which would kill the infection of the wounds and could be applied to the inside of the *khora-kema* leaves.

Although Mazar-e-Sharif was only two days' walk to the north, the Russian boy was too weak to sit as a passenger on the motorcycle. And even if Abbas could master the motorcycle and somehow keep the boy seated behind him, once in Mazar-e-Sharif the boy's throat would be cut by mujaheddin, even by Hazara loyal to Baba Mazari. Only one hope for the boy: Abbas must ask Abdul Ali Mazari himself to spare him and return him to a Russian commander.

Abbas left the boy in the shade while he searched higher up the mountain for better shelter. He found an overhanging rock that covered a broad enough area to keep the sun away. In the winter it would be a home for wolves. He cleared the ground and made a bed for the boy and wrapped his wounds in *khora-kema* leaves. The boy had no fever. Infection had not taken hold. If infection came, Abbas would make use of manna from the leaves of the camel-thorn, but to find camel-thorn he would have to climb further up the mountain and even then he would have to hope for guidance from angels. The camel-thorn only made manna in certain years, and usually only in the height of summer.

The boy slept for an hour at a time but whenever he woke he screamed. To Abbas, he was no more than a child, although tall. His eyes were blue. Above one eye an old scar in the shape of the Dari letter *geem* stood out. But there was something that troubled Abbas more than the wounds. The boy had injected heroin into his left arm many times. The soft flesh of his elbow crease was scarred and blue. He knew from many tales that the Russian soldiers craved heroin and opium and drank foolishly. Some inhaled petrol fumes if nothing else was available. In Kabul, it was said, Russian soldiers wandered the streets offering anything they possessed for heroin. It was considered no sin to sell them what they wanted, since they were invaders. Many went mad.

It would be a week or even two before the boy could ride on the back of the motorcycle to Baba's village. The food and water in the goat-hide bag would barely last. Abbas prepared himself for a time of patience. He prayed more often than he usually did, and not always prayers from the Holy Book; many he fashioned himself, asking God to lift the scourge of war from Afghanistan. For Abbas, war was like a barren field that gives no grain, no wildflowers for the bees to rob, no melons, no grass for animals to graze. It was like a famine that settled on the land. Instead of fruit, Kalashnikovs and missiles. Abbas had noticed other evils. War drove people back into their tribes. It was not Afghans who fought the invaders, but Tajiks under Tajik commanders, Uzbeks under Uzbeki commanders, Pashtuns under Pashtun commanders. And of course, Hazaras under Baba Mazari. And when the invaders were gone – for they would surely be defeated – the tribes would turn their new weapons on each other. Abbas was Hazara, but he had lived long enough to see great kindness in those of other tribes. It was a Pashtun who had saved his life on his visit two years past to Kabul, pulling him from the path of a Russian vehicle. The man who had shown him the shining valley near Herat where the leaves turned silver in the sun was a Tajik. The flowers of those trees, as big as a plate, gave nectar in such abundance that Abbas' bees returned to their hives almost too laden to fly. And it was an Uzbeki who had married his sister Maria and made a fine house for her with his own hands. In his heart, Abbas was Hazara, but if the price of peace in his country was that people forgot their tribe and could never recall it, then let it be. He had seen less of war than many other Afghans, but he was sick of it forever.

When he was not trying to reason with God, Abbas turned his mind to the problem of the vacuum flask. The tragedy of Konrad's death was that his mother and father would never find comfort again in life. A smaller piece of the tragedy was that Abbas would never learn more about the molecules. For he sensed that the molecules were at the heart of the problem of the vacuum flask. They clung to each other like the cells of a beehive, and surely passed information to each other. But what was that information?

Four days came and went with the Russian boy still too weak to lift himself from the blanket on the floor of the shelter. Sometimes he lay staring with his blue eyes at the overhanging rock above him. Sometimes he stared at Abbas. He made no objection when Abbas fed him, or helped him to relieve his bladder and his bowels. He accepted spoonfuls of broth. His eyes were either full of fear, or full of nothing. Once Abbas saw him lift his hand and touch the place on the inside of his arm where he had injected heroin. Abbas thought, 'Soon a craving will come. How I can restrain him, I don't know.'

The craving came on the morning of the fifth day. The boy's eyes darted all over the shelter. Twice he spoke something in his language – a language that sounded to Abbas like the bleating of a calf when it is first born. He said to the boy, 'Rest.' In the afternoon, the boy began to swing his head back and forth on his bed. He spoke his strange calf-language and his eyes were now full of pleading.

Abbas pointed to the needle scars on his arm. He said, 'No more,' and shook his head. The boy spoke the Dari word for 'please': *lotfan*.

Abbas said, 'No more.'

Then the boy lay still for hours, sometimes with his eyes open, sometimes shut. He ate broth and dried apricots. He allowed Abbas to inspect his wounds.

In the night, Abbas was awakened by a rustling sound in the shelter. He saw the shape of the Russian boy bent over the goat-hide bag. He moved swiftly to the boy and helped him back to the bed. The wound on his neck had begun to bleed again. Abbas stopped the bleeding with moss and matted cobwebs from the walls of the shelter then covered the wound with fresh *khora-kema* leaves.

The boy said, '*Lotfan!*'

Abbas shook his head.

'*Lotfan!*' said the boy, and began to cry.

Abbas gave him the milk from the stripped stem of *khora-kema*. The boy calmed down for an hour, but then began to cry out in pain. The muscles of his arms and legs were cramping. Abbas bathed the boy's limbs with warm water and massaged the muscles of his shoulders. The boy wept all night and Abbas had to sit by him and hold him still whenever he began to writhe.

Two more nights passed in this way.

Abbas became used to the sounds of the darkness whenever the boy's sobbing stopped for an hour. He heard the distant rumble of trucks on the highway, the more distant murmur of Russian bombers on their way south-east to Herat, sometimes helicopters flying high overhead in swarms. And he heard owls calling to each other in their hunt for mice and desert rats and scorpions and the small snakes of the region with their golden bellies. He heard the songs of nightingales and the cry before dawn of a little bird he'd noticed with a white breast that fed on the gnats that rose in clouds to find shelter away from the light.

He no longer thought of his family. It caused him pain to picture his son Esmail waiting to catch a glimpse of his father returning along the track that led over the Sangan Hills. Nor could he picture Sabah in her beauty when she uncovered her hair and teased him by letting the tips brush his face. Nor could he think of love-making, nor of the breakfasts his daughters prepared for him on the one day a week he stayed home and slept late. He did not expect to see his family again.

In these mornings of late spring the sun came over the mountains at first slowly, then suddenly it was in the eastern sky, white and fierce. The shadows it threw were a deeper shade in late spring than in early spring. Its heat was so strong that even grasshoppers found the shade. Abbas worried that the water would run out, and he drank little himself. Most was needed for the Russian boy's wounds, and to massage his limbs when the cramping came. Food, too, was a worry. Abbas ate little of the food, but he had always been a small eater and could survive on next to nothing. The boy needed nourishment every day. Abbas said to himself, 'Such a burden this foolish boy has become!' Then he said, 'Well, so be it.'

On the morning of the eighth day, the boy smiled. He reached for Abbas' hand and squeezed it. He spoke in his own language of Russian. Abbas thought it safe now to leave the boy alone for an hour or so while he searched for a spring. He also hoped to find the plant known as *gaz* in my language of Dari, but known as tamarisk in English. He wanted to harvest *gaz-anjabin*, which is the manna of the *gaz*, for the manna would act more powerfully on the boy's cramping than the *khora-kema* milk.

He made the boy understand that he would be gone for an hour, and the boy nodded his head.

Abbas followed a *wadi* up the mountain until he came to a place where the red sand changed to pink. This sometimes meant that the water that flowed in the *wadi* in early spring could still be found an arm's length down. He dug with the implement he'd fashioned to make graves for Konrad and the false mujaheddin. He found water at the depth he'd expected and drew it up with a metal cup and poured it into empty plastic bottles. Its taste was bitter, but the bitterness meant that it contained a natural enemy of infection that would benefit the Russian boy's wounds.

Abbas filled six bottles with the bitter water, then went in search of *gaz*. He stood on a high rock and looked for the tips of the trees growing up from shade into sunlight. By good fortune he found a grove and cut the black bark to make the sap flow. He collected the sap on the blade of his knife and made more cuts and gathered the manna on the blade and more and more, and put the tip of his blade to the wound in the bark and let the sap run down to the hilt. He took sap from the tamarisk until he had a full tin. He fitted the press-lid to the tin and made it secure. *Gaz* is full of salt and even the manna has a salty taste, but once he heated it in water the best part of the manna would come to the surface, while the salt would sink. The salty water could be used to wash the boy's wounds, while the manna could be chewed and its nourishment would pass into the boy's body.

He was walking back to the shelter full of success when he

heard an engine come to life. For a moment he was baffled, then he thought, 'It is the motorcycle.' He ran through the rocks with all the skill he'd taught himself chasing sheep and goats in the mountains as a boy. He saw the Russian faltering along on the motorcycle – unsteady at first then finding his balance and speeding away.

Abbas dropped the goat-hide bag and chased the motorcycle. He shouted at the Russian, '*Estadah! Estadah!*' But the boy didn't stop and Abbas chased only the noise of the engine until the noise of the engine came to an end.

He found the motorcycle and the unconscious Russian lying in a tangle on the ground. He lifted the motorcycle and freed the boy and with great effort dragged him back to the shelter. All of his wounds had opened again and blood was flowing. Abbas boiled water and washed the wounds and treated them with moss and matted cobwebs until the bleeding had ceased. The boy became conscious again and immediately began to weep.

'Find your courage!' Abbas shouted.

When the boy continued to weep, Abbas pulled his ears.

'Find your courage!' he said again. Then he said in great anger (not that the boy could understand), 'Should I not leave you in the sun to cook? Why do I not? What madness has brought you to Afghanistan? Did you come to make a nuisance of yourself? For surely you have succeeded!'

If the boy could not understand the words, he could see the anger. He stopped weeping.

Abbas boiled the manna, the *gaz-anjabin*, in water. He cleaned the wounds again with the cooled water, taking care that he was not cruel in his anger. He made the boy understand that he had to chew the *gaz-anjabin* and swallow it. While he chewed, the boy stared at him with his blue eyes. Abbas felt he was instructing a child.

On the day that followed the boy's madness with the motorcycle he fell into a fever. But Abbas could see from the colour of the healing wounds that the fever was not from infection. No, the boy's body craved heroin and opium and was struggling with itself. Not a true fever, but a time of sweating and shivering. Abbas sat by the boy and bathed him with warm water and massaged his limbs and fed him milk from the *khora-kema* and chewed manna in his own mouth until it was soft and made the boy swallow it. He sang songs to the boy, songs he had sung to his own daughters and to his son. He recited poetry he had learnt from his grandfather Esmail. He recited the words of the Prophet from the Holy Book. He told the Russian boy stories of the Bandit King of long ago, Ali Hazari, who scorned the rule of Cruel Shah Hamal and stole money from the Shah's palace and gave it to the poor people of Hazarajat. These were children's stories and the Russian could not understand even a single word, but he listened.

The fever passed, the shaking passed. The Russian boy's wits returned. He had more than one word of Dari, it now seemed. He could say, 'thank you', and 'water' and very strangely, 'birdseed.' He attempted to tell Abbas a story in sign language. It appeared that he had kept a bird in a cage in his barracks, and had gone into the market to buy birdseed. That was what Abbas understood. It also appeared that he had six brothers and sisters. His name was Lev. His city (here he made the shape of buildings) was Kursk.

Abbas told his own story to the boy. He made the shapes of

three children, each one taller than the one before. He showed with his hands and with sounds the flight of a bee. And he showed with his hands a flower opening, and the bee gathering nectar. The boy Lev wore a puzzled expression for a long time, but then understanding came, and he laughed. 'Pchela!' he said, and made the sound of a bee. Then he touched a finger to his lips and showed pleasure, as at the taste of something sweet. 'Med!' he said. 'Pchela, buzz buzz buzz! Pchela! Med! Pchela, med!'

When he judged the boy strong enough to travel on the motorcycle, Abbas dressed him in an Afghan shirt and trousers and turban. With the goat-hide bag and fresh water from the wadi and the remaining flat-sided container of petrol, Abbas and the Russian walked to the site of the motorcycle.

This was the dilemma. If Abbas took the boy to the Russians, the Russians would shoot Abbas. If Abbas took the boy Lev to the mujaheddin, the mujaheddin would shoot the boy, or something worse, and might even shoot Abbas too. Only Baba Mazari could make sure that both the boy and Abbas were kept from harm. Abbas had tried to make the boy understand, and the boy had nodded his head, but he was probably puzzled. He trusted Abbas. That was enough.

More than the mujaheddin, and more than the Russian helicopters, Abbas feared the motorcycle. He knew how to operate the machine but steering it seemed a nightmare. The Russian boy knew more of the machine's ways but his wounds restricted him. Abbas would steer the machine.

He practised driving the motorcycle over the sand. It was not difficult if he drove slowly. He prayed to God for a journey of charity with few collisions and drove due west through Samangan finding trails away from the roads. The Russian boy held him by his waist. But the boy Lev could only hold on for twenty minutes before he needed to rest his arms.

Abbas made the machine move at only half the speed that Konrad had driven it. Even then, his fear was enough to make him stop twice to vomit into the sand. Such a strange thing that he should so fear the machine when he was unafraid of more dangerous things. A snake could glide across his body when he slept on the ground and he would only say, 'Greetings to you!' Once he had wakened from a short sleep in the honey fields with a big camel spider on his head but had remained still while the spider found its way to another place of rest.

For the whole journey Abbas feared the mujaheddin and the false mujaheddin and the Russians and the communist soldiers of the Afghan army.

South-east of Sar-e Pol he stopped for the night and fell onto the sand and slept without first making the boy a bed. He woke in panic, fearing that the boy Lev was dead. But the boy had also fallen asleep on the sand and was breathing well. Abbas lay on his back looking up at the night sky. The stars were brighter than ever he could recall and were strewn in multitudes down to the western horizon. Between the stars the sky was not black but the blue of midnight. A lizard slept beside his head.

It was the afternoon of the following day when Abbas reached Baba Mazari's village in the north. He raised his head in great relief and praised God's mercy and praised God's charity. All of the scourges he'd feared had been avoided.

Three guards walked down from the house with their rifles in their hands. They were not the guards who had watched Abbas depart twenty days earlier. One guard called to Abbas, 'Abbas Behishti of Tayvareh?'

'From Sangan, brother. Tayvareh is to the west of my village.'

'Who is this?' the guard asked, jutting his chin towards the Russian boy.

'I rescued him from false mujaheddin near Pol-e-Khomri.'

'Is it a Russian dog?'

Abbas was embarrassed by the guard's bad manners. He said, 'Brother, mind your speech. I will talk with Baba.'

'You will talk with the worms in the earth if you rouse my temper, *sadah*,' replied the guard gruffly. ('*Sadah*' means 'hillbilly'.)

Abbas lost his temper. This did not happen often. He seized the guard by his beard and pulled it hard. 'You cannot remember the manners your mother taught you? Then shame!' He turned the guard around and slapped him hard on his behind. He glared at the other guards as he led the Russian boy Lev to the house.

Baba was away in the north for three days, as Abbas discovered. But Baba's wife greeted him as if he were of the family. She called him 'honoured man' and was polite to the Russian boy Lev. Privately she asked Abbas, 'What has happened? Is Konrad no longer with us?'

'It is my sorrow to tell you that he has lost his life to the Russians. A helicopter killed him with a rocket.'

Baba's wife nodded. She touched her heart and her forehead to show her own sorrow. Then she said, 'Who is this child?' and Abbas answered, 'You may think of him as my prisoner. He is one of the Russians from their city of Kursk.'

Baba's *hawoo* (his second wife) brought in melon juice, then hot tea made in the Turkish fashion, then small cakes of nougat. Abbas yearned to wash himself and to trim his beard, which had become untidy, and to cut his fingernails and toenails, but first he asked Baba's wife to call a surgeon for the boy Lev. When the surgeon came he agreed that the boy's wounds had escaped infection but he opened the gash on the boy's neck again and stitched it carefully so that the scar would not disfigure him.

It was thought unwise for the Russian boy to see who came and went from Baba's house and thus he was kept in a second house in the village where Abbas visited him each day. This second house was that of Khalid Turkman. Despite his name, Khalid was not a Turkman but a Hazara who had lived and worked in Turkmenistan under the Russians. He had attended the university in Ashgabat and held certificates to show that he understood mathematics of many kinds. He understood Russians too and spoke their language and had come back to Afghanistan to give advice to Baba Mazari about the Red Army.

Khalid Turkman spoke with the Russian boy Lev in his own language and told Abbas what he'd learned.

'He is nineteen years old,' said Khalid Turkman. 'He was at the university in Kursk when he was sent to the army.'

Then Khalid said, 'He does not like the war. He hates the army.' And, 'He doesn't want to die.' And, 'He says you are like an angel who came into his life.' And, 'He is sorry he tried to run away from you. He says he doesn't want drugs anymore.'

Abbas spoke. 'If we let him free in Mazar-e-Sharif he would have a needle in his arm in ten minutes. Ask him what he studied at his university.'

Khalid spoke to the boy for some minutes. 'He says he studied physics. Do you know what is meant by that?'

Abbas sat up straight in his excitement. 'Ask him if he understands the molecules.'

'If he understands the molecules?'

'Yes! Ask him, it would be a kindness.'

The Russian boy indeed knew about molecules. Abbas asked Lev why a vacuum flask can keep hot things hot and cold things cold. The boy Lev himself seemed as excited as Abbas. He asked for some paper and a pencil. On the paper he drew small circles with symbols attached. Through Khalid, he explained about the transfer of heat between molecules. And he said that a vacuum flask has two layers of glass, and between the two layers lives a vacuum. In a vacuum there are no molecules and the transfer of heat is greatly reduced. If a hot liquid is poured into the vacuum flask, the temperature of the liquid will remain the same for a long time. If a cold liquid is poured into the flask, in the same manner the temperature of the cold liquid will remain the same for a long time.

Abbas asked, 'Everything is molecules?'

'Everything,' the Russian boy replied.

Abbas sat back in his chair smiling with happiness. This was something he thought might be true! God had made the world with molecules! It gave Abbas pleasure to think of the molecules joined by their small arms, each with its symbol. He thanked the Russian boy with all his heart.

When Baba returned from the north, he pulled his beard and covered his head when he learned of Konrad's death. 'I fear to tell his mother!' he said. He stood and walked up and down in the court-yard for some time, shaking his head and striking himself on the chest where his heart dwelt.

Then he seated himself again. 'As God wills,' he said.

He listened to Abbas' story of his meetings with Khalid Naseri. He nodded his head at the news of his death. Then he asked about the Russian boy, Lev, and heard all that Abbas had to tell.

'What would you have me do with him?' he said.

'I would have him returned to his people,' said Abbas.

'Then you mean that you would have him hanged,' said Baba. 'How did the false mujaheddin capture him, Abbas? I will tell you. In the way they capture many others of these Russian fools. By putting a pistol to his head when he was pleading for opium. The Russians will know how he was captured. They will hang him or shoot him.'

Baba again stood and paced in the courtyard. He touched his jaw and asked his *hawoo* for oil of cloves. 'I will take a hammer to this tooth,' he said. 'The surgeon told me that it would take two days to fix my mouth. Two days! Have I such leisure?'

Then he said, 'It matters to you that this boy is saved? I would shoot him now.'

'He is a child,' replied Abbas.

'Yes, he is a child. He is a Russian child trained at Ashgabat to kill our children.'

Baba poured more clove oil onto a small piece of cloth and dabbed his afflicted tooth again.

'Very well,' he said. 'The boy can live. But in two weeks he will be back in the market trying to sell his Kalashnikov for twenty American dollars' worth of heroin. Yet if it is your desire, my brother, he will live. I have a prisoner – a Russian officer – in Mazar. The Russians love him, he is the son of someone important. I will give them the officer and this fool of a boy and tell them that the boy must be spared. Will that satisfy you?'

Abbas crossed the courtyard and kissed Baba's hand.

'And now let me ask you this,' Baba said. 'Will Khalid Naseri return to Hazarajat and lie in our soil?'

'Baba, with my blessing,' said Abbas.

'Is this from your heart, brother?'

'From my heart,' said Abbas.

At their parting, the Russian boy Lev wept until his face was soaked. He swore a sacred oath that he would never touch heroin again. Abbas did not believe him, but he pretended to. He said, 'My good wishes to your mother and father, and to your brothers and sisters. Thank you for the story of the molecules.'

Once the boy was gone, Abbas was ready to return to his own family. But he would not ride the motorcycle back over the Sangan Hills. No, he would walk. Baba Mazari embraced him and called him a hero of the Hazara people. Abbas said, 'Will Konrad's mother call me a hero of the Hazara people? I wish he were here.'

He made the journey back to his home with his head full of molecules and their strange ways and his heart full of sorrow for the death of Konrad. He stopped many times on the path to his home to commend Konrad's soul to God, and to pray for some sense to come into the head of the boy Lev.

Past the Sangan Hills, on the track that crossed a small tributary of a river that joined the Helmand, he found his home safe, and his children safe and his wife smiling.

The day after his return, Abbas took his son Esmail with him on a journey of half a day to the grave of his grandfather, Esmail Behishti. He dug in the earth close to the headstone and placed the ball given to him by Khalid Naseri in the hole, wrapped in the pennant. He packed the earth firmly into the hole and placed a small stone on top of it. He spoke these words: 'The sinner Khalid Naseri offers these to you.'

Abbas had told his son the story of the ball and the pennant and the reason for their burial. He had told him what little he knew of the game of baseball, of the two teams that strove against each other to be champions of America. Now as Abbas and his son prepared to leave the grave and return to their home, the boy said, 'Will our grandfather accept the ball of the Americans?'

Abbas did not answer immediately, and the boy asked again, 'Papa, will our grandfather accept the ball of the Americans?'

Abbas said, 'Yes, I think he will accept it.'

11

The Richest Man in Afghanistan

The hills and mountains near Sangan rise in every direction and no matter where you stand, you can see mountains beyond mountains. In the hills it is possible to find valleys sheltered enough to provide grass and thorny bushes to feed goats and sheep, but in many places there is nothing. And yet in this nothing, Jawad Noroosi one day found his fortune.

I say 'one day found his fortune' but in truth his fortune was his luck, which had been with him from birth. It was in the hills that his luck first revealed itself, and might have made him the richest man in Afghanistan if it had not also been a curse. Not that it mattered. Jawad had little use for money, living the simplest of lives, with no family to lavish gifts on, and no wife to fill a house with ornaments.

230

Jawad Noroosi was only seventeen years of age when his luck became a legend. Up until that time, he was thought of as a boy afflicted with a mad mother and a father almost as mad. The husband had told everyone that his wife was the Messiah of a new religion that honoured the moon. He said that his wife could make blackbirds fly as high as wild geese and return with apples made of gold. But years of waiting for this miracle only ended in disappointment and the few followers that the Woman Messiah had gathered drifted away.

A boy of seventeen is considered a young man when it comes to work, as I have said before, although no more than a child in other ways. He might sweat beside his father in the fields for twelve hours a day, but we would still say that such a boy was too young for marriage. And we would still say that a boy of that age needs his mother. At this difficult age, Jawad's mother the Woman Messiah and his father the mullah of her new religion disappeared. They had been seen on the road to Kandahar and had told a traveller they met that the people of Sangan were too fickle to live amongst. Jawad, their only child, was left to care for himself in the small house his parents had owned.

Jawad's mother the sorceress (for that was how the villagers thought of her) had left him a stone for good luck wrapped in his second shirt. And a note: 'The stone is from the moon. Guard it well.'

Jawad had always shone with happiness, but now he was overcome by despair and wept for a week. An old man of Sangan, Baba Khadem, took him into his care and reported that the boy sat staring at the piece of rock his mother had left him and talked of jumping to his death from the top of the town hall – not a very tall building, but the tallest one in Sangan at the time of this story, seventy years before today. That would be a shame, because the boy had certain gifts that promised a better future: he spoke twelve languages and could tell by his nose where water was to be found under the earth. Amongst the languages he spoke were Uzbeki, Baluchi, Pashtun, Turkmen, Nuristani and a dialect of Persian spoken only by the fire-worshippers. The boy said he'd learnt all of his languages from his mother, the sorceress or Woman Messiah. Apart from his human languages, the boy could also converse with Baba Khadem's mule in a tongue that sounded like a saw cutting through timber.

And Jawad had a further gift: that of working hard. Baba Khadem gave him the task of making bricks for the summer cottage he was building in the hills close to the snowline. The boy not only made the bricks, he loaded Baba's mule with forty at a time and led the beast into the hills and back twice a day before nightfall.

It was on one of these journeys into the hills that Jawad discovered topaz. He showed the stone to Baba and asked, 'Is there a use for this?' To which Baba said, 'Surely!' and told the boy to bring back all he could find. The next day, Jawad returned from the hills with a block of stone in which green garnet could be seen, a very rare gem. He asked Baba, 'Is there a use for this?' Baba said again, 'Surely!' and told the boy to bring back all the topaz and all the garnet of any colour he could find.

The boy came back each day with so much topaz and green garnet that Baba Khadem began to worry about his own soul. He had made many journeys up and down the hills and mountains of Sangan and had never found so much as a fragment of topaz or green garnet. And yet God had led this smiling boy with a mad mother and a mad father to a trove of gems. To Baba, this meant that God intended the riches for the boy to make up for foolish parents. He said to Jawad, 'These riches are your own. I want none of them.' And from that day, he closed his mind to the boy's gift.

The gift mattered little to the boy. Once all the bricks for the summer house had been carried up to the snowline, he didn't even bother to search for more gems. Instead he took over the occupation of well-digger when the town's well-digger of many years was bitten by a fox with the foaming disease and died within a week.

The first well to be dug took him through a layer of familiar rock. He recognised topaz by the light of his candle without bothering to harvest the gems. But he told the owner of the well, which was soon turned into a quarry. He unearthed more gems in the construction of his second well and that well too became a mine. His great gift became so well known that he was followed everywhere by men of the town waiting for him to put his pick to the earth. So many hungry faces around him made Jawad uneasy, and he gave up well-digging.

Since the house left to Jawad by his mad mother and mad father sat on a piece of land just big enough to enclose a garden, the young man, or boy, if you prefer, decided to make his living by growing corn and broad beans. He purchased corn seed and bean seed and set about turning the soil. In great excitement, men and boys and even a few women of Sangan raced to the site of Jawad's labour, thinking that he would quickly be up to his neck in topaz and green garnets. But no, he dug only nine shallow furrows for his seed (an uneven number for good luck) and all the people waiting for riches went home unhappy. Baba himself came to see what the boy was up to and informed him that the earth was too poor to support even weeds and that the project was certain to fail.

Within a week, the shoots of the corn and beans had risen above the ground. Within two weeks, the beans were climbing the stakes Jawad had driven into the earth. Within three weeks, the corn stalks had reached the height of an ass. Within four weeks, against all nature, bean pods had appeared. And again against all nature, corn ears were fattening on the stalks. In six weeks from planting, Jawad Noroosi's garden flourished with corn stalks twice as high as a horse, while each bean in its pod was the size of the giant ruby on Zahir Shah's famous coronation ring. The wonder of what the poor earth of Jawad's garden had produced drew sightseers from all over the province of Ghowr, and even from as far away as Farah and Herat.

A mullah from Tayvareh studied the garden and declared it impious. 'The devil has had a hand in the raising of the corn,' he said. 'And the beans.' Anyone who ate the produce of Jawad Noroosi's garden would be carried to hell by witches and goblins. All the same, people ate the beans and the corn, sold for a very modest price by Jawad, and sang their praises.

But Jawad's success soon made him bitter enemies. In Sangan many farmers relied on growing corn and beans for a living. But who would pay for their produce when Jawad gave ten times the weight for half the money? The mayor of Sangan came to Jawad's garden with five deputies and a demand that he switch to turnips, which nobody in Ghowr Province cared for anyway. And stories were told of women growing beards after eating Jawad's corn and beans. A farmer's wife appeared in the marketplace with a beard that reached to her waist, claiming that she shaved each morning only to have the beard grow back within hours. It was plain to see that the beard was false, made of bark and dried grass, but many chose to believe her. Another woman, also the wife of a farmer, swore that she'd left a plate of Jawad's corn on a shelf in her kitchen where it was eaten by rats. 'The rodents grew to the size of a grey wolf!' she said. 'Aiee! Who will be safe?'

Jawad's spirits, which had taken so long to return after his abandonment, now ebbed away. His good fortune seemed a worse affliction than ill fortune. Like his father and his mother the Woman Messiah, he asked himself if he could remain in Sangan where he was so scorned. He said, 'I will go to the hills and live the life of a hermit.' He could always use his nose to find water, and as for food, he would be content to live on beetles and grasshoppers.

He said goodbye to Baba Khadem and set off one morning carrying few possessions: a pot and a pan, a metal cup, a metal plate. He also took his pick and his spade, in case he should need to excavate a hole in the hillside in which to live. It was a mistake to take the pick and spade. Word quickly spread that the moon-worshipping son of the Woman Messiah was heading into the hills to dig for gold. All over Sangan, farmers and brick-makers and bakers and butchers chased after Jawad with picks and spades. Even the old men who loitered near the mosque polishing the boots of those at prayer threw their rags and shoe-black aside and hurried along the path taken by the fortunate young man. Whenever Jawad stopped for a rest, the crowd following him stopped and watched. When he spread his bedding on the ground and slept for the night, the crowd camped a short distance away, studying the poor fellow as a falcon in the sky studies the movement of a field mouse below. In the morning, Jawad could not even empty his bladder in private. It was thought that he might secretly cleave the earth with his pick and steal away with a sack full of gold.

In the hills on the afternoon of his second day of travelling, Jawad found a cave in which to take up his life as a hermit. He settled in the entrance with his legs crossed and prayed to the God of our faith for the crowd before him to go far away. He prayed with his eyes shut, but when he opened them again, a hundred people called in one voice: 'Jawad, when will you dig for gold?'

Jawad replied, 'Never! Go home!'

And the crowd cried out, 'Jawad, when will you dig for topaz? When will you dig for green garnet?'

Nothing was left of Jawad's smile, nothing was left of the laughter that he had once been known for. In his anger, he picked up a stone from the floor of the cave and threw it at the crowd, and then another stone, and another.

People in the crowd cried, 'Aiee! He has gone mad!' Then the baker of Sangan picked up one of the stones that Jawad had cast and peered at it closely.

'*Lazhuward!*' he shouted. 'It is *lazhuward* that the moon-worshipper has found!'

'*Lazhuward*' is our Dari word for the stone known in English as lapis lazuli. But of course, Jawad had been seeking no such stone. He had only grasped what lay closest to him on the floor of the cave.

A stampede followed the baker's words. Every man and woman in the crowd – and most shamefully, even some children – knocked Jawad aside in their haste to dig lapis lazuli from the cave. Those who had no digging implements made use of Jawad's own pick and spade, and even his metal plate and cup, his pot and pan. When Jawad climbed to his feet he noticed that the mullah of Tayvareh who had declared his beans and corn impious was digging furiously for the precious stone.

Jawad left the crowd far behind as he climbed into the mountains. His face was wet with tears. All that he had left to him was the stone from his mother, once a part of the moon. That stone he kept close to his heart. He now understood why she had left Sangan.

High in the mountains he came upon a parrot of bright red and blue and yellow with a tail as long as the leg of a man. At the time of meeting the parrot Jawad was making his way north-east, thinking that he might settle in the land of China. But the bird disagreed with his plan. Perched high on a boulder with its bright tail hanging down, the parrot called to Jawad, 'Young man! Turn your face to the south!'

'To the south?' said Jawad. 'But I am on my way to China.'

The bird shook its head. 'I advise against China,' it said.

Jawad frowned and scratched his chin. 'What will I find in the south?' he asked.

'What will you find in the south?' said the bird. 'Use your head! Your mother and father were bound for Kandahar.'

'Do you mean that I will find my mother and father in Kandahar?' Jawad asked in amazement.

'Who knows?' said the bird, and it beat its wings and flew out of sight.

Jawad thought it would be wrong to ignore the bird's advice. He might wander for fifty years without meeting such an intelligent bird again. So he turned his face to the south and came down from the mountains into the valley of the Helmand.

He had lived on beetles and grasshoppers for months by the time he reached the banks of the great river and so he thought he would try his hand at fishing. But he had never fished before in his life and was ignorant about the means of catching fish. He was not far from the town of Zin and fishermen were to be seen on the banks. Jawad called to one of the fishermen, 'Brother, how will I catch a fish for my supper?'

The fisherman laughed. He whispered to a friend before calling to Jawad, 'It's easy!' he said. 'Say, "Fish, fish, I am waiting for my supper!" One will jump into your lap!'

Jawad did not truly believe what he was told, but he had no better advice. 'Fish, fish!' he cried out, standing on the bank of the Helmand. 'I am waiting for my supper!'

Within seconds not one but twenty fish had leapt from the water and landed at his feet – bream, barbel, silver carp, gudgeon, and the biggest of all, a pike. The fisherman who had told him the means of catching fish came running with his friend.

'A wonder!' said the fisherman. And his friend said, 'I have fished here for thirty years and never seen a pike of such size!'

'Keep it,' said Jawad. He picked up a barbel to eat for his supper. 'This will be enough for me.'

The fishermen did indeed scoop up the fish that were left. But even as Jawad was cooking his barbel on the riverbank, many more fishermen came shouting for him to call pike from the river, or at least sweet bream. Jawad called more fish, even a pike bigger than the first, but that was not enough for the fishermen. They plagued him with their demands until at last he stole away while the crowd was fighting over the bounty. He had not eaten his barbel and had to satisfy himself once more with brown grasshoppers.

Jawad made his way steadily south, keeping a distance between himself and the Helmand for fear he would be asked to empty the great river of fish. He crossed another river, the Arghandab in Zabol Province, without any thought of fishing, and came at last to the highway. With his heart full of hope that he would again see his mother and his father he began the final stage of his journey to Kandahar, the city of the south where pomegranates grew at their sweetest – the city where the world itself began many ages past.

He stood in the great bazaar of Kandahar where a thousand shopkeepers shouted the merits of their wares. He said in despair, 'How will I ever find my mother and father in a city of so many souls?' He asked a man who wore the turban of a tribe he had never come across before, and the man said, 'I don't sell mothers and fathers, I sell brass lamps!' Jawad next questioned a seller of enamel chamber pots, saying, 'I seek a woman with an earring of amethyst and the white stone of the moon-worshippers on her forehead, have you seen her?' The chamber pot seller said, 'May all moon-worshippers be taken by the devil!' Hoping for more courtesy amongst the fruit sellers, Jawad approached a man who sold pomegranates the size of melons and asked if he had heard of a woman and a man who performed miracles with blackbirds. This time he was successful. The pomegranate seller said, 'The moon sorceress? Oh yes. I followed her until my wife forbade it.'

'Then where can I find her?' said Jawad in relief.

'You will find her in Korooshi Square at eight o'clock tomorrow morning. They're hanging her.'

'Hanging her? In God's name, what reason could they have?'

'The moon-worshippers usually escape with a warning. And the lizard-worshippers. Maybe she offended the mayor in some way. Go to the jail and ask her.'

Jawad found his way to the jail after many twists and turns. He pleaded with the sentry for admission, saying he was the son of a woman waiting to be hanged in the morning. The sentry was moved by Jawad's tears and called the turnkey, who permitted Jawad to say goodbye to his mother the sorceress.

Jawad's mother sat in her cell with her head bowed to her chest. Beside her sat her husband, who was also destined for the scaffold. Jawad called through the sturdy iron bars of the cell, 'Mother! Father! It's Jawad your son come to comfort you!'

Jawad's mother and his father crawled across the floor of the cell, since it was forbidden to stand upright. Jawad asked for his mother's hand to kiss, and his father's.

'What a fate awaits us, dear son!' said the Woman Messiah. 'We are to be hanged.'

'But what is your crime, mother?'

'Ah me, dear son! The Mayor of Kandahar says we must pay a million afghanis in taxes!'

'Aiee! Why did he name such a sum for you to pay?'

'Dear son, I told the mayor that I could command blackbirds to fly as high as wild geese and return with golden apples. The mayor said, "How many golden apples have the blackbirds fetched to you?" I said, "One hundred" and the mayor said the tax on one hundred golden apples was one million afghanis. Arithmetic, dear son. I never mastered it.'

It was plain to see that the sorceress was a broken woman. It was plain to see that the sorceress's husband was a broken man.

Jawad said, 'So...no golden apples?'

'No golden apples, dear son.'

'You must tell the mayor that you made a mistake. You must tell the mayor that you cannot command blackbirds to fly as high as wild geese and fetch golden apples back to you.'

'Dear son, I did.'

'What did the mayor say?'

'That I must hang. And your dear father, too.'

Jawad's mother began to weep. Jawad's father helped her return to her corner of the cell. Then he crawled back to speak with his son.

'Dear son,' he whispered, 'we have come to the end of the road. Your mother, alas, is mad. I have always known, but my love for her clouded my judgement. We abandoned you and that was a sin. Can you forgive your parents?'

Jawad answered, 'A thousand times over.'

Jawad went from the prison to the mosque of our faith and asked to see the Imam. A mullah looked at Jawad's untidy beard and ragged clothes and broken sandals, saying, 'The Imam sees beggars on the third day of the week,' and turned away.

Jawad called after him. 'Sir, in the name of our faith, heed me for a single minute. I have not come to beg. I have come to borrow a pick!'

'A pick?' said the mullah. 'What a curious man you are. Is the house of our faith a place to find a pick?'

'And yet,' said Jawad, 'if you would search about, you may find one.' Then he added, in the ancient Persian of the fire-worshippers, 'If you would so trouble yourself, the bounty of Heaven will surely come to you.'

The mullah was an educated man. He had studied in Qom. He was amazed that a ragged man like Jawad had mastered such a difficult tongue. 'Wait here,' he said. While he was away the afternoon shadows crept almost to the eastern side of the square. But when he returned, he had a pick in his hand.

'I bid you joy of the pick,' said the mullah, and handed the implement to Jawad.

To the outskirts of the city went Jawad with all the haste he could manage. Once there, he knocked on the door of a dwelling that was held up with hope, such a house that a poor man would live in. And to answer the knock an old man appeared, as ragged in his clothing as Jawad himself.

Jawad said, 'Brother, let me dig at your doorstep. A great reward awaits you.'

The old man looked at Jawad, looked at the pick, and looked at Jawad again. 'Dig if you will,' he said.

Jawad swung his pick at the hard earth, and again. Each time he struck the ground, nuggets of gold came to the surface.

The old man watched in wonder. 'Were you sent by the Prophet?' he asked. 'I prayed for you many times over.'

Jawad gathered the gold in a threadbare blanket provided by the old man, paying him with five nuggets each as big as a sweet plum. He carried his cargo of gold to the mosque where he returned the pick to the mullah, leaving five nuggets each the size of a persimmon. Then he hastened to the palace of the mayor, calling over the fence to the esteemed man walking in his garden, 'Sir, I come with ransom for the Woman Messiah!' A command was given for the gates to be opened, and at the feet of the mayor Jawad poured out twenty gold nuggets, each the size of a pomegranate.

The mayor, who in his time had come to know gold when he saw it, studied Jawad with great interest. 'And what is the sorceress to you?'

'Sir, she is my mother, but alas, she is mad.'

'And how did you come by this bounty?'

'Sir, I prayed to the God of our faith and He sent it to me.'

The mayor considered for a minute more, thinking, 'Better gold than a fee for the hangman.' Finally, he gave orders for the release of the sorceress and her husband, and that very day, Jawad and his mother and his father walked out of the gates of the prison.

Under the blue sky, Jawad's mother put her hands to her face and wept. Jawad's father comforted her in his embrace.

'I cannot send blackbirds into the sky as high as the wild geese and make them return with golden apples,' Jawad's mother said through her tears. 'I have lived a foolish life.'

Jawad's father comforted her. 'But you did not lose the love of our son. Is that not the thing of most importance?'

And Jawad said, 'Mother, there must be some greatness in you, for the stone you gave me from the moon led me to topaz and green garnet and lapis lazuli and fish by the bushel and nuggets of gold.'

'Oh dear son!' Jawad's mother cried. 'It was only a stone I found on the road, nothing more!'

'Is that the truth?' said Jawad. He took the moonstone that was not a moonstone from his pocket and gazed at it in amazement. Then he threw it away.

'Our gift,' he said, 'will be this: that we have no gifts but the life God has given us, and each other.'

12

The Cookbook
of the Master Poisoner
Ghoroob-e-astab of Mashad

Some princes are never nervous; some are nervous every day. And it can happen that even a bold prince on the battlefield will suffer certain fears. Mirwais Hotak of Kandahar was a nervous prince. He was both ferocious and clever in combat, but he had studied history and knew that most princes die with a knife in their throat. He himself had become Prince and Emir of Kandahar by this means, killing with his own hands the Safavid Prince of Persia who had ruled before him. And so Mirwais Hotak only ever walked about the palace guarded by six powerful soldiers specially trained to kill quickly.

The leader of the bodyguards in the Kandahar palace was a man known as Thunderclap, for his sudden way of dealing out punishments. He had given thought to all of the methods an assassin might employ to murder his prince and had taken steps to avoid such calamities. Confident though he was of preserving the Emir's life from violence, Thunderclap remained worried about poison. He persuaded Hotak to employ not one but twenty food tasters, each one obliged to eat a spoonful of anything destined for the Emir's table. Twenty food tasters each taking a spoonful from every one of the prince's dishes took time but at least the plan ruined the opportunities of any poisoner.

Any poisoner except for one, a certain Ghoroob-e-astab, meaning 'Nightfall' in English, the greatest poisoner of his age or any other. Over a lifetime of distilling and mixing, Nightfall had so mastered his craft that he could prepare poisons that were almost an honour to die from. And victims died not by digesting his poisons only; Nightfall fashioned mists that drifted on the breeze and sought out one man alone in a gathering of a thousand. At the height of his powers, he could command a cloud of poisoned gnats to float from his home in Mashad, Persia, to a city as distant as Kabul and settle on the sleeping lips of a prince and all his court.

So against the craft of the poisoner Nightfall there was no defense. If the intended victim concealed himself in a guarded chamber surrounded by servants, still he was not safe. And if he lived only on water and wild berries and his body was washed in warm water and oil twenty times a day, still he was not safe. If he sat in the sunshine or the moonlight under a fine gauze fashioned of Isfahani silk, still he was not safe. Sunshine and moonshine, the air itself – all were allies of Nightfall.

The captain of Hotak's bodyguard understood this. With the king's permission, he travelled secretly to Mashad in Persia and offered Nightfall gold in exchange for counter-poisons. Nightfall was charmed by the thought of making money by curing the very people he had poisoned but the difficulty was this: there were no antidotes for his poisons; that was part of their beauty. Yet the great poisoner was reluctant to give up the captain's gold and so he took a day to write out a number of elaborate recipes for Persian dishes. If these dishes were prepared in exactly the manner described, he told the captain, they would guard the Emir against all the poisons in the world.

Now it was far from true that Nightfall's dishes would guard those who ate them from poison. But since Nightfall's craft had cleared Persia and Afghanistan of any rivals in the fraternity of poisoners, there was little risk that the Emir would be assaulted in such a way. He would be free to think that the recipes were preserving his life. And Nightfall's scheme went much further: he would trade his recipes for gold to every court in Persia, to every court in Afghanistan. It would become known that the master poisoner had set an infallible shield between princes and poisons, and that commissions to kill by means of potions were now a waste of time. Nightfall would retire, as he should, for he was by this time an old man with troublesome wives to deal with and bickering sons and daughters.

The myth of the recipes lasted fifty years, well after the master poisoner had gone to his reward. The dishes were carefully prepared in palaces and mansions for all of that time, and even in small households when the secrets of the first cookery book in the history of Afghanistan were smuggled out by kitchen workers. Only one copy of the book still survives. It has passed through many hands over the centuries and is now kept in a vault in Kabul together with a document revealing the ingredients of Nightfall's two thousand poisons.

With the permission of the Governors of the Bank of Kabul, Nightfall's counter-poison recipe for *khoresht aaloo* is displayed below. The dish is to be prepared by an adult male.

Khoresht Aaloo

Let the chicken be brown of feather with a proud bearing. In life it must feed on the seeds of wild grasses and insects such as the harlequin beetles that live on the leaves of the *castanea sativa* and hazelnut. Take care that the bird does not dine on ants or green locusts! See that it is slaughtered one hour past sunrise on its first birthday. Organs and head are not employed in the recipe. Allow the cleansed body of the bird to stand in the morning sun on a plate of white porcelain for fifteen minutes and no more. Be precise! Employing a blade with a keen edge, cut the bird into ten pieces. Be sure that the blade in its history has had no contact with undomesticated flesh such as that of the hare. Wash the ten parts of the bird separately in rain water. Do not make use of water that has run in a channel but only water that has been gathered from Heaven.

Take two onions each the size of a green apple of Naishapur. Let the skin of each onion be identical in hue to that of the feathers of the bird. Remove the skin of each onion in one piece. If the skin breaks, take a new onion and peel it. Place the peeled onions in the sunlight on a plate of white porcelain for fifteen minutes and no more. Again, be accurate! Slice each onion into three pieces. Warm each piece of onion between the toes of a white camel mare for one hour. If a white camel cannot be found, it is acceptable to whiten the coat of a brown camel with clay. Wash the onion pieces in rain water. Do not make use of water that has run in a channel but only water that has been gathered from Heaven. Slice each piece of onion as finely as the width of the Line of Saturn on the palm of the hand. Use a keen blade. Be sure that the blade in its history has had no contact with vegetables that grow above the soil, such as the pumpkin, or with fruits that grow from trees with a divided leaf, such as the pomegranate.

Pause to soak twelve prunes in a white porcelain bowl. Do not make use of water that has run in a channel but only water that has been gathered from Heaven. Let the prunes come from the upper branches of a sloe gage such as those that flourish on the banks of the rivers flowing from the Elburz to the Caspian. Build a cooking fire outdoors of walnut wood.

Take a frying pan with a heating surface the width of the left and right hand outstretched with the tips of the thumbs touching. Scour the interior of the frying pan with sand until no blemishes remain. Be warned! A single blemish, whether of rust or of char, will mar the potency of the counter-poison.

Place the scoured frying pan on the walnut fire. Pour a quantity of sesame oil into the scoured pan sufficient to cover the heating surface to the depth of a caraway seed. Allow the sesame oil to heat for two minutes and no more. Place the onion slices in the oil in arabesques. After one minute of cooking, turn each onion slice. The onion must be the gold of a bangle on the wrist of a Shirazi palace dancer. Fry the chicken pieces with the onion for twenty-five minutes and no more. The flesh of the bird must now bear comparison with the dusky skin of the Adyghes of Syria, known falsely as Circassians. Now pour the water in which the prunes have soaked onto the chicken and the onion. Do not be foolish. There would no longer be any point in preserving the arabesques. Add salt from the Desert Land of the Tuaregs. Let the grains of salt be numbered and not exceed four thousand. Allow the chicken, the onions, the prunes and their water to simmer on the walnut fire.

Make a selection of six potatoes from the fields of Sherbaghan. Let each potato equal in size the fist of a child of the age of five years. Wash the six potatoes in rainwater. Do not make use of water that has run in a channel but only water that has been gathered from Heaven. Place the six potatoes in a white porcelain bowl in the sunlight for fifteen minutes and no more. Be exact! From the six potatoes select the most perfect two. Peel the most perfect two potatoes with a keen blade. Make sure that the blade has not in its history come into contact with fruits or vegetables that grow in stalks, such as rhubarb. Slice each of the two most perfect potatoes into segments no greater than the distance between the Head Line and Heart Line on the palm of the right hand. Place the segments of the two most perfect potatoes in the scoured frying pan with the chicken, the prunes of the sloe gage and the juice in which the sloe gage prunes soaked. Just so.

Now take a quantity of the saffron that the Buddha-Worshippers of Bamiyan use in their ritual of the New Moon and sprinkle it on the potato slices. Within one minute the potato slices will take on the gold of spring daisies in the mountain pastures of the Reshteh-ye Alborz. (If the potato slices do not take on the gold of spring daisies in the mountain pastures of the Reshteh-ye Alborz, start again with a fresh bird.) Allow the potato slices to simmer for twelve minutes in the scoured frying pan and no more. Be scrupulous!

Prepare Basmati, in the Afghan manner. Wash your body from head to toe with rainwater. Do not make use of water that has run in a channel but only water that has been gathered from Heaven. Dress in garments freshly laundered. Recite what verses you know of the Gulistan of Abu-Mohammad Muslih al-Din bin Abdallah Shirazi, known as Saadi. Serve the *khoresht aaloo* and Basmati. Eat.

13

Thoughts on Growing

and Eating

Growing

In my country of Afghanistan everything is arranged in such a way that your heart is broken again and again. It is not only wars that break your heart; it is the arguments that last a thousand years, the age-old jealousies, and of course, the poverty.

Not that Afghanistan is without beauty; not at all. I could take you to places in the north close to the Oxus River that would steal your breath away; places that you would not believe could exist as I lead you through an arid landscape of broken rock and red sand and stunted bushes. Then you would suddenly find yourself gazing down from a mountain pass on the river shining under a blue sky and a green carpet climbing up the slopes. And you would think, 'Ah! This is Paradise!' I could take you to Faryab in the spring; to the plain of Dasht-i-Laili and show you wildflowers of a hundred colours spread so densely over the sand that it would only be the giant dunes rising above the flowers that would make you believe that this was a desert. Or I could take you to Kandahar in the early morning, approaching the city from the west, and the sky would be so broad above us and the air so crisp that you would believe what I had whispered to you: that the walls of mud-brick coming into view were built only a generation after Adam and Eve left Eden.

I could show you many other types of beauty: the smiles and laughter of children who might have little to smile about, nothing to laugh about; the courage of women who gather their children about them and teach them what they will need to know in life, even when the rice bag is all but empty and the sheep are bleating in hunger; I could show you five hundred feasting at a wedding in Mazar-e-Sharif, toasting the groom, singing in praise of the bride, and not one of the five hundred confident of lasting through a further year of war. We are a people who should never have survived our history of five thousand years; we are a people who should no longer exist. And yet we do, and there is beauty in that fact alone.

Most importantly, what of the mystery of our Afghanistan? Is there not great beauty in the mystery? For we are a very mysterious people, we Afghans. We come from the long-ago, our roots go down so deep in the sand and soil and rock that we can be said to be as much a part of the land as the gundy trees and marsot bushes; we are both wild and gentle, full of anger and full of love. This is where the world began, in Afghanistan. The world of townships, at least, and I say it was an Afghan who first put brick on brick, and an Afghan who first sowed soil with wheat.

But when you are an Afghan, you want your land to flourish and instead you are faced with arrangements, as I say, designed to break your heart. I am about to speak of the food of Afghanistan, and since food comes from the land, let me first speak about land. Few Afghans own any land, or few as a proportion of the total. Most farmers are what we call *gharib kar*, or sharecroppers, who are permitted to cultivate a few *jeribs* that are owned by another, keeping one fifth of what they produce. Another type of sharecropper, a *baz kar*, may be allowed to keep one quarter of his crop by a more generous *Bai*, or landlord. A tenant farmer of another sort, a *khistmand*, keeps fifty per cent of his crop but has to provide the seed, the oxen, the plough and, of course, all of the labour. Many landowners in Afghanistan have never laid eyes on the soil they own. The land came to them as gifts from powerful people or as rewards for deeds done. Their land is handled by an agent, while the owners sometimes live far away.

Oh, the oxen and the plough. Afghanistan is a country in which the most up-to-date weapons have been employed over the past thirty years by the Soviet Union and by the United States; weapons worth billions of dollars. Aerial bombardment in some provinces has created huge craters in the soil. But in 1990 in Faryab Province – to single out just one region – the soil of the fields was turned by the oxen and the plough, and by one tractor. One tractor in the entire province. The cost of a single two thousand kilogram bomb of the type dropped on Herat and its outskirts in 1984 – and hundreds of such bombs were dropped on Herat – would have paid for nine tractors, while the total cost of aerial bombardment over the period of the war against the Soviets could have provided eight hundred tractors for every province in Afghanistan. Do you see what I mean about heartbreak? No nation on earth knows more about modern munitions than Afghanistan. And hardly any nation knows less about modern farming practices.

I am a man who hates waste in all its forms: the waste of soil that is turned not by ploughs but by bombs, the waste of clean water polluted by dead bodies, the waste of energy in murderous bickering. The most frustrating thing of all for me is knowing what plenty the soil of Afghanistan can produce when it is given the chance. Our fruits are amongst the finest grown anywhere on earth, our grains are full of sunshine, our vegetables grow plump to the point of bursting. The seven per cent of land in which things can grow in Afghanistan could feed the population many times over, and still leave surplus to sell overseas. And is that not the first task of any nation's people – to grow the food that feeds them?

Eating

The food of Afghanistan, including the dishes mentioned in these stories, was first the food of Persia. And the food of Persia is a version of the food of India. Before India, who can say? Afghanistan has never known peace and security such as the Persians experienced under their emperors, when people with an interest in food had the leisure to explore and experiment. In Afghanistan, especially for the Hazara, eating is what keeps you alive, not something you write poems about. And so the dishes we prepare are versions of those first prepared to the east, in Isfahan and Shiraz, in Mashad, Tabriz, Kerman, Yazd, Rafsanjan.

More than any other people in Afghanistan, the Hazara have kept what they eat very simple. My ancestors carried the meat of goats and sheep under the saddles of their horses on long journeys to battlefields – a trick that kept meat tender and lent the dish made from it a pleasant flavour of horse sweat. Nobody ever accused the Hazara of fussiness when it came to food.

However, it is the eggplant that the Hazara praise; that all Afghans praise; or the tomato, the potato, the pomegranate, not so much the dishes that employ them. If a woman of a village in the Hazarajat is able to prepare delicious *badenjan*, she will be congratulated, of course, but the eggplant that forms the basis of *badenjan* will be considered to have made the greater contribution to the success of the dish. When I eat *badenjan*, I do not pay my wife the sorts of compliments you hear on television cooking programs, speaking of a delicate aftertaste, or the way in which the potato slices have 'adopted' some of the flavour of the baked tomato. Instead, I congratulate her on a successful visit to the market, and on having a good eye for eggplant. Okay, for her cooking too, but in few words, heartfelt words.

Let me explain. In the West, cooking is spoken of as an art, and art itself is considered something borrowed from God. But it is different amongst the people of my faith. For us, art is something men do – men and women. It has nothing to do with God, Who may watch and applaud, but does not whisper suggestions into the ear of the artist. God made the eggplant, God made the capsicum, God made the plump ear of corn. What act of creation by a man can compare with the creation of the eggplant? Look at the world. The eggplant in its beauty is but one of a billion of God's creations. This is a world of such beauty and such diversity that God can well leave to us what we call art, including the art of cooking.

It is the eggplant we praise, as I say. If Afghans of my faith are asked to talk about food, we will think of individual items of food, of the places within Afghanistan that are famous for that item of food, and of God Who gave us hunger and the foods to satisfy our appetites. We think of the pistachios of Badghis in the west close to Turkmenistan; the wheat, barley and red beans of Samangan in the north; the oranges and olives of Nangarhar on the Pakistan border; the grapes of Charikar; the potatoes of Balkh; the pomegranates and mangos and apples of Kandahar; the almonds of Oruzgan; the mulberries and tomatoes of She-berghan; the sesame oil and the Karakul mutton of Aqcha. And think of this: in Helmand, where most of the opium for the world is grown, we also grow peanuts, and wonderful peanuts they are. We have very little soil left to us in Afghanistan, but that which we have is blessed by God.

I have said that Afghans of my faith think of God when food is placed before them, but it is not only the marvel of the eggplant that moves us to think of Heaven. In the scriptures of Islam, many verses remind us that greed of every sort is ruin; a blight on the soul that settles like mould on grapes that receive too much sun and water. The Holy Book has nothing good to say of those who pile wealth upon wealth and adorn their palaces and mansions with ornaments of gold. Islam is a faith of those who would flour-ish without great indulgence. The Prophet Himself has said this: 'Man fills no vessel worse than his stomach. It is sufficient for the son of Adam to have a few mouthfuls to give him the strength he needs.' People of my faith would be embarrassed to spend their lives talking of food. In our world, many people go hungry for every person who can eat his fill each day. God is closer to the hungry man than the man who satisfies his appetite at will.

But having said all this, I must tell you that the recipes we have inherited from India and Persia reach perfection in Afghanistan. Small changes have been made; certain herbs added, certain spices. The changes are important, particularly in dishes that include meat. For my taste, Indian dishes go a little too far with spices. You could be eating crocodile, including the skin and the teeth, and all you would taste is spice. The Persians, for their part, developed the art of preparing rice and great honour is due to them for this accomplishment. Afghans have taken the preparation of rice a little further. I have said that the Hazara are not fussy eaters, but when it comes to the preparation of rice we are very fussy indeed. And so are all Afghans. On top of the small changes, the ingredients we provide are superior to those the Indians or the Persians employ. I am not boasting; what I say is simply a fact. I will soon give you the recipe for a *qorma* that makes use of a shoulder of Karakul lamb from Aqcha. Unless you have tasted Karakul lamb in a *qorma*, your experience of good food is incomplete.

Halal and Haram

Before I speak of Afghan dishes, I must explain what is meant by *halal* and by *haram*, since these two terms are very important to all people of my faith in the preparation of food. To people of other faiths, except for Jews and Hindus, the idea of some foods being lawful (*halal*) and some being unlawful, or forbidden (*haram*), must seem strange. Even to Muslims, the idea of certain foods being forbidden is puzzling, if we think about it. But mostly, we don't think about it.

This is what is written in the Holy Book:

God only prohibits for you the eating of animals that die of themselves, blood, the meat of pigs, and animals dedicated to other than God. If one is forced to eat that which is prohibited, without being malicious or deliberate, he incurs no sin. God is the Forgiver, Most Merciful.

So people of my faith do not eat any animal that is found dead. The animal may have died of natural causes, it may have choked, it may have fallen off a precipice. Okay, that creature is *haram*. Or think of this: a creature is held sacred by the people of some other religion, maybe by a religion of snake-worshippers. If the snake is dedicated to their God, people of my faith leave it alone. Except for cows, which are held sacred by the Hindus. We still eat cows. Creatures that bleed – except for fish, which are *halal* even when you catch them – become *halal* in the killing process. Animals cannot be killed by means of electric shock, they cannot be killed by boiling, but must be slaughtered in the old-fashioned way, which is to say, with a knife. The person who slaughters the beast must speak the name of God.

Once the beast is slaughtered, it must be bled until all running blood has been drained. People of my faith are not permitted to consume blood in its fluid form at all. Of course, a certain quantity of blood remains in the flesh of the slaughtered animal, but this is not considered *haram*. The slaughtering must be carried out by one of our faith, or at least by one of the People of the Book, meaning those mentioned in the Holy Book: all Muslims and all Jews, and those of certain faiths that have disappeared from the world. A Muslim may eat any food that Jews consider 'kosher', or 'clean'. Neither Jews nor Muslims may eat the flesh of the pig. A pig cannot be made *halal*. Why the pig should be singled out in this way is a mystery to both Muslims and Jews. Maybe some story from many ages past, some story now lost could explain why pigs are *haram*. It's no great loss.

The Preparation of Rice

Rice is not exciting, held in the palm of our hand. But it deserves respect. It has its own special beauty. For Afghans, rice is best eaten with each grain separated. When it is placed in a mound after cooking, the grains should tumble down the sides like pebbles. I have seen rice sticking to a wooden spoon like the glue that carpenters heat in a pot and use in their craft. Cooking rice in that way does it no honour. As for the grain itself, we choose long grain Basmati rice from Pakistan. It is a shocking thing to say, but Afghans who have brought the preparation of rice to its highest stage of development do not themselves grow the very best grains. Such a shame! Nevertheless, the Pakistanis are happy to sell us their rice and we are happy to eat it. Pakistani Basmati grains – and Indian Basmati, too – are the royalty of rice.

The Basmati must be soaked in clean, cold water for thirty minutes before cooking. The rice is not added to the bowl of water, but instead the water is poured onto the rice. Each ten minutes, the rice is moved gently in the water with a spoon. After thirty minutes, the rice is drained in a *chalow saffi*, the utensil known as a colander in English. In fresh cold water the rice is boiled in a pot, allowing the level of the water to exceed the depth of the rice, but not too greatly. Once the water boils, the rice remains submerged for five minutes only, and must be stirred briefly twice in the space of those five minutes. The rice is again drained in the *chalow saffi*, and once drained, it is rinsed and allowed to stand in the *chalow saffi* for a short time. At this stage, if the Basmati has been treated without abuse, each grain will stand separate. In a dish or bowl suitable for use in an oven, and better that the dish should be pottery, a small amount of oil and butter is heated. The Basmati is poured onto the melted oil and butter and turned with a spoon while salt is added. The quantity of salt should not destroy the taste of the rice. The Basmati is baked at a temperature that is judged not to be excessive for a period of twenty minutes.

There is a tale of the Woman of Naishapur that I will use to end this story of Basmati and its preparation.

Many ages past, in the time before our faith came to Afghanistan, Kabul and the lands around were ruled by people of the north. The town in those days was called Kabul-Shahan and belonged to Hindus who worshipped many gods. The Prince of Kabul-Shahan was called Shahiya, a man of luxury, and cruel. For the sake of his vanity this Prince took it upon himself to discover the best rice in the world so that he might boast: 'My intestines have digested the choicest grain granted us by Heaven.' Many nervous cooks passed through the Prince's kitchens for it was his habit to fling those whose rice disappointed him into the river with their hands tied to their feet. With the passing of time the Prince came to hear of a woman of Naishapur, where our faith had blossomed, and this woman's rice was considered a wonder. The Prince sent his soldiers on a great journey into Persia to capture the woman and bring her to his palace. The soldiers were successful; the woman stood before the Prince in chains. The Prince asked the woman of Naishapur if her rice was the wonder of Persia and she said, 'It is.' The Prince commanded her to prepare rice for him and the woman said, 'Leave me in your kitchens for a day and night.' Busy sounds could be heard in the kitchens when the woman went to work. Saucepans clashed against saucepans, cutlery rattled, and the kitchen cat mewed loudly. Reports were brought to the Prince of all this activity, so that his appetite was roused more and more with every hour that passed. In the morning, the kitchen doors were thrown open and the woman came forth with a golden bowl under a golden cover. She placed the bowl before Shahiya with the words 'It is done.' The Prince lifted the cover and saw a single grain of rice in the bowl. He said, 'Do you mock me?' The woman replied, 'In the Holy Book it is written that we must not waste by excess, for God loveth not the wasters. Prince, more than one grain of rice would be a waste on one such as you.' So shocked was the Prince, so shocked were his guards that the woman walked from the palace without a hand being raised to stop her.

Herbs and Spices

I have read that in the kitchen of a master cook of China you may find two hundred herbs and spices. We are more frugal in Afghanistan. Perhaps twenty herbs and spices are used in our cooking. We buy herbs fresh and add them to our dishes as needed. Spices we buy from the market in big quantities and grind them up when the time comes.

Ginger

Stories are told of the strange power of ginger, be it fresh or dried. Even pious people of my faith still hold onto ancient beliefs about its benefits either in dishes or taken as a medicine. It is thought to cure so many ailments that you could almost think, 'I will go into battle with my pockets full of ginger. Whatever fate befalls me, I will fix it with ginger.'

Dill

Of course. Dill is always on hand. It is also supposed to cure various ailments, but I don't believe it. Let it do its job in a *qorma*, that's all I ask of it.

Turmeric

Turmeric is used with meat and vegetable dishes. Wherever there is rice, turmeric in the *qorma* adds something special to the rice's flavour. And there is always rice. What sense is there in doing without it?

Nutmeg

We use nutmeg with meat dishes, together with cumin and coriander. Not too much nutmeg. Don't be crazy.

Cardamom

You can flavour beverages with cardamom. The Arabs use it in their coffee, their *gahwa*. Have you tried the coffee of Arabistan? Madness.

Sumac

It's like lemon. Better you use lemon.

Baharat

This is another word from Arabistan. A mixture of spices. *Sebah Baharat* means 'seven spices'. It's handy. You can add it to everything. Maybe not to chicken.

Cumin

For lamb and beef dishes. More for lamb. Or goat. Other herbs appeal to me more. Some people enjoy it. If you leave it out and you have ten guests, one will stand up and cry out, 'Aiee!' So best add it if you do not know your guests too well.

Saffron

Good to sprinkle on potato slices when they are cooking. Good for making yellow rice. Too much saffron and you don't feel like eating anything. There is a phrase in English, 'to be heavy-handed'. Don't be heavy-handed with saffron. It's like a good friend you enjoy seeing for an hour at a time. And it's expensive. Certain good friends you can enjoy an hour at a time are also expensive.

Paprika

Best for lamb. Also fish. But not carp.

Nigella seeds

This is what the Prophet of our faith says of nigella seeds: 'There is healing in the black seeds for everything but death.' Headaches –

no. Trust me. So, not for everything. Nigella seeds produce the same flavour as pepper. Be sensible.

Fenugreek

A strange thing, but fenugreek is both bitter and sweet. Who can explain it? Perfect with chicken.

Caraway

Tastes like anise. If you are good with *baklawa*, have caraway seeds in your kitchen.

Cayenne

Hot. Too much heat, the taste is destroyed. You wish to eat food, not heat.

Cloves

Grind the cloves. A whole clove cannot be digested. Use it in *baklawa*, certainly. And with kid.

Coriander

Grind the seeds with a pestle and mortar. Use in salads and everything else. Not so much with lamb.

Fennel

With meat and vegetables, if you are attracted to it. I am not.

Black pepper

Grind your own black pepper. Do not purchase it in powder form from the supermarket. Don't be lazy. Who can cook properly and be lazy at the same time? No one.

Sesame seeds

Best if you roast them. Then use them in everything.

Tabil

A mixture of garlic, coriander, caraway and cayenne.
Know what you are doing before you reach for the *tabil*.

Garlic

Yes and no. That which garlic suits, it suits perfectly.
That which it doesn't, it ruins.

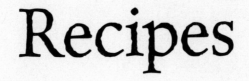

Recipes

Lamb Qorma

Refrigeration is uncommon in Afghanistan. Meat is often preserved, but if it is to be eaten unsalted, it is used quickly. In parts of Hazarajat where the snow remains on the ground for six months, meat is packed in ice. But two days after slaughtering, and no freezing – that's when meat is at its best. My brother Abdul Ali was a butcher, a very good one. He taught me about meat. Away from Afghanistan, you know, I never enjoy meat of the quality I knew in my village and in Mazar-e-Sharif. But this is the world. Not everyone can find freshly killed Karakul lamb. A pity. For this qorma, use the best lamb you can come by – the meat from the top of the foreleg starting just below the neck, without the bone. You will need more than a kilogram of meat so judge the piece you are offered carefully. We will feed four or five people with this qorma. Maybe six.

Here is what you will need:

Lamb (see above).

Four big tomatoes. Not *almost* big, but truly big. And very ripe.

Eight cloves.

Enough peppercorns to fill the bowl of a medium-sized spoon.

One nub of ginger, about the length of your thumb.

Cardamom, maybe five green pods.

Three brown onions.

Two garlic cloves.

One small spoonful of cumin seeds.

One stick of cinnamon, pounded into a powder, or a medium spoonful of ground cinnamon.

One medium spoonful of coriander seeds.

A pinch of paprika, such as would cover the palm of your hand.

One small spoonful of turmeric.

Oil for frying. Sesame is best.

Plain yoghurt.

◈ Okay, cut the lamb into many equal pieces so that a single piece can be taken in the mouth comfortably when it's cooked. Set the meat aside and turn your attention to the tomatoes. Cut the tomatoes into pieces about the size of the lamb pieces then set them aside with the meat.

◈ Now the herbs and spices that will become part of the dish. First crush the cloves in your mortar. The crushing should leave the smallest fragments of the cloves you have the patience to produce. Next in your mortar crush the peppercorns. Grate the ginger, not too coarsely, until you have enough to make a small mound that covers the middle of your palm. Crush the cardamom in your mortar. The cardamom will not suit everyone. It will be your judgement. Now it is time for the garlic, but don't crush the garlic cloves until you have completed the next step, which is the chopping and frying of the brown onions.

◈ Okay, the onions. In Afghanistan, we rarely fashion a meal without onions. What the world was like before onions were invented, I cannot imagine. So, the onions, three of them. Peel them to preserve as much of the outer flesh as possible. I am talking of course of brown onions. Onions of another colour may be substituted, but I wouldn't advise it. Once the onions are peeled, chop them up but not too fine. You need chunks of onion, not thin slices. Now heat some cooking oil in a big saucepan. I am serious when I say a *big* saucepan. For dishes like this, a big saucepan is your friend. Do you want to fill a smaller saucepan to the very brim? No.

◈ Heat some oil in the saucepan. I am going to suggest sesame oil, but this is not vital. If you have canola in your cupboard, use canola. Use olive oil if you choose, but the flavour of the *qorma* will gain in the cooking if you can find some sesame. Please don't permit the oil to burn! Keep the flame low. Add the onion pieces to the oil and stir them until they turn gold.

◈ The remaining spices (cumin, cinnamon, coriander, paprika and turmeric) are now added to the onions. Turmeric first, only what will fill a small spoon. As you add the turmeric, stir it in quickly. Then the other spices in any order, including the garlic, which you should have crushed by now. Let the onions and spices heat for maybe two minutes, not too much heat – if you burn the onions you will have to start again. Who has that much time?

◈ Add the tomatoes to the saucepan for, let's say, four minutes – one minute for each tomato. Not too much heat. Keep stirring. If the tomatoes are not mushy after four minutes, cook for longer.

◈ Time to put the lamb in the saucepan. Let the lamb pieces mix in with the spices and onions and tomatoes for three or four minutes. Now add tepid water, two-and-a-half cups, stirring as you go. Now yoghurt, proper yoghurt, no flavouring, nothing fancy, just yoghurt, one cup and another one-third of a cup, stirring, stirring. Good. Put the lid on the saucepan, keep the heat low. This is going to take two hours. Read a book. Every fifteen minutes, put the book down and stir the saucepan. In this last hour, you are stirring the *qorma*, and you are reading your book. You started at two-thirty in the afternoon. Now it's five in the afternoon. Turn off the *qorma*. If you are of my faith, wash and pray. If you are not, do whatever you must. But at five forty-five, prepare the Basmati in the fashion I have described. At six-thirty, serve the *qorma*.

Sabzi Gosht
(Lamb with Spinach)

This is a dish always served at weddings. But what am I saying? Almost every traditional Afghan dish is served at weddings. The wedding ceremony and celebrations last for three days and in that time we eat a lot of food. It has to be this way. The success of the marriage, the blessings of Heaven, the lasting goodwill of friends, the reputation of the bride and groom and of the bride and groom's family and relations, all depend on a big, extravagant wedding ceremony. The quality and quantity of the food provided will be discussed for years after the ceremony. Someone will say, 'Ah, the wedding of the carpenter Rousal Ali and the girl from Sar-e Pol – what was her name? Now that was magnificent, ah, the kofta nakhod, *sublime! Ah, the* aash. *Never in my life have I tasted the like!' And if there were disappointments, 'The* qorma – *were they trying to poison me? Dear God!'*

Ok, lamb with spinach. This is what you will need:

The **lamb,** of course. Take trouble to find good lamb.
   With this dish, your jaws and teeth get a holiday.
   The lamb has to melt in your mouth and just the pressure of your
   palate will bring out all the flavour that the meat has absorbed from
   the spices and herbs. So, good lamb, no excuses, cut from the leg,
   one-and-a-half kilos.

Brown onions, half a kilo.

Garlic, four cloves.

One cup of **beef stock**. Best if you make it yourself and have it ready.

A pinch each of **turmeric, cardamom, cinnamon**
   and **nutmeg.**

Some **ground black pepper,** maybe a teaspoon.

Salt.

Sesame oil or **olive oil.**

One good bunch of **fresh spinach.**

Fresh yoghurt. This must be proper yoghurt, not that foolish
   yoghurt that is sometimes sold with bananas
   in it and strawberries and sugar.

Grated lemon peel. Not so much, maybe what will fill
   a teaspoon.

Five big **tomatoes,** very red.

Roasted pine nuts. Enough to fill an eggcup.

◈ Divide the lamb into pieces, each about the size of a small potato.
You must quickly sear the lamb in a big cast-iron casserole dish,
with a small amount of sesame oil or olive oil. By 'a small amount'
I do not mean next-to-nothing. We want some of the flavour of
the oil to pass into the dish. Next add the brown onions, chopped
into small pieces. Sauté the onions with the lamb for two, maybe
three, minutes; you judge. Then put the crushed cloves of garlic
into the pan and sauté the garlic for a shorter time, say a minute.

◈ Now add all the spices, one spice at a time, and sauté for another two minutes. But concentrate: if the onions blacken, if the garlic burns you will have to make a difficult decision: throw everything away or eat a ruined dish. In Afghanistan we can't afford to throw food away so we make sure we don't burn the onions and the garlic. Now add the tomatoes, chopped into chunks, and the beef stock. Okay, now the casserole dish goes into the oven. We don't want the lamb to cook too quickly, so keep the temperature down to maybe two hundred degrees centigrade. Cook the lamb for one-and-a-half hours, or even longer, but not too much longer or you will kill the natural taste of the lamb and be left with nothing but the taste of the spices and the garlic.

◈ After cooking in the oven, the lamb will be falling to pieces. Let the casserole cool for a few minutes before you add the spinach. You will have washed the spinach and drained it by this time and you will have torn it up with your fingers. The heat of the casserole will cook the spinach as you add it. Blend the spinach in, add the lemon rind and the yoghurt and keep stirring. Now some salt, not so much. Sprinkle the roasted pine nuts on the casserole, then put the lid back on and let the dish cool for fifteen minutes before you serve it with Basmati prepared in the Afghan manner.

Aash

Aash is for anytime; at weddings, certainly, but even for breakfast if you choose. Okay, maybe not for breakfast because the noodles must be freshly made and who wants to make noodles early in the morning? In Afghanistan, breakfast is a quick meal, and then you work. You eat some naan, you drink some tea, maybe some honey on your naan. But I didn't want to talk about breakfasts, I wanted to talk about aash, which is our pasta. We learned about it from the Chinese, who may have taught it to our ancestors in Mongolia, although it is difficult to teach something to a man who is holding an axe above your neck. One way or another, noodles came to Afghanistan. A good thing. Who can live a life without aash? Who would wish to?

This is what you will need:

Plain flour, enough to twice fill the small bowl in which you serve pistachios.

About half a cup of *daul nakhud* (yellow split peas) from the market.

One-and-a-half cups of red kidney beans from the market.

One big bunch of fresh spinach.

Olive oil. You will need quite a bit. Half a cup for the meat and a little extra for the noodles. (Not sesame for *aash*!)

One big brown onion.

Almost a kilogram of beef or lamb ground up with a mincing device or finely minced with a sharp knife.

A generous pinch of turmeric and a pinch of cinnamon.

Ground black pepper.

Salt.

Four big tomatoes, cooked and reduced to a puree.

One-and-a-half cups of good fresh yoghurt.

One very hot chilli pepper, chopped very finely.

A pinch of dried mint.

Your biggest spoon full of ground coriander.

◈ First make the noodles with the plain flour and salt and water. What could be simpler? Add water and a pinch of salt to the flour, which you will have sifted into a bowl. Make two (or even three) balls out of the dough, and please don't roll and knead the dough too much or you will end up with something good for making house bricks but not good for eating. Wrap the three balls of dough in cloth, just a fraction damp, and leave them alone for maybe half an hour. Read a book, a good one, not a book about vampires or serial killers or anything like that. A peaceful book.

◈ Now roll out the dough nice and thin on a surface dusted with flour. Then take your knife with a sharp point and slice the dough into strips – and that's your noodles. Thin strips, of course – I'm sure you know how wide a noodle should be. Spread out a broad cloth and lay the noodles on it. Dust the noodle strips with flour, not too much. Now leave the noodles on the cloth and give your mind to the *daul nakhud*. Wash the yellow split peas to get rid of any debris – bits of grit, that sort of thing. Then put the peas in a saucepan with enough water to cover them and then some extra. Boil the water, turning the heat down once the bubbles begin. It will take maybe thirty-five or forty minutes to soften the peas.

◈ Now, the kidney beans. These you should have left soaking for two hours in enough water to barely cover them. I should have mentioned this earlier. My apologies. Okay, the flavour of the kidney beans will have seeped into the water in those two hours that I failed to mention. Add the beans and their soaking water to the yellow peas and let them all simmer together for a few minutes.

◈ Now fill a big pot with water. Maybe not fill the pot to the top; it depends on how big the pot is. Let's say about seven or eight or nine cups of water. Now bring the water to the boil. Add salt to the water, enough to make a small mound on the palm of your hand – not too small, not too big. And some olive oil, enough to fill one of your medium-sized spoons. Lower the noodles into the boiling water, not too many at once, and keep stirring. Let the noodles boil for five minutes, then add the spinach, chopped very finely, like leaves of grass. Let the spinach and the pasta cook together for another five minutes.

◈ So now the noodles are cooked and the spinach has given some of its flavour to them. Take the pot off the flame and drain the water away in a *chalow saffi*. Back in the pot go the noodles and the spinach, together with the yellow peas and the red beans and the water in which they have cooked. Now throw the whole mess about in the pot, and with a wooden spoon blend it all together. Keep it all warm, but only warm; don't let it burn.

◈ Now to the frying pan and the meat. Heat olive oil in the frying pan – quite a lot of oil, don't be a miser. But don't go crazy with the oil, either. How much? Let's say half a cup of olive oil. Fry the chopped-up brown onion in the oil, but don't burn it, by any means. Now add the minced beef or lamb – whatever you have settled for. Don't let the meat form into clumps. Use a knife or a cleaver in a continual stabbing motion to break up the minced meat. You want small fragments of mince; the smaller the better. Add salt and ground black pepper, still using the knife or cleaver to break the meat into fragments. Add all of the spices once the meat is browned, blending them in. Now add the tomatoes, which will look like a paste, blending it all together. Finally add two cups of tepid water; maybe two-and-a-half cups, blend it all once more. Put a cover over the frying pan and let the meat sauce simmer for ten minutes, then remove the lid and turn off the heat.

◈ Now the *chakah* – the yoghurt sauce. This is simple. Add the yoghurt, the dried mint broken into fragments, the chilli pepper, and maybe two spoonfuls of ground coriander – small spoons, like teaspoons. Toss the noodles and *chakah* ingredients until they are nicely mixed.

◈ When you are serving, keep to the Afghan custom of allowing your family and guests to fill their bowls at the table, or from the cloth spread on the floor. For the *aash*, use deep bowls. Provide more than enough *naan*.

Kofta Nakhod

This is a recipe in which chickpeas play a big part, as they do in many Af-ghan dishes. And this being so, you might think that Afghanistan has many, many fields of chickpeas under cultivation. But no, we don't, and this is a disappointment. Our chickpeas come mostly from India, and the Indians first saw the chickpea when a traveller from their country brought it back from Afghanistan. In fact the Indians call the variety of chickpeas they grow kabuli, which in their language of Hindi means 'from Kabul'. Chick-peas need more rainfall than most regions of Afghanistan can provide, or if not rainfall then irrigation. Most irrigation in Afghanistan is of the old-fashioned sort, with channels that are forever becoming clogged with de-bris, and the shadoof in place of a pump. If you wish to see how Adam cultivated his fields, come to my country.

But back to business. For *kofta nakhod*, you will need:

One cup of dried **chickpeas**.

One big brown **onion**, grated.

Ground black pepper.

A small quantity of **cinnamon** and **dried mint**.

Salt.

One kilo of **ground beef**.

Enough **plain flour** to cover the palm of your hand,
sifted three times.

◈ You have to think ahead to make this dish. The chickpeas must be soaked in hot water for ten hours, then drained in your *chalow saffi*. Next, grind up the chickpeas either with an electrical device or with the tines of a fork, as most women do in Afghanistan. (The electrical device is much easier, of course. If I had my will, every wife in Afghanistan would be given one of these de-vices. But then there is the problem of electricity.) You must grind the chickpeas very finely, so if you are using the old-fashioned method, be patient. Now mix the chickpea meal with the flesh of the grated brown onion. Do you know the method for preventing your eyes from filling with tears while you are grating onion? If you do, please contact me at the address of the publisher. Add the pepper, cinnamon and the mint, making sure that the mint is crushed into fragments. And a certain amount of salt. How much salt is 'a certain amount'? More than too little, less than too much. Now mix the seasoned chickpea meal with the ground meat and the sifted flour. Be very thorough in mixing the meat and chickpea meal. Now make the meatballs, taking care that you do not roll them too firmly. You be the judge. By the way, it is the custom in some parts of the world to roll meatballs in the armpit. But not in Afghanistan. The meatballs should be just the right size to make a mouthful.

◈ Okay, now boil water in a deep saucepan. Drop the meatballs into the boiling water one by one, with maybe five seconds between each meatball. When all the meatballs are in the saucepan, turn the heat down so that the water is only simmering. Some people swear that the lid should be on the saucepan during the time of simmering – that's about forty-five minutes – some swear that the lid should be left off. Whatever your prejudice, the meatballs will still be perfectly cooked in forty-five minutes.

◈ The *kofta nakhod* can be served with soup, but not *in* the soup. That is not our custom. Or they can be served with Basmati prepared in the Afghan way. Plenty of *naan*.

Boulanee

These are versions of what in England would be called 'pasties' or 'Cornish pasties'. Actually, types of boulanee are found everywhere. But the original and best come from Afghanistan. Is there a case for us to patent boulanee, as the French and Italians have patented their wines and cheeses? Maybe not. Who cares? Boulanee are delicious; you eat one, you eat two, you decline a third, remembering what Our Prophet said of excess in eating: 'What will feed one man will feed two; what will feed two men will feed three.' Then you eat the third.

Now, promise me this: you will make your own pastry to enclose the boulanee filling. If you wished to, you could go to the supermarket and buy sheets of pastry prepared in a factory, or packets of eggroll envelopes. No. If you are going to enjoy boulanee, enjoy the preparation too. When you eat them, you can think, 'These are from my own hand.' If we are to enjoy food, let it be an enjoyment we earn.

This is what you will need to make *boulanee*:

Three-and-a-half cups of **plain flour**.

Olive oil, or **sesame**.

Maybe two **potatoes**. Better that they should be red-skinned, each about the size of the fist of a child of three years.

A few fresh **spring onions**.

One handful of fresh **coriander leaves**, chopped very finely.

Salt.

Ground black pepper.

◈ Start with the pastry. Sift the flour into a bowl. Add some salt – a sensible quantity, not too much; you are seasoning only the pastry at this stage. Blend the salt in with the sifted flour. Now very gradually add a cup of water. The water should not be too cold, and it shouldn't be warm. Once the water has been added, pour in the oil. Bring everything in the bowl together and knead it with your fingertips, not too violently. If you feel the dough is a little too dry, add more water but very, very little at a time. Fashion the dough into a ball then knead it on a surface dusted with flour for maybe ten minutes, maybe eleven. You want the dough to become a breathing thing, not a dead thing. Once you are satisfied that the dough is alive and well, return it to the bowl and cover the bowl with a tea-towel, a little damp. The dough is going to develop its flavour over the period of an hour under the damp cloth. Do not be tempted to hurry this process along. Have a book to read, or a magazine. Not a magazine about film stars and diets and scandals. A sensible magazine. Not too many pictures.

◈ Okay, put the magazine or the book aside and boil the two red-skinned potatoes. Keep an eye on the potatoes as they boil. Remove them from the water just as they are beginning to shed their skins. Peel the skins off completely. Put the naked potatoes into a mixing bowl and turn your attention to the spring onions. Slice the onions from the bulb upwards to the green leaves very finely – a single slice of the white bulb should be so thin that you can almost read your magazine through it. Do not use the very tips of the green leaves, just the healthiest part. Add the spring onions to the bowl, and the coriander. Did you know that the leaves of the coriander bush are spoken of in the stories of Scheherazade – in *One Thousand and One Nights*? Yes, they are said to have the power to arouse in those who eat them thoughts of romance. If you wish to be aroused in this way, my best advice is to eat a great deal of coriander. Back to business. You add the arousing coriander, cut very finely as I say, to the mixing bowl, and the ground black pepper, as much as will sit in the centre of your palm, and some salt (enough to season two potatoes) and two big spoonfuls of olive oil or sesame oil. Then mix it, mashing the potatoes thoroughly.

◈ Now take an amount of dough from the ball of dough, about as much as would equal the size of one of the potatoes you used, or a little smaller. On a surface dusted with flour, roll out the dough nice and thin, no thicker than the band of the wedding ring on your finger. The dough will spread to almost one-and-a-half hand spans. From this rounded shape of dough, cut circles one-and-a-half times the length of your middle finger. You will get maybe three circles from your larger circle of dough, and some left over, maybe enough to fashion a fourth small circle. Now make another large circle of dough, and more small circles, until all the dough is used. Spread an amount of the seasoned potato mix on each shape, not all the way to the edge, then fold each in half and seal the edges by pressing the dough together with the tips of your fingers. Heat a good quantity of your olive or sesame oil in a broad pan until it is good and hot. Now brown each *boulanee* on both sides. The *boulanee* is ready when the pastry has turned a friendly golden colour.

◈ Let the *boulanee* cool for fifteen minutes. Clean up the kitchen. Read another page of your book, maybe. Then eat a *boulanee* and thank God that you have the tastebuds and the appetite to do justice to what you have fashioned.

Chelo Nakhod

A stew made with chickpeas and chicken. Wonderful. I thank God for the invention of the chicken.

What you will need:

A **chicken**, above all. A fat, happy chicken – one that has spent her life eating harlequin beetles and earthworms and grass seeds; a free-range chicken, as they are known in the West. In Afghanistan, all chickens are free-range. It would come as a shock to any Afghan chicken to hear of enclosures that prevent a fowl from flapping her wings and digging in the dirt. Chickens and cows and sheep and goats live happier lives in my poor, Third World country than many of the people. Nobody drops bombs on them.

Five or six **bay leaves.**

A quantity of **dried chickpeas**, enough to fill the bowl from which you eat your porridge in the morning.

Three stalks of **celery**, including the leaves, cut finely across the grain.

Two big **brown onions**, chopped into small pieces.

A nice **carrot**, sliced lengthways and then sliced into small pieces.

A big **zucchini**, sliced lengthways into four sections then each of the four sections sliced into three sections lengthways.

A pinch of **cumin seed.**

A few spoonfuls of **fresh dill**, chopped finely.

A few spoonfuls of **fresh coriander**, chopped finely.

The juice of two good **lemons.**

Ground black pepper.

Salt.

Basmati rice.

Sesame oil.

◈ It is the night before the day on which you will make this *chelo nakhod*. Take the chickpeas and soak them in a big bowl of hot water overnight. Read your book before you go to sleep. If you are married, be sure to kiss your wife or your husband before you close your eyes. Speak some loving words, if possible.

◈ Use the big pot that you have so much trouble fitting into your dishwasher for this *chelo nakhod*. Fill it two-thirds with water, place it on the heating surface and bring the water to the boil. Place the whole chicken in the pot then add the bay leaves. Cook the chicken for one hour with the lid on the pot, but every ten minutes take the lid off and skim away anything that has formed on the surface. Read your book while the chicken is boiling, or do a crossword puzzle. Not a Sudoku.

◈ After an hour the chicken will be falling away from the bones. Take the pot off the heating surface and remove the chicken, without burning your fingers. On another surface, one you can wipe down, pull the flesh of the chicken from the bones, including the flesh on the legs. Remove the skin, too, which will be loose and will come away readily. Make sure you get every last piece of chicken flesh!

◈ Now skim the surface of the water in which the chicken cooked one more time. Remove the bay leaves. Return the chicken pieces to the pot and to the water in which it cooked. Into this big pot, tip the softened chickpeas, the celery stalks, the brown onions, the carrot, zucchini, cumin seed, fresh coriander, dill, the lemon juice and salt – just enough. Also the ground black pepper; just a little more than enough. Let the pot simmer for one hour.

◈ Now the rice. We will do this a little differently to normal. Find a pot almost as big as the chicken pot. In this pot, boil five cups of water with a certain amount of salt added. Now pour into the boiling water enough Basmati rice to satisfy your family and your guests. Let the rice cook for a sensible time, not long; if you are a grown man, for about the time it would normally take you to shave, or if you are a woman, the time it would normally take for your husband to shave. Next, drain the rice and rinse it with cold water. When the rice is reasonably dry, transfer it to a broad frying pan and pour the sesame oil over it. Cover the pan with a lid and cook the rice on a very low heat for half an hour. In this way, the rice will become crisp on the bottom of the pan and fluffy on top. Now call your family members and your guests. Allow them to serve themselves, covering the crispy rice with as much of the magnificent chicken stew as they can possibly wish for. Accept the congratulations of your family and guests. Eat.

Glossary and Notes

Abdul Ali Mazari

A revered Hazara political leader, Abdul Ali (or 'Baba' – 'Father') Mazari founded the Hezbi Wahdat party that championed the rights of Hazaras in Afghanistan. He died at the hands of the Taliban in 1995, aged forty-nine.

Afghani

The basic unit of currency in Afghanistan. One AUD is worth approximately forty-four afghanis.

Ashak

Afghan appetiser of leeks and minced lamb wrapped in a crust of dough.

Badenjan

Afghan crushed eggplant and yoghurt dip with herbs and spices.

Barakzai dynasty

A Pashtun family that provided twelve of the thirteen Afghan 'khans' (or kings) between 1826 and 1973.

Bichak

Afghan appetiser, either sweet or savoury, served as a triangular pastry typically stuffed with pumpkin and herbs or with minced fruit and jam.

Bolanee, or Boulanee

Afghan baked pasties typically filled with mashed potato and herbs.

Chalow

Rice prepared in the Afghan manner, parboiled then cooked in an oven.

Dari (language)

Official language of Afghanistan derived from ancient Persian and similar to Farsi, the language of Iran.

Dogh

A yoghurt drink, often served chilled, with mint.

Gosh feil

Afghan 'elephant ear' biscuits, made with egg-dough and spices, sprinkled with crushed pistachio nuts.

Gundy tree

A type of wild olive tree.

Hazara

The third-largest ethnic group in Afghanistan, making up around twenty per cent of the population. It is widely accepted that their ancestors came from Mongolia in the thirteenth and fourteenth centuries during the period of the Mongol Empire. The Hazaras are the most oppressed minority in Afghanistan, being Shi'a in a largely Sunni Muslim country and facing longstanding discrimination and persecution from other ethnic groups.

GLOSSARY AND NOTES

Hijra

The journey made by the Prophet Mohammed and his family to Medina in Saudi Arabia in the year 622 (Western calendar).

Husseiniya

A house designated as a mosque, often found in small villages in Afghanistan and elsewhere in the Muslim Middle East.

Imam

A priest of the Islamic faith, usually of high standing.

Jihad

An Arabic word meaning 'struggle' or 'strive' and most commonly used amongst Muslims to mean 'striving to practise one's faith'. It can also mean struggling against enemies of Islam.

Kashk-e baadenjaan

The whey of cheese, used in many Middle Eastern dishes.

Khameerbob

An Afghan pasta dish.

Khan

A Central Asian title for a sovereign or military ruler.

Khoresht aaloo

An Iranian dish popular in Afghanistan made with chicken and prunes.

Koo-koo-yeh morgh

A chicken omelette.

Kuchi

A nomadic tribe that has traditionally travelled through parts of Afghanistan, often herding sheep and goats.

Lavash

Thin, flat bread, usually soft, popular throughout the Middle East and elsewhere.

Maghrib

Evening prayer for Muslims.

Mantu

Dumplings, sometimes savoury, originating in Armenia but widely enjoyed throughout the Middle East.

Mecca

A city in Saudi Arabia that houses a memorial to the Prophet Mohammed. The Grand Mosque is considered the most holy shrine of Islam.

Mujaheddin

Loosely aligned Afghan guerrilla groups, which came to prominence when they fought against the pro-Soviet Afghan government during the late 1970s. In 1979, when Soviet troops entered Afghanistan at the request of the Afghan government, the mujaheddin forces fought both the Russian and Afghan government troops with marked success. After the Soviet Union pulled out of the conflict in the late 1980s, the mujaheddin fought each other in the subsequent Afghan Civil War.

Mullah

A religious teacher or leader, trained in the doctrine and law of Islam; the head of a mosque.

Naan

A type of bread.

Palao

Any of many Afghan dishes served with rice cooked in a savoury broth.

Qabil palao

A rice dish made with mutton or lamb.

Qorma

A name given to any of a number of Afghan dishes of rice and meat.

Ramadan

The ninth month of the Islamic calendar, during which participating Muslims fast from dawn until sunset each day.

Rubab

A short-necked string instrument that has a deep resonant sound; similar to a lute, it is made of wood with a goatskin covering. The rubab (also 'rabab'), sometimes considered the national instrument of Afghanistan, is often called the 'lion' of instruments; it has a double-chambered body carved from mulberry wood, three main strings and a plectrum made from ivory, bone or wood.

Russian invasion of Afghanistan

Fifty thousand Soviet military personnel entered Afghanistan in December 1979, at the request of that nation's Marxist-Leninist government. Ten years of fighting between the Soviet armed forces and mujaheddin forces ended when the last Soviet troops withdrew in February 1989.

Sha'ban

The eighth month of the Islamic calendar.

She'er berinji

Afghan rice puddings.

Shadoof

An ancient device consisting of a bucket held by two ropes which, when swung, scoops water from one channel and deposits it in another; a man-powered water pump.

Shi'a

One of the two major branches of Islam – Sunni and Shi'a – which formed after a split in the early years of the faith, and based on fundamental differences in beliefs. At times, these differences have led to major conflicts between the followers of the two major branches of Islam. Shi'ites make up only about twenty per cent of Muslims worldwide.

Sunni

Numerically, the dominant Muslim denomination. The Hazara are Shi'a but the majority of the population of Afghanistan is Sunni.

Tambor

An ancient stringed instrument with a long slender neck. It is known throughout Central Asia and dates back to 1500 BC. Today it is mostly played in Afghanistan and Kurdistan to accompany popular music, but it was traditionally a holy instrument used by Sufi mystics and poets in Afghanistan.

Tamburlaine, or 'Timur', the Great

A warrior of Turco-Mongol ancestry, Tamburlaine established a vast Middle Eastern empire in the fourteenth century. Renowned for his savagery, he died in 1405, aged thirty-five.

Toichek

The most common sort of Afghan bed; consisting of blankets covering a thin mattress, the whole bed is designed to be packed away during daylight hours.

Tribes

The four major ethnic groups of Afghanistan are Pashtun, Uzbek, Tajik and Hazara. Uzbeks and Tajiks also have homelands outside Afghanistan, in Uzbekistan and Tajikistan respectively. Strictly speaking, each of these ethnic groups include up to seventy individual 'tribes'.

Tula

Traditional Afghan musical instrument similar to a large recorder. It has six finger holes and is played by blowing into, or across, the mouthpiece.

Turbat

One of the names for the prayer rug on which Muslims kneel at times of prayer.

Wu'du

The ritually prescribed preparations for prayer amongst followers of Islam, and the sequence of actions carried out during prayer, including washing of parts of the body.